BLOODSTONE

TIM MACKINTOSH-SMITH
BLOODSTONE

دار جامعة حمد بن خليفة للنشر
HAMAD BIN KHALIFA UNIVERSITY PRESS

Hamad bin Khalifa University Press

P O Box 5825

Doha, Qatar

books.hbkupress.com

TPB: 9789927118562

eBook: 9789927118579

Typeset by York Publishing Solutions Pvt. Ltd., Noida, India
Printed and bound in Doha, Qatar by
Al Jazeera Printing Press Co. L.L.C.

Qatar National Library Cataloging-in-Publication (CIP)

Mackintosh-Smith, Tim, author.

Bloodstone / Tim Mackintosh-Smith. – Doha : Hamad Bin Khalifa University Press, 2017.

Pages ; cm

ISBN : 978-9927-118-55-5

1. Terrorists – Fiction. II Title.

PR6061.A724 B56 2017

823.914 – dc 23

For Abdulwahhab, Ashwaq, Shayma', Muhammad, Shadha,
Ruqayyah, Ghayda' and Umm Muhammad
who heard this story first

Contents

Main Characters

The Travellers
Sinan, slave of **Abu Abdallah**
Abu Abdallah Ibn Battutah of Tangier, former judge and globetrotter

In Seville
'El Bermejo', properly Muhammad son of Isma'il, Sultan Muhammad VI of Granada (by usurpation)
Don Pedro, King of Castile, known as 'the Cruel' or 'the Just'
Abraham Ibn Zarzar, physician and confidant of **Don Pedro**
Solomon of Seville, dealer in gemstones
Cristóbal the Moor, goldsmith of Seville

In Granada
Lisan al-Din Ibn al-Khatib, Grand Vizier of Granada
Ali the Alchemist, scientist and libertine
Lubna, *qaynah* (female singing slave) and concubine of **Ali the Alchemist**
Sergeant Hamid of the Mamluk guard
Ibn Zamrak, Sultanic Secretary to the Sultan of Granada
Zayd, Clerk of Works in the Alhambra
Umm Ahmad, a decayed old woman
The Chief of the Night, head of the Granada constabulary
Sultan Muhammad son of Yusuf, Sultan Muhammad V of Granada

The Lions
Layth, leader of the Lions (a group of conspirators)
Dirgham
Hattam
Sarim
Haydar
Jassas

Prologue

By the ruins of Itálica, Seville, 29 Jumada 'l-Thani 763 (25 April 1362)
He knew he was going to die. Here. Now. The Christian, his killer, was behind him.

He rode on, staring into the shimmering emptiness ahead, counting out his life in heartbeats. The only sounds in the rising morning heat were the creak of harness leathers and the hoof-falls, muffled in dust, of his mount. If it could be called that: a donkey, for a Sultan! He smiled his last smile. At least this cloak of scarlet was a fitting funeral pall for him, for Muhammad son of Isma'il, Sultan of Granada, Commander of the Muslims.

His killer, the young king, called him 'El Bermejo'– the Red One. Red cloak, red hair, red beard. And in the pouch about his neck was something redder than the rest, redder than the blood that would soon be shed. He felt it, cold and insistent, knocking at his breast.

A question came: who would wash him, pray over him, bury him?

No one. He'd be hacked up, hung up, a warning.

A lark cried falling far and high through the sky above the plain. Then, at last, it came, the hard dry drum of hooves. He turned to face it.

Death hit him in the breastbone at the point of King Pedro's lance.

There was no pain. Just everything splintering, and the spring sky somersaulting.

Pedro's face in the blue, ice-blue eyes smiling down. 'So, *No one wins but Allah*, eh, Bermejo? Isn't that the family motto?' The young king laughed and kicked him in the head.

'So . . . much . . .' he heard a voice say, 'for Christian . . .chivalry.' The voice was his own. There was still no pain, but he knew he was going.

'Oh, and I'll have this, too,' Pedro said, still smiling, reaching down to rip the bloody pouch from his neck. 'Payment. For screwing me up with Aragón.'

He saw Pedro take the stone out of the dripping pouch and turn it round and round against the blue: distillation of crimson, redder than anything in creation. He opened his mouth to tell him it was cursed. He wanted to die with Pedro's fear in his eyes, not Pedro's smile. But the words wouldn't come.

It didn't matter. Pedro would find out about the Ruby in time. Just as he himself had, and those before him.

Then everything went red and he knew no more, not even when they came and finished him off.

Chapter 1

The Alhambra, Granada, 22 Safar 770 (5 October 1368)

The three men climbed in silence. Looking up, Sinan saw bastions and battlements leaping skyward through the forenoon light. The road rose, and he realized that the towers sprang from a ruddy cliff of wall that seemed to have no end. He thought of the storytellers back home across the Strait, and of their fabled City of Brass. This was no less fabulous: a citadel of iron, bearing down on the brow of the hill like a rusted crown. He wondered what lay inside.

'Master,' Sinan whispered at last to the small man by his side, 'will your friend make you a vizier?' He looked at the figure lumbering ahead of them, just out of earshot.

'He'd better,' Abu Abdallah replied under his breath. 'By God's grace, you know as well as I do, Sinan, how bad things are.' The lines on his gallnut face creased into a frown. 'Short of stumbling across a crock of Gothic gold, a vizier's salary is our only hope of ever paying off the debts.'

And, Abu Abdallah thought, peering beadily up at the fortress-palace like a squirrel surveying an unharvested wood, there were the other perks of high office: titles, robes, estates, embassies to far lands . . . social heights his modest Moroccan forebears could never have dreamed of climbing. Abu Abdallah's name already appeared, grafted on by marriage, in the dynastic family trees of Coromandel and the Maldives. In the old globetrotting days, before his luck deserted him, he had married royal wives, and divorced them; he had played chess with sultans, and beaten them; he had dabbled in the more dangerous games of coup and counter-coup, and kept his head while all around him were losing theirs. A vizierate at Granada– a seat in the Sultan's ministerial cabinet– wouldn't just pay off his debts. It would be the resurrection of his career, his life and, almost literally, of his body . . . It had quite slipped his mind, until he'd turned up unannounced the day before and seen the shock on his old friend's face, that he was, after all, not meant to be here. Or indeed anywhere on earth.

Yes: *I will rise again*, Abu Abdallah said to himself with a smile. And the image brought to mind one of the other perks of the high life . . . a stream of women flowed across his memory – Greeks, Turks, Mongols, Tamils, Marathas, fair, dusky, cool, musky, slave-concubines of so many remembered beds. Strange, he thought: *I was born just across the Strait, in sight of Spain, and I've never had a Spanish girl. Everything but.*

'And, master,' Sinan said, breaking into his reflections, 'when you do become a vizier, you will remember your promise, won't you?'

'What? Oh, that . . . Sinan, who else but you could be my Secret Secretary?'

Who else indeed? Sinan might have been Abu Abdallah's slave, but it was he who was the real master of the old man's life; he who had saved that life, back in the bloody chaos of Fez in 'sixty-two . . .

They followed their host round another bend in the road and were confronted by a great gateway. Sinan stared up at it, and a shock ran down his spine.

At first sight it might have been part of the architecture, a decorative cresting on the summit of the gate. But no; they were heads. Human heads. And they were attached not to bodies, but to poles.

Lisan al-Din, Grand Vizier of Granada, looked up at them and cleared his throat. 'May God Almighty damn this skull,' he intoned,

> 'that Satan's skill
> Inspired with every form of foul skulduggery!
> May it inspire within the mouths and minds of men
> No mite of mercy, and no mote of memory!'

He folded his arms, resplendent in embroidered sleeves, over a brocade-hung paunch. The words hung heavy in the forenoon air. 'Though I say so myself, that second couplet in particular is rather good, is it not.'

It was not a question. Abu Abdallah, much smaller and less splendid in his hooded travelling burnous, said nothing. He carried on squinting up at the row of heads. Their long-dead grins added a frivolous note to the severe stonework of the Alhambra's main gate. One of the heads had fallen askew; it seemed to be cocking a snook at the world of the living.

'I composed the verses apropos of the head in the middle,' Lisan al-Din said. 'The head of . . . El Bermejo.' Silently, Sinan mouthed the alien syllables: *El Bermejo*. 'It's way past its best, I admit,' the Grand Vizier continued. 'Been up there more than six years, pecked by the ravens and tanned by the elements. But it still does the job. Puts the rebels off.'

'May I ask a question, sir?'

Lisan al-Din turned in surprise at the sound of the words, uttered in beautiful Arabic, as if wondering where they had come from. It was the third member of the group who had spoken. The slave. *But slaves didn't speak* . . . The Grand Vizier's eyes, hooded and shadowed by chronic insomnia, opened wider than they had for a long time.

Sinan took this as a sign of permission. 'Was he a Christian, sir? I mean, the former owner of the middle head? I can see some traces of a red beard. And his name sounds Spanish: *El Bermejo*.'

3

Lisan al-Din studied the slave. Like his master, the young man was still dressed in a traveller's burnous. If he had noticed anything else about him, it was only the disturbing fact – uncommon, almost unknown, in Granada since the events of fourteen years before – that he was black. Now he saw a face.

He had seen plenty of Blacks during his years of exile in Morocco; must have seen this one, if he was in his friend Abu Abdallah's household that far back. But he had never actually looked at a Black. What he saw here took him aback: the features were as surprising, as perfect, as *beautiful*, as the man's Arabic. Planes of complex darkness, framed by darker beard that softened hard diagonals of cheekbone. Skin cool as jasper, warm as Egyptian velvet. And the eyes – liquid shot with light and dark. The slave might have been half his age, if that; but the eyes seemed to regard him from a distance of time as vast and unknowable as that continent of his across the Strait, beyond the desert. For a moment Lisan al-Din, Grand Vizier of Granada, literary prodigy of the age, was lost.

The call of a guard up on the battlements brought him back. 'Sharp eyes he's got, this boy of yours,' he said to Abu Abdallah.

Abu Abdallah grinned. 'Sharp eyes, sharp brain. Sharp name, too, ha ha!'

'My name is Sinan, sir,' the slave said. '*Spearhead* . . . sorry, sir. You of all people need no explanation.' Abu Abdallah twinkled and nodded, as one would to a clever son who has said the right thing. 'But if I'm not mistaken,' Sinan went on, looking back at the head on the gate, 'the redness of the beard is unnatural. It is the result of dyeing with henna. Which suggests that, despite his foreign name, its owner was probably a Muslim.'

'Goodness,' Lisan al-Din exclaimed. 'I see what you mean. Amazing perspicacity, especially for a Black. Where did you pick him up?'

'On a bend in the Niger, past Timbuktu,' Abu Abdallah said. 'He was knee-high to a locust at the time, weren't you Sinan? A hospitality gift, he was, from the viceroy of the Mansa, or Emperor, of Mali.'

'Only you, my old friend, only you . . .' the Grand Vizier said, shaking his heavy head. 'Most people would have said in the slave market in Fez.'

'Yes,' said Abu Abdallah, suddenly solemn. 'Only me.'

Again, Lisan al-Din was lost for words. In the seven years since he'd last seen him, he'd forgotten the extent of his friend's magnificent singularity. *And has it really been seven years?* he asked himself. *Abu Abdallah doesn't look a day older* . . . 'Hmm. Well. In response to Master Sinan's hypothesis, I can inform him that the . . . *thing* up on the gate was indeed a Muslim. Or rather, in theory a Muslim, but in deed a worshipper of the devil. I cannot bring myself to utter his real name, so I refer to him by the name the Christians gave him – El Bermejo, the Red One, so called from the inordinate use of henna which you remarked upon, Sinan. You may also be surprised to learn that he was, for a time, the usurping self-styled Sultan of this blessed land.'

'The *Sultan*? How . . . how come, sir?' Sinan said. Abu Abdallah was pleased his slave had asked. He knew the beginning of the story well: he had heard it from Lisan al-Din's own mouth during the Grand Vizier's exile in Morocco. But of its ending, no more than rumours had reached that godforsaken Moroccan province where he himself had spent the last years in virtual exile.

'Oh, the usual reason,' Lisan al-Din said. 'Greed. For money. For power. For all the glittering baubles power and money bring.' The noon prayer call sounded, at first distant from the plain below, then closer, from the walls above. Sinan looked up at the mighty citadel. 'Yes, Master Sinan. *Greed*. For titles, robes . . . concubines.' He glanced at Abu Abdallah, who was fiddling with the tassel of his burnous. 'Perhaps, above all, greed for a stone: the Great Ruby.'

A question began to form on Sinan's lips, but the Grand Vizier turned away and led them onward up the road, towards the gate's dark mouth.

5

'When I was serving the Sultan of Delhi as Malikite judge of his capital,' Abu Abdallah said as they approached the gaping portal, 'he used to have a whole avenue of corpses, hung, drawn, quartered, halved, filleted, whatever cut you wanted, lining the entrance to his palace. *Uggh*. They used to spook the horses.'

'So you have told me,' Lisan al-Din replied over his shoulder. 'On several occasions. You have also told me how you nearly became one of those corpses yourself.' The Grand Vizier smiled one of his rare and gloomy smiles as he pictured Abu Abdallah's scrawny body dangling in the Indian sun, the grin twinkling even in death ... His own smile vanished. That image of his friend, dead, had reminded him of the extraordinary question he had to ask. For Abu Abdallah, who had made a career out of wheedling favours, had now, it seemed, wheedled the greatest favour of them all – from Time itself.

But for now the question would have to keep, until they reached somewhere private; somewhere more congenial to the imparting of shocks. And shocks there would be ... Lisan al-Din glanced warily at his friend; Abu Abdallah grinned back, a skeleton on the loose from his own cupboard. They crossed the shadow-line of the gate, into the dark.

Chapter 2

Across the valley from the Alhambra, the noon call to prayer sounded through the alleyways of al-Bayyazin. Its thin spirals of sound wound into the deepest corners of the hillside suburb. Ali the Alchemist did not hear it. For him, it was a sort of involuntary noise that the city emitted at regular intervals. It had been many years since he had answered that call.

But he heard the knock on his street door. It sounded through his courtyard, waking for a moment the long grey tabby cat that dozed in a patch of autumn sun, and it sounded in the rooms that opened off the yard. In one of these Ali sat hunched over his work, flecked by dusty light from the lattice that looked on to the street and surrounded by cauldrons and braziers, crucibles and mortars, alembics and albarellos. The knock sounded right inside his head. 'Damn,' he murmured. 'Who is it now?'

Then he remembered that he had invited a few old friends to lunch – a lunch he knew would turn into an all-afternoon booze-up. They drank like drains, this lot. How many jars of Malaga wine would they empty this time? And then – damn again! – the coppersmith was due with the new apparatus, after the afternoon prayer. He needed paying. They hadn't settled on a price, but Ali knew it would be high. 'It's a one-off, your honour,' the man had said, slowly shaking his head. 'Never made anything like it in my life.' He certainly hadn't. Thank God Layth would come tonight with more funds.

Layth. He rolled the name round his mouth, like a shot of arsenic. He loathed Layth, loathed the sight of those green zealot's eyes, that beard that didn't look quite real on a face that had stayed too pretty too long. At least he knew Layth loathed him too. And, thank Heaven, he hardly ever came; apart from anything else, that made it all much safer. When he did come, it was always under cover of night. *I've never seen Layth by daylight*, Ali suddenly thought; *maybe he's a ghoul, not a son of Adam.* And he would never come further than the lobby. To Layth's sanctimonious nostrils Ali's house stank of scandal and of wine, the mother of mortal sins, and he always fled it like a raped nun.

And yet neither could do without the other. Layth needed Ali's brains. Ali needed Layth's cash.

He heard loud drinkers' voices going through the courtyard to the guest room. Oh, they were OK. They were fun. They kept the mental flab of middle age in trim . . . carefully, he added the last measure of white powder to the liquid in the beaker . . . He'd go and join them, have a bite and a few cups – not too many, not with the work he was doing – then leave his guests in Lubna's capable hands.

Lubna could cope with anything. They still talked about the sparring match she'd had with the blind poet of al-Mudawwar. He'd tried to grope her, pretending to feel his way, and she'd hit back with words: 'Filthy old man! But what can you expect from someone brought up in al-Mudawwar with the billy-goats, where they think that piss is perfume and shit is sugar-candy?'

'What woman's voice is this?' the blind man had asked, feigning surprise.

'The voice of an old hag – like your mother,' Lubna hit back.

He'd turned his verses on her, but she'd repaid him in kind – and got the better of him. How did it go, Lubna's famous response?

> *'You goad me with your virile rhetoric,*
> *Because I'm of the sex that's fair and tender.*
> *Beware, blind one, my poems have a prick,*
> *For unlike me they're masculine in gender!'*

8

Off the top of her head, it was. For a while, all Granada was quoting the brilliant riposte of Ali the Alchemist's singing-girl.

It was, therefore, no surprise that Ali's boozing, versifying friends were under Lubna's spell – and not only the spell of her words. She must have been all of thirty by now; but she had borne Ali no children, and her body was still firm and taut from the girlhood years of herding on the high sierras, before her capture. Her voice, too, still had the rough and sexy edges of her Spanish mother-tongue . . . here it was, calling him now . . . Yes, they were all under Lubna's spell; yet Ali felt no jealousy. Lubna was his slave, his *qaynah*, his singing-girl, but the possession was mutual. She was his, in legal terms. He was hers in every other sense of possession, every sense that was meant by love.

She loved him fiercely back, this girl stolen from a mountainside. But the fierceness was shot through with sadness. Sadness that she had given him no children. And the darker sadness that haunted the happiest slave.

' . . . *Ali!* Come at once and deal with this bunch of ne'er-do-wells! Skulking in that stinking den of yours . . .' She was almost at the door. At the last moment, he remembered the couscous sieve – the latest in a series that he had 'borrowed' from the kitchen and gone on to ruin with his new process – and tried to hide it.

Too late. Lubna stood there, light and dark. Dark from the shadowed doorway; dark eyebrows and dark peak of hairline framing a frown. But the darkness could not veil the light in her face, her voice. Ali drank her in, sight and sound, with a thirst that he knew would never be sated. Lubna. *White-as-milk.* And that was only the half of her.

She saw him try to hide the sieve and smiled through her frown. Dark lips, bright teeth – *Like silver*, the song went, *at the bottom of a well.*

Chapter 3

Inside the gateway there was a clatter of arms as the guards saluted the Grand Vizier and his guest – then a silence, as they eyed the slave. Sinan had already found the looks more penetrating here in Granada than they ever were back in Morocco. There was a barbed edge of hatred to them. He ignored them and looked up at another massive archway, and a half-seen inscription – of welcome, or warning? He couldn't make it out – and then the gloom swallowed them. They doglegged upwards through the darkness, then emerged into day again, inside the Alhambra.

Into day; but Sinan felt that the light here, within the walls, had a distinct quality, a shade of darkness felt rather than seen. It was almost as if they had come to another country, islanded by the great red walls, with its own sky. And its own population: there were functionaries in embroidered robes and caps, younger and less exalted versions of Lisan al-Din, purposefully shuttling across the forecourt; there was a small knot of religious scholars or judges, distinguished by their nodding turbans, awaiting entrance into some inner sanctum; and, stationed at intervals round the periphery, soldiers whom Sinan knew from their dress and complexions to belong to the sultan's elite Mamluk guard – *mamluks*, slaves like himself, but captured in the Christian territories then converted to Islam and a culture of fervent militarism. He could feel several dozen pairs of eyes on him.

One of the functionaries, a scribe with a bronze pencase in his waist sash, came and drew Lisan al-Din aside. 'You must excuse me,' the Grand Vizier said to Abu Abdallah after a short whispered exchange. 'I am summoned. But I will be back shortly to show you round. Not the full tour, I'm afraid, as His Presence the Sultan is in residence. I have some interesting sights to show you, however, which will more than make up for the ones you may not see. Meanwhile, I'll get someone to take you up the Watchtower. We always start there with our . . . more distinguished visitors.'

Abu Abdallah inclined his head at the compliment. Before leaving them, Lisan al-Din spoke to the scribe, who spoke to a lesser official, who spoke to a Mamluk sergeant with a crooked nose, who spoke to a lesser Mamluk, who marched through another gate. Sinan had the impression of being in some elaborate colony of insects, a pyramid of multiple hierarchies and concentric walls, ever more impenetrable. He wondered if he would ever get to see the man, the Presence, at the centre of everything. He also felt uncomfortable, smothered by stares and by the sheer density of it all.

A few minutes, later his claustrophobia was blown away. An officer led them through the inner gate, across a bridge over a small ravine, along a narrow street that passed between the Mamluks' barracks, up a wide dark staircase – and on to what Sinan could only think of as the prow of a ship sailing through the sky.

'*Glory to the Creator!*' Abu Abdallah exclaimed, panting from the climb as he looked over the parapet. Above him the red standard of the Nasrids, the dynasty founded, like this tower, by the sultan's ancestor five generations before, flapped a brisk tattoo in the breeze. Sinan joined his master and tried to take in the view.

To the east the great outer wall of the Alhambra curved round – the hull of the ship – reinforced by the stark square bastions. Immediately beneath this, to the north, wooded green waves of hillside rolled and plunged down to a deep cramped valley. Beyond the valley rose another steep roller of hill, its lower levels covered by a tightly-packed, tumbling flotsam of houses, its treeless crests burnt yellow by a long hot summer. The upper end of the valley was enclosed by more sere peaks and by the serpentine line of the outer city wall. On the near side of the wall, on a steeply terraced slope, Sinan could just make out the regular piles of stones that marked a cemetery.

He turned – and gasped. Before him, to the west and south, beyond a foreground of city punctuated by the exclamation marks of minarets, lay a plain. At first it seemed as vast and as infinitely green as the Encompassing Ocean, but then Sinan saw that it was dotted with farmsteads and mansions and framed by a far shoreline of hills. Further to the south-east, the hills swung in and swelled into jagged mountains, backlit and glowering and even now, in early autumn, streaked with last winter's snow. He tried to take the view in, and couldn't: it was too big, too strange. It all had the vivid unreality of a landscape seen in a dream.

'So what do you think of that, my boy?' Abu Abdallah said, softly. 'I said you'd see some fine sights when you took to the road with me.'

Sinan had no answer. They stood there for minutes on end, silenced by the panorama before them; even Abu Abdallah – who, as the cook-slave back home once said, uncharitably, but with some truth, made a noise even when he wasn't making a sound.

At length Abu Abdallah spoke. 'He's a fine fellow, Lisan al-Din. Historian, poet, orator, biographer, calligrapher. You name it, he does it, with style. *Lisan al-Din*, "the Tongue of Religion" . . . Hah, no one ever remembers *my* honorific – *Shams al-Din*, "the Sun of Religion"; but then, we "Suns" are two a penny. Lisan is the one and only, the silver tongue with the golden pen . . . unlike your old master, who was blessed with a tongue like a banana skin and a pen that ties itself in knots. The gift of the gaffe, that's what I've got, Sinan.' The silence cut in again, but only for a moment. 'Not that it matters, of course, when one is universally acclaimed as the world's greatest traveller. But to be a stylist *and* a statesman

13

like Lisan is something of an achievement too. Although . . .' Abu Abdallah turned to Sinan and lowered his voice ' . . . between you, me and the flagpole, he's a bit pleased with himself.'

Sinan thought of pots and kettles, and had to look down to hide his smile. 'But then who wouldn't be, running this lot?' He spread his arms to take in the Alhambra, the plain, the mountains. 'The sultan merely reigns. Lisan al-Din's the one in charge.'

The breeze suddenly dropped; the red standard of the Nasrid dynasty wilted and fell silent. 'Master,' Sinan said, 'will he really make you a vizier?'

Abu Abdallah drew himself up to his full, diminutive height. 'Undoubtedly, by the grace of God. And if not Lisan al-Din, then . . . someone else. Sometime soon.' He looked at the distant hills, his billy-goat beard jutting over the battlements. 'I may be getting on in years, but one's as young as one feels. And one's credentials are impeccable: Malikite Judge of Delhi, Ambassador Plenipotentiary to China on behalf of the Sultan of Hind and Sind, Chief Justice of the Maldivian Archipelago, brother-in-law to the Sultan of Coromandel . . .'

Sinan's mind glazed over until the familiar litany was finished. 'And master, when you do become a vizier, you *won't* forget your promise, will you? I mean, to appoint me . . .'

' . . . my Secret Secretary?' Abu Abdallah said, completing the equally familiar question. 'Sinan, how many times have I told you? No one else on earth could fill that position.'

The wind rose again. Sinan could see a dark army of clouds appearing over the far rim of hills, the vanguard of storms. For the first time this year, he shivered.

❁

The Mamluk with the crooked nose led them back across the forecourt. Lisan al-Din was waiting for them by a doorway. It was an undistinguished doorway in a discreet façade. But Sinan felt that something momentous lay within.

14

He followed the Grand Vizier and Abu Abdallah along shadowed passages and through low chambers – in all of which he could sense, rather than see, the eyes of Mamluk guards – until they entered a large room. Its full dimensions were at first invisible in the latticed light. But as his eyes adjusted, Sinan made out the dancing patterns and colours of tile mosaic on the walls, and slender marble columns burgeoning into carved and painted capitals that supported a coffered wooden ceiling, richly inlaid. The ceiling seemed to bear down on them, like the lid of an elaborate jewel-box; or coffin. Sinan thought of those caverns, haunts of thieves and *jinn*, that he'd heard the storytellers describing back in the market in Fez – dark, glittering, dangerous.

'The Chamber of Counsel,' Lisan al-Din said. 'We must come back when His Presence is sitting in public audience and the shutters are open. In his blessed wisdom he greatly beautified it a few years ago. But much of what you see now was the work of his late father, Sultan Yusuf, of sacred memory, who as you will have heard was murdered while at prayer –'

' – *by the hand of a black slave*.' The words came from a shadowed corner, soft, insinuating, enunciated. They were followed by a face – that of a tall thin man in a robe almost as stately as Lisan al-Din's. The face was angular and pallid; it had a sheen of sweat, or oil. The nostrils flared and twitched, as if scenting decay. The eyes were fixed on Sinan. For the second time, the slave shivered.

'Yes. Absolutely,' Lisan al-Din said with deliberate flatness. 'Allow me to introduce my esteemed colleague Ibn Zamrak, the Sultanic Secretary.' The newcomer nodded almost imperceptibly. 'And this is my most honoured friend and guest, Abu Abdallah Ibn Battutah of Tangier, the renowned traveller. No mortal man has seen so much of God's earth, as you are doubtless aware . . .' If the Sultanic Secretary was aware, he showed no sign. So Lisan al-Din continued, reciting his friend's achievements with quiet but pointed pride: 'Abu Abdallah devoted thirty years to seeing

15

strange lands, to witnessing the wonders and marvels of creation, to seeking the bounty of sultans and the blessing of saints, from the far west of the Land of the Blacks to the easternmost capes of China. He has trodden both ends of the earth; he has sailed upon the Circumambient Ocean. And few men have suffered so many vicissitudes as he – shipwreck, kidnap, piracy, war, deadly illness, the spells of sorcerers, the wrath of tyrants – and lived to tell the tale. And, for that matter, to write it down. In short, one might say that Abu Abdallah is the embodiment, in our age, of the immort–' he stopped short; then cleared his throat and continued ' – *of the immortal Khadir.*'

There was a silence. In it, Abu Abdallah, eyes downcast with at least a modicum of modesty, contemplated the compliments; Lisan al-Din contemplated his friend – and his own unintentionally disturbing comparison: al-Khadir, the great traveller of Islamic legend, was one of a handful of humans who had been granted earthly immortality. Abu Abdallah, like al-Khadir, had defied distance. Had he also defied death?

At last, and with evident reluctance, Ibn Zamrak extended a pale and bony hand across the silence. 'I have indeed heard of you, sir, and of your vicissitudes . . . or should one say, *escapades*?' There was no warmth in his words, and even less in his handshake. Nor did he attempt to conceal the small cloth which he drew from his sleeve and with which he carefully wiped his shaken hand; as he did so, Sinan noticed a distinct and unaccountable smell – of *vinegar*. The Sultanic Secretary then turned to Lisan al-Din and spoke in a low but audible voice. 'I urge you most strongly to keep an eye on that Clerk of Works. Time is running out. Money *has* run out – he's way over budget. In fact, he's so much over that I can't think where the excess has gone, except –' the voice diminished to a hiss ' – into the innermost folds of his capacious sleeves.' And with that the Sultanic Secretary turned and walked away, throwing another look of undisguised contempt at Sinan.

16

'I do apologise,' Lisan al-Din said when he was out of earshot. 'Most indelicate of him, talking shop like that . . . But one has to make allowances. Ibn Zamrak's origins are somewhat humble, and he has a plebeian chip on his brocaded shoulder. Not to mention a lot of ticks in his turban, as they say. Oh, and some *very* strange obsessions about hygiene. But he also has a point. This palace may look like a piece of paradise on earth, but it is poxed with corruption, riddled with rats – not to mention moles and other forms of vermin. Rotten, in a word. *To the very core.*'

The Grand Vizier had silenced himself by his own vehemence.

'When I was Malikite judge of Delhi,' Abu Abdallah chipped into the silence, 'I found the best policy was to rise above it all.'

Lisan al-Din did not respond, but continued his own train of thought. 'That said, even if he does supplement his salary with the odd bit of peculation – and God is the one who knows – Zayd the Clerk of Works is a highly reliable and efficient man. You'll meet him later. But first . . . come.' He led them through a small door into a small high-walled courtyard. The long sides were blank; in contrast, the far end was a barely controlled riot of carved and painted inscriptions and geometry and vegetation that framed two further doors. They approached the doors, then stopped. 'We may go no further,' the Grand Vizier said. 'His Presence is within.'

Sinan could feel that presence. He felt it suddenly, in his guts, just as long ago, far away, he had felt the presence of . . . the *boliw* – the word rose from the deepest chambers of memory, from a tongue he had almost forgotten – the *boliw* that dwelt beyond the door of a painted house of mud where his father had once taken him. Long ago, far off, in a life beyond reach. What were the *boliw*? He no longer knew. The meanings and memories of that life had receded like ghosts at dawn; the dawn of another existence. Except for the one sharp terrifying memory that never went away.

'*Wa la ghaliba illa 'llah*,' Abu Abdallah said, reading an endlessly reduplicating inscription in the plasterwork. *No one wins but Allah.*

'The motto of our glorious Nasrid dynasty,' Lisan al-Din said. 'But now, follow me. I want to show you my ... *new baby*.' For a moment, another of his rare smiles lit the Grand Vizier's gloomy features.

The three men retraced their steps and left by that first, discreet doorway. There were many more people outside now. The same officials and Mamluks – there again was the Mamluk sergeant with the crooked nose – but also others who looked like ordinary citizens going about their ordinary business. Sinan realized that here, outside the palace proper but within the great defensive walls of the Alhambra, was a whole city within a city – or rather above a city, poised above Granada proper on the edge of its plain below. Lisan al-Din led them east, away from the citadel with its Watchtower. They passed a woman – a *qaynah*, or high-class singing slave-woman, to judge by her coquettish gait and the cloud of scent and servants she trailed behind her. Abu Abdallah's head swivelled round to follow her; Sinan noticed an answering turn of the woman's head, and an almost imperceptible narrowing of the eyes above the veil.

Lisan al-Din noticed too. 'It's good to see you looking so young at heart, my old friend,' he said. The Grand Vizier sighed inwardly. He knew only too well that he himself was not young at heart, or at anything else. Certainly not in body. Abu Abdallah was in his mid-sixties, ten years older than him. But he acted like a man in his twenties. Then again, what was the point of desire when you couldn't ... follow through? Perhaps he should pick Abu Abdallah's brains, which he knew to be well stocked with exotic aphrodisiacs, recipes picked up on his travels.

Still, Lisan al-Din thought as they arrived before another doorway, at least he had *this* to keep him going. Inside the door they passed through semi-darkness, following the scent, damp and dusty, of fresh plaster, then ... For a few moments they were blinded: light bouncing off marble and cascading through columns, light so intense that it eclipsed the sky above them. Then Sinan began to make the details out. They were on the edge of a rectangular courtyard, perhaps thirty yards long, which seemed at once both vast and intimate. It was lined by slender marble pillars, a hundred of them or more, that met in groups then moved apart in an elaborate and rhythmic dance of light and dark, shafts and shadows. The blinding white marble paving – where did all this light come from? the sky was growing visibly more overcast – was cut by shallow dry channels. Sinan saw one channel leading from the mid-point of each of the four sides of the court to . . . a *tent*, planted in the exact centre of the court. It could not have been more incongruous.

Then Sinan realized why the tent was there. The porticos behind the colonnades were filled with wooden scaffolding, and with movement, subdued but purposeful. Men worked in almost total silence, plastering, inscribing, carving, colouring – each quadrant displaying a different stage of the process of encrustation. It was like watching bees at work on a honeycomb. That central tent must conceal more workers, Sinan thought. Were they preparing a chamber for the king bee – for the sultan?

'*This* is my baby,' the GrandVizier said, surveying the view before them. The doleful face beamed with pride. 'You are seeing it in the foetal stage, so to speak,' Lisan al-Din went on. 'But I hope you will be able to stay and see it fully formed.'

'When will that be?' Abu Abdallah asked.

Sinan saw the usual gloom return to the Grand Vizier's face. 'That is the question . . . But it must be finished by the birthday of the Prophet, peace and blessings be upon him, in less than three weeks. Time, as Ibn Zamrak just reminded us, is running out.'

'But why the hurry?' Abu Abdallah said. 'After all, Cairo wasn't built in a day.'

'Because with the Prophet's birthday coincides another event of even greater importance – God forgive me – I mean, of great importance for the future of this sultanate.'

He clearly was not going to say what the impending event was. They stood for a while, unasked questions hanging in the air with the plaster dust. Then Lisan al-Din beckoned and led them into a side chamber.

The chamber was filled by a forest of timber scaffolding. Sinan's gaze followed it upwards, into a dome; beneath this was a platform, on which a number of men lay or squatted. They were busy with brushes, painting. Sinan was surprised to see that the painters' features and complexions resembled those of the soldiers of the Mamluk guard. Were these men also Christian slaves? He followed Abu Abdallah and Lisan al-Din to the far side of the hall. Above this was a smaller dome, where the painters had already finished. On the dome's inner surface he could see men, and animals – a representation of a hunt. Sinan had never seen anything remotely like it. Not in his present life.

'We've borrowed the painters from our neighbour Don Pedro, king of Castile,' Lisan al-Din explained. 'That old misery Ibn Zamrak, whom you have just had the dubious pleasure of meeting, objected to the scenes they are depicting, "*on theological grounds*".' Abu Abdallah grinned. It was a fair imitation of the Sultanic Secretary's sibilant voice.

Sinan knew why Ibn Zamrak had objected. The depiction of living beings was seen by some as an encroachment on God's prerogative for creation. But the beings on the dome fell far short of divine perfection. 'With your permission, sir,' he said to the Grand Vizier, 'that horse is much too small for its rider.'

Lisan al-Din turned to the slave. God, he had a nerve! But he admired the Black's intelligence, and his cheek.

'And in fact, sir,' Sinan went on, 'all the animals are the wrong size . . . Although it might be that the painters were trying to create an illusion of relative distance and nearness.'

Lisan al-Din shook his head in disbelief. 'He's a gem, this Sinan of yours!' he said to Abu Abdallah, without taking his eyes off the slave. 'May I make you an offer for him?' Sinan felt his stomach leap – even though he knew what his master's response would be.

'He's not for sale,' Abu Abdallah replied. Sinan relaxed. 'Not at any price. He looks as if he was brought up on crocodile bollocks and human flesh, I know. But I couldn't do without him. Apart from anything else, he can rustle up a lamb tagine fit for paradise. And he can even read and write. Three different scripts, and a finer hand than the Mufti of Fez!'

Sinan smiled to himself. His master was always boasting about his abilities as a scribe. But Abu Abdallah had been a good teacher. Sinan thought back to his first lessons in reading – when? Fourteen years before, perhaps. And he remembered how those lessons had taken him back to even earlier ones, now so dimly recalled – out hunting, tracking, with his father. Reading was tracking, hunting a quarry of meaning.

'Well,' Lisan al-Din said, 'if you ever change your mind . . .' He led them out, back into that glittering court.

As he did so, a man in his thirties wearing the robes of a middle-ranking official appeared from a slit in the central tent. Sinan studied his features – broad, fair-complexioned face; hazel eyes; auburn beard – and knew at once that he had Berber blood. He had seen approximations of that face all over Morocco. 'Ah, Zayd the Clerk of Works, with your usual perfect timing,' Lisan al-Din said, not trying to hide a note of condescension. He introduced the younger man to Abu Abdallah. 'And how is our Sultanic surprise progressing?' the Grand Vizier asked the clerk.

'I think we'll have it ready in time, sir, by the grace of God.'

'Don't *think*, man,' Lisan al-Din said. '*Do*.' He had hardly raised his voice, but Sinan suddenly knew why his master's friend was the one in charge.

Zayd the Clerk shrank visibly. 'As your eminence commands,' he said in a thin voice, before taking his leave.

'A good man, as I said,' the Grand Vizier confided when Zayd had gone. 'He's a descendant of the Zirids, the Berber dynasty who founded

Granada, and he tries his best to live up to his grand antecedents. I'm a little hard on him, I know, but I like to keep him on his toes.'

'I dare say,' Abu Abdallah murmured. 'But come on, Lisan, don't keep me dangling. What's inside this tent? What's this "Sultanic surprise" of yours? It sounds like some new kind of pudding. Perhaps it is . . .' He turned and made for the slit in the fabric.

The Grand Vizier clamped a weighty hand on the small man's shoulder. 'Don't even think of it, my friend. Until it is unveiled on the Prophet's birthday, it is absolutely top secret.'

'Oh, go on, Lisan,' Abu Abdallah said, released from the grip. 'You know you can trust me. Besides, you must be so proud, with all this work you've been putting into it. Solomon himself, peace be upon him, could hardly have done better . . .'

'Well,' Lisan al-Din said, softening, 'I admit that the actual choice of subject for the sultan's surprise was that of Zayd the Clerk. However, the all-important original concept was mine alone. Again, that ghoulish old woman Ibn Zamrak objected to it on the grounds of religious propriety, but . . .' The afternoon call to prayer sounded, first faint from the mosque outside the new court, then louder, relayed around the palace by reedy, penetrating voices. *Where did time go these days?* the Grand Vizier asked himself. *Time is a sword: if you don't cut it, it'll cut you . . . unless you're Abu Abdallah,* he thought, staring at his friend. *The man who seemed to have come to terms with Time. His own terms.*

'I'm all ears, Lisan,' Abu Abdallah said, smiling encouragement. 'And you know me. I won't tell a soul.'

The Grand Vizier ignored his friend. The extraordinary question would keep no longer. 'Abu Abdallah, there is no way you will prise this secret from me. Your flattery may work on barbarians like the Sultan of Hind and Sind. I am immune. Instead, pray permit me to delve into *your* secret.' The Grand Vizier looked his friend straight in the eye. 'Are you not supposed to be dead?'

Chapter 4

Across the valley in al-Bayyazin, Ali heard the last of his guests staggering out of the street door. The sunset prayer must have been called a while before; twilight had spun webs of gloom in the corners of his laboratory. For the first time that year, Ali realized the evenings were drawing in. He touched a taper to the glowing coals in the brazier, then lit the lamp that stood on the shelf above his work bench. There was nothing else to do but wait a little till the solution dried. He went back to his other task, that of committing the final version of the Remedy to verse.

It had been a brilliant idea of his, to conceal it in the veil of poetry. The details of the Remedy were too precise, too dangerous, for memory alone. To write them out in naked prose would have been madness. He could of course have put it into code. But then it would have only needed to fall into the wrong hands – and there were plenty of those in Granada – to attract every devious brain in the Secretariat.

No. Poetry was safest. With poetry you could disguise the most dangerous secrets in the sweetest, most meaningless nothings, and have them delivered by the fair hand of your singing-girl . . . He hated himself for using Lubna like this. But, as a slave and a woman, she was that ideal tool of conspiracy – an all-but invisible messenger. At least she had no contact with the loathsome Layth. It was all done at a remove.

He went back to this, the last, the crucial message, in *rajaz* metre, tapping the rhythm on the bench while the words formed. Time limped past in syllables. *Tum-taa-ti-tee, tum-taa-ti-tee . . .*

The laboratory had faded to black. Only an island of lamplight remained, in which Ali silently shaped the words. He was almost there, at that elusive perfection. Perhaps he should give up: perfection, they said, was for God. The lamp flickered. Words, thoughts flickered. Something flashed through the lattice – lightning, it must have been; yes, there was a distant rumble of thunder. And Ali was just conscious of another flicker – an unseasonable moth, chasing the lamp-flame – then yet another – the soft flash of a grey paw, chasing the moth. Ali silently cursed the cat. Then another lamp, and Lubna's voice.

'Come on. Where is it?'

Ali knew exactly what she meant. It was best to come clean. 'OK. I've wrecked another one.' He held out the couscous sieve, its holes blocked by black, dried-on gunge.

'How do you expect me to feed you when you destroy my kitchen? Making mud pies again . . . Anyone would think you were four, not forty.'

'It's the last time,' he said, knowing that, this time, it probably was. Lubna looked at him, unconvinced, then turned to go. 'Wait,' Ali said. 'Listen to this.' He recited the verses he'd been working on.

When he had finished, Lubna closed her eyes and silently repeated the lines, her lips shaping the words. She possessed the ability – remarkable, but not unknown among true poets – to memorize verse on a single hearing. 'There's one syllable too many in the line that ends with "Aragón".'

He looked at her, awed by her own alchemy: he'd given her the tricks of verse, and she'd left him far behind.

She seemed to read his mind. '*You taught me every day the bowman's art,*' she said, smiling in the lamplight.

'*And when your arm took aim,*' he said, completing the ancient couplet, '*you pierced my heart.*'

Lubna put her hand inside his open collar and let it slide down the line of hair that led to his navel. It rested there, cool and smooth.

24

He snaked his arm round her waist, above the jut of her hip. 'Your poem,' she said suddenly, pulling away, 'what does it mean?'

'It means what it says, and a lot more besides, like poems should.'

She nodded, and held her hand out for the ruined sieve. The muezzin's voice floated in from the nearby minaret. 'Listen. There goes the call for the last prayer. Don't be long.'

'I'll try. Oh,' he called after her, 'and can you do something about this cat of yours? It's already lost one of its seven lives. I made sure of that, when it knocked that water over the other day and ruined my work.'

And if it hadn't, he thought, *I'd never have known* . . . The thought jogged his memory. 'We'll be needing a good long length of wick,' he said to the beloved figure in the doorway. He held out a rat's-tail of twisted cotton. 'For the lamps. This is all we've got left. The evenings are drawing in.'

Lubna shivered, and called the cat. It stayed where it was, as deaf to its mistress as Ali was to the mosque, entranced by the dance of the moth round the flame.

Chapter 5

Back across the valley, in a place known to few, the man they called Layth concluded his evening prayers with a silent list of requests to his God. As usual, one of them concerned himself. The rest were all curses.

When he had finished, he turned to face the other Lions, some of whom were still kneeling and whispering their own private requests to the Almighty. But the two lines of men soon broke and formed a circle, rearranging their limbs to sit cross-legged on the rough hard ground. Often at this time he would speak to them – of violence and worship, martyrdom and purification – in his gentle, melodious voice. He electrified them, and made them ready to die – for God, they thought, but in reality for Layth.

But tonight he could no longer ignore their growing anger. It had been growing for days; weeks, even, while he had tried to shut it out. Tonight, though, he could almost physically smell it: black bile, festering in their livers, overpowering his charisma. He would let them speak first. He looked at them, smoky torchlight flashing in his green eyes, and stroked the beard that looked as if it didn't belong to the elfin face. His gaze wandered round the circle, then fixed on another pair of eyes; immediately, they looked at the floor. 'Come on, Dirgham . . . What's on your mind?'

A half-formed, boy's face dared to glance back. 'Nothing, Shaykh Layth.'

Layth nodded. It was an honest answer. The one they called Dirgham was from a poor artisan family of al-Bayyazin, like himself.

Unlike himself, there wasn't much up top. Except loyalty. When it came to it, Dirgham would be the first to sacrifice himself.

Layth turned to another face, this one long and grim. 'And you, Hattam?'

As usual, tall, cadaverous Hattam needed no prompting. 'Shaykh Layth, just look at where we are.' He threw up his hands, palms pointing at the low rock ceiling. 'We call ourselves lions. So why are we hiding in a hole, like foxes?'

Layth heard no murmur of agreement; but he felt one. Even if your heart was set on martyrdom and paradise, there were limits to what the rest of your body would endure on earth, or under it. They had been here for months now, seldom emerging from these tunnels and chambers that stank of piss and rats and bats. At least this central part of their underground headquarters was dry; dry as a hayloft. But they shivered in the cold and fumbled in the dark, and when they did go up and out, to replenish supplies, it was always at night. Hattam had a point.

'Because, Hattam,' Layth began slowly, looking into the man's disconcerting, death's-head eyes, 'the prudent lion conceals himself in his den until the moment is right. And we could have no better den than this, thanks be to God — and to Asad. But for him, we would never have known of this place.' Layth looked round the other faces. 'Here we are safe. We are invisible. We are under their very noses. And where else would we find such supplies of our most vital ingredient, here for the taking? Without this place, there would be no Remedy.' He gazed up and through the rock. 'A little bodily suffering is part of the rent we pay on an eternity in Paradise.'

'What you say is true, Shaykh Layth.' It was the schoolmasterly voice of Sarim, the oldest of the Lions. 'But the question we should encourage ourselves to ask is, *For how much longer?* You know what the poet said:

> *No arrow, unreleased, could win the day;*
> *No lion that spurned the hunt could catch its prey.'*

Sarim was the learned one, passed over for a job at the Secretariat. Disappointment, Layth knew, was often the sharpest spur to vengeance. 'You bring us reports from Asad,' Sarim continued, 'from the very heart of the Alhambra, about the rampant ungodliness that is rotting Granada from its core; of the building of yet another pleasure-palace on a site that had been set aside for a *madrasah*, a college for the teaching of the word of God; of the depiction in it of living beings, even – I seek refuge from the accursed Satan! – of the sons of Adam . . .' His voice trailed away, dumbstruck by such irreligion.

' . . . pictures painted, Asad tells us, by the foul and idolatrous hands of Cross-worshippers sent by that ally of devils, the tyrant Pedro!' Hattam spat the name out. 'This friendship of our self-styled sultan with the Nazarenes, *this* is what will be the ruin of Granada, of al-Andalus, of Islam! *We must do something, now!*'

Beads of spittle arced through the torchlight. Even Layth was silenced. Hattam alarmed him: he existed at the tipping-point between sanity and madness. But at least he and the other Lions were growling, hungry for the hunt. They were living up to their name. To their names: again, Layth looked from one to the other – crazy emaciated Hattam, angry poetical Sarim, gormless faithful Dirgham and the rest of them. The ten men here before him, together with himself and the absent Asad, had all adopted different Arabic names for the king of beasts. It made it safer that only he knew all their true identities. The lion was said to have over a hundred such names in all, more than the ninety-nine Most Beautiful Names of God.

'We are twelve,' Layth said softly. He paused. 'But we are worth twelve hundred of the ungodly . . . and twelve thousand of the infidels!' His green eyes flashed – and saw that they were with him now, to a man, to a Lion. 'The strength of our group, our *pride*, is not in numbers, not in brute force, but in our solidarity, our cunning. Or do I need to remind you that the mere assassin's dagger is no use these days?' The dagger had of course been of excellent use, back in the days when court security was lax, in eliminating the current sultan's father, Sultan Yusuf . . .

For an instant, Layth let his mind begin to wander back, to the part he had played in that glorious, sordid piece of history – then stopped himself. He knew where those memories would lead.

'No,' he went on. 'As you all know, we have another way of . . . of attaining the Red One.' He smiled at the men, then focused his green gaze on Haydar. 'What news?'

Haydar was their back-room boy, the quiet one with the tiny, precise gestures, exact mind and steady hands that were perfect for measuring and compounding (and embezzling: unlike Sarim, he had landed a government job – then lost it for failing to share the loot with his superiors). 'Our daily production rate has increased, Shaykh Layth. Stocks of the Remedy, as you have seen, are well up to expectations.' Haydar's head twitched minutely in the direction of the raised side-chamber. 'That is all I can say, for the time being. Now, of course, I do not wish to press . . .' his eyelids fluttered slightly, 'but I can do no more than follow the Syrian recipe . . . that is, until the Alchemist fulfils his promise.'

And there was the problem. Exact, efficient Haydar was no more than a follower of recipes. He lacked the spark of brilliance – or luck – that ignited the true scientist; that fired Ali the Alchemist. And so it was the Alchemist, that notorious wine-swilling *zindiq*, on whom the whole wheel of their fortunes pivoted. It was he who had discovered the improvement to the recipe, the refinement that would make the Remedy devastatingly, horrifyingly effective.

'By God's will, we haven't long to wait,' Layth said. 'The Alchemist's most recent communication said he needed only a few more days. And, for your information, I am going now to see him in person and to ... to exert a little pressure.'

'Hah, *pressure*!' It was Hattam. 'What you mean is that you're going to press some gold into his stinking hand, to spend on wine and hashish and whoring and –'

'The end,' Layth said, quietly, silencing Hattam with an unblinking stare, 'justifies the means.'

Layth wrapped his *taylasan* – half shawl, half cowl – tighter round his neck. The year had turned a corner and let the cold in. Especially here, where a shiver ran down the dark defile, riffling the invisible stream and the leaves above him. Still higher above him rose the walls, their massive presence felt, not seen – except now, for a moment, in a flicker of lightning. Layth wound the *taylasan* tighter and increased his pace.

The end justifies the means. It certainly had, fourteen years before. In fact two ends: the death of the old sultan, and the death of the sultan's killer – Mabruk, the black slave who had given him, Layth, such pain.

And such pleasure ... now Layth let his memories loose, felt the blood thrill through his body until every vein was pulsing with the name: Mabruk, *Mabruk*. It didn't matter how much his brain repented, and sometimes even his heart. His body, this vile heap of dust and ashes, bone and blood, could never repress the memory of that pleasure. It dwelt in every cell.

So did the guilt. Layth had found it was easier, much easier, to do to death a human enemy – even a human lover – than to kill his own relentless remorse. So he had learned to live with that remorse, and to enjoy it.

Soon, though, all would be purified ... Layth quickened his pace again, wrapped the *taylasan* tighter still. A few more days, the

31

Alchemist had said, and then the new Remedy would be ready, and they would have purity, and power.

The power to destroy the ungodly and the infidels. The power, perhaps, to rule the world – if not to destroy it too.

Chapter 6

'This is the life!' Abu Abdallah set down the heavy goblet. Instantly, a silent Christian house-slave appeared and refilled it. Blood-coloured sherbet, made with pomegranates from Lisan al-Din's estates and snow from Jabal Shulayr, winked in the light from a score of lamps. 'I told you we'd be orbiting in high circles, my boy.'

Sinan, who was still sitting in the place on the floor where he had prayed the evening prayer beside Abu Abdallah, looked around. He'd never dreamed that such circles even existed below the seven heavens. The long wall of Lisan al-Din's guest pavilion was a firmament of crystal lamps in niches, flanked by large gilded jars in alcoves. The side walls were hung with rich textiles – Egyptian velvets, Sicilian silks embroidered with leaping gazelles and looping Arabic script, Damascus brocades. Other costly fabrics covered the plump mattresses and cushions that lined the walls. On a low brass table in front of his master, superbly carved chessmen were deployed on a marquetry board, ready to do battle. The large folding doors that occupied the fourth wall of the pavilion lay open. To tell the truth it was a little too cold; but, as Abu Abdallah said, the scents that drifted in from the garden beyond the doors were worth a sultan's ransom – Indian jasmine and stocks, clipped myrtle and honeysuckle, the last late roses – scents that mingled with the sound of a fountain fed by the nearby Ayn al-Dam', the Spring of Tears.

'One day,' Abu Abdallah said, 'when I'm elevated to my vizierate, I'll build a place like this. And I'll get some decent white slaves to replace you, Sinan . . .'

Sinan's mouth opened.

'...when you have become my Secret Secretary. Fear not, Sinan, you too will undergo elevation.' The sherbet jug rematerialized. Abu Abdallah waved it away. 'I'll lack nothing money can buy. And power will get me anything it can't buy. Anything except −' He stopped abruptly, stared into the fragrant darkness.

Suddenly the fountain sounded deafening against the unsaid words.

'Except what, master?'

'You know, Sinan.'

Sinan nodded.

In his attempts to piece together from his master's jigsaw ramblings a picture of the old man's former family life − if it could be called that − Sinan always lost count after about wife number ten. He was pretty sure that, during Abu Abdallah's travelling decades, there had been five known children, littered across Asia from Damascus to Delhi. Littered, abandoned, and probably now all dead. As for the fifteen stationary years since he himself had entered Abu Abdallah's household, there had been three more wives − divorced, like all the rest − and two more children, dead in infancy. Of those three women who had occupied the same house as him, Sinan naturally knew nothing. For him they had existed beyond a social chasm as deep as the gulf the separated hell and heaven. What was surprising was that he also knew nothing of his master's feelings towards those women. His only conclusion was that there had been no feelings.

Sinan thought he knew why. As a personal slave, he was his master's sounding-board. And just as a well-made lute that starts as a passive resonator begins, with time, to respond actively to its player, so he too had begun to think, sometimes even to forethink, his master's innermost thoughts.

It was all to do with the concubines. If he had given up counting Abu Abdallah's wives, Sinan had never even tried to enumerate

34

the slaves of his bed. Given or bought or swapped along the road, these were the women his master talked about. They were the ones he'd found moving, in every sense; wives tied him, left him cold. Abu Abdallah's life had lurched between poles: motion and stasis; pleasure and duty; abandonment and entanglement. Somewhere, where the opposites met and touched, there was perfect happiness. That transient point was only to be found on the road, and Abu Abdallah had only ever been there once.

'Just that once, you know,' the old man sighed, their thoughts touching. 'In the Maldives. I can still hear her laughing ... And then I buggered things up and had to run.' He stared into the scented dark beyond the doorway. "How long," he recited, in a low clear monotone,

> ' "*until my overburdened heart-strings start*
> *to fray and sever?*
> *Ah me! Each day I love and lose, desire and part;*
> *and so . . . for ever?*" '

Ah, but you wouldn't understand, Sinan. You never ... feel the urge. How many times have I offered to buy you a nice little wife? Black. White. Striped, if you want. And you just shake your woolly head.' Suddenly he turned and grinned mischievously. 'I sometimes think you must be a Secret Eunuch, not a Secret Secretary ... Come to think of it, it's never too late to have the chop. You'll be worth a lot more without your balls when I flog you off in the slave market.'

'Master!'

Abu Abdallah laughed and shook his head. 'Oh Sinan, you know me better than the back of your black hand, but you still can't tell when I'm winding you up. Anyway, enough of this moping. Let's go for a stroll into al-Bayyazin. You know what the Prophet, peace be upon him, said: "Ward off old age by walking." '

Sinan was about to mention the likelihood of rain, but thunder growled the warning instead.

'Sounds like we might be in for a soaking,' Abu Abdallah said. 'But you never know, we might bump into my perfect woman. Hmm; I quite fancy what I've seen so far in Granada. And if we don't find her . . . well, we can come back and have a game of chess. You could even let your old master win for once.'

Sinan went out to fetch a covered lamp from the slaves' quarters. Outside, beneath the heady perfume of the night, there was a subtler note. It was a scent he'd hardly known in his life with Abu Abdallah, a life lived mostly in the harsh parched outer provinces of Morocco: the smell of earth, damp from the fountain's spray. And in an instant quicker than a thought it transported him – back to the bank of the Great River and to the memory that never let him go.

Abu Abdallah said Sinan didn't understand. He did. He too had loved, once. Unlike Abu Abdallah, he knew he could never love again.

There were few other people about. It wasn't just the hour and the dark that kept the Granadans indoors, but also the threat of the storm. Sinan thought back to the morning, to the top of the Watchtower, when they had seen the clouds simmering over the rim of hills. Now the storm was loose on the plain below, shaking sheets and throwing forks of lightning. A distant trident hit Jabal Shulayr's snowy head, silhouetting the towers of the Alhambra with a lurid backlight. '*O most generous God!*' Abu Abdallah exclaimed. 'Looks like we're in for a real downpour.' A delayed grumble of thunder reached them, as if the mountain had groaned under the blow. Granada was in suspense, awaiting the deluge.

But still no rain fell as they trod the steep and intricate alleys of al-Bayyazin, negotiating steps and piles of manure by the feeble light of Sinan's borrowed lamp. Other faint lights came from piercings in the long blank walls of houses, together with faint voices, complaining, cajoling, praying. The handful of people they met all had lamps too. With their faces uplit by flame and downlit by lightning, they looked to Sinan more ghoulish than human. He pictured them rising from those ranks of graves that he had seen from the tower . . . Then he wondered how he looked to them. Worse than ghoulish, to judge by the expressions of fear and one man's muttered charm against the accursed *jinn*. It must all go back to that killing of the old sultan – 'by the hand of a black slave', Lisan al-Din's disagreeable colleague Ibn Zamrak had said. So, all black slaves were now tarred with the murderer's brush.

In the daylight however, Sinan recalled, his unwonted appearance had also provoked other reactions – sly glances from above face-veils, and once an appraising stare from behind the twitched curtain of a litter. He had even caught a comment in a girlish voice, underlined with a nudge by the speaker in her friend's ribs – ' . . . and you know what they say about Blacks . . . I mean, their *things* . . .' – followed by a ripple of giggles. Sinan thought of the giraffe sent as a curiosity to the sultan of Morocco by the emperor of Mali, and knew how the animal must have felt. *God*, he consoled himself, *is with those who are patient*.

But in this beautiful threatening city Sinan had never experienced anything like the look that lay in wait for him. He and Abu Abdallah had entered a particularly narrow passage, a deep shadowed slot between tall walls. They were picking their way gingerly, avoiding the detritus at their feet. And then a shadow moved, and became a man. He carried no light. But for a moment he was exposed in close-up by Sinan's lamp, like some nocturnal predator caught hunting through the houses – a man with a *taylasan* wrapped round his neck, a heavy beard worn on a strangely delicate face, and eyes of a green that took Sinan back to his recent first journey by sea, across the dreadful bottomless waters of the Strait. And in that moment, in those lamp-lit eyes, Sinan saw disgust – and lust.

They heard footsteps hurrying away. *'God protect us!'* Abu Abdallah whispered. 'You wouldn't want to bump into that thing at night in a dark alley.'

'Master,' Sinan said, 'we just did.'

Abu Abdallah's nervous chuckle made him feel calmer. It also made him realize just how shaken he'd been by that look of utter loathing, and longing. There was something else, too, in those green eyes, something that drew him down into the deepest recesses of his past, beyond memory.

They walked on. The alley opened out. In another flash of lightning, Sinan saw that the houses here looked more prosperous. Boxy lattices projected from blind walls, dappling the street with fitful light and turning it into a nocturnal negative of a forest glade. Something in the scene took Sinan back . . .

A cry came, sudden and sharp, from one of the lattices. A shutter shot open. A long lithe creature leapt across their path.

The rest happened in a moment so overloaded that it seemed to miss its step, stagger, stop.

A thunderbolt struck right by them in a flash of sound and light and fire that sent them reeling. Sinan caught his master and fell with him just as the heavy lattice smashed into the wall where they'd been standing. They lay there motionless, not even breathing, in the horrid timeless silence that followed.

Sounds began: the beating of their hearts – they were alive – their first heaving breaths, a patter, hard, of falling splinters, soft, of falling rain.

They lay there, waiting for time to regain its balance.

Then there was a scream. It was a woman's scream, and it seemed to break loose and run raving up and down between the houses. They both jerked up at the sound and saw her standing in the flamelight that licked at the hole where the lattice had been, hair uncovered, flying, electrified, her hands clutching at her head as if to hold it on to her body, her white face ripped open by a silent black gash of mouth. She disappeared; reappeared on the street, looked about her, frantic, left and right, as if to see where her scream had gone, then flew noiselessly after it and was swallowed by the dark.

Abu Abdallah was sitting up, looking in the apparition's direction, towards the narrow alleyway from which they'd come. Then he seemed to pull himself together. 'Quick. Into the house. There may be someone still alive.'

Sinan rose, groggy; something heavy had hit him on the back of the head. He found the entrance of the house wide open, the massive door and its frame blown clean out of the wall.

He went in, calling. 'Is anyone there? *Anyone there?*'

There was no answer; only a smell, like the smell of . . . of hell, Sinan thought. A stink of brimstone and burning bone.

The fire was in the room on the street side of the interior courtyard. Sinan made it in through the doorway, but no further. He shielded his face against the heat – and saw from beneath his hand that there *was* someone here. A man. On the ground. Staring up at him.

He could get no closer. The heat was too great, the flames closing in. But it didn't matter. The man's stare was sightless. Sinan knew he was dead from the angle of the head. And – *why?* – there was a puddle of blood on the floor, winking in the glare of the flames as it inched towards him from the corpse.

In the last moment before the heat became too great to bear, Sinan saw why the head was askew, and where the blood was coming from – from a savage diagonal gash that had ripped with bestial force through the man's neck, all but severing the head from the body.

Chapter 7

María's feet had once been so tough. They had been hardened by goat-tracks and threshing-floors, and by the beaten earth of the hut where she and Jaime had found shelter after the Death took their mother and father. With those feet María could out-run and out-climb her brother any day. Jaime was younger than her, of course, but not much, and he was a boy.

Now she realized how much they hurt, those feet that used to be María's. Until tonight she'd never run in her life as Lubna. María's feet had turned into Lubna's, cocooned in Cordoban slippers, caressed by carpets, tucked under her when she sat, neat as a cat on a cushion, her fingers chasing *taqsims* up and down the lute-strings.

Tonight, though, Lubna had run, run until the rock had ripped her bare feet ragged. Where she had run to she didn't know. All she knew was that her feet hurt so much that she tried to think them off her body. *They are no longer Lubna's.*

But, in truth, she knew that the pain was everywhere, and that none of her was Lubna any more. It was Ali who had called her by that name, given his purchase an identity. It was the word he'd tried to whisper, staring up into her eyes while the blood drained from that gash in his neck: Lubna, *White-as-Milk*. Her name had ebbed away with his life.

She stared into the night. There was nothing to measure the blackness, nothing to make it pass. Even the *Pater Noster* wouldn't come. So she lay there, lost to time and place.

41

If Lubna was no more, she wondered, then was anything left of María?

There was still someone left who had known María: her little brother, Jaime, stolen with her off the mountainside. The boy she'd looked after when their parents were gone, hugging him to keep him warm; cleaning him up when he'd fallen off that wall, smack on his face . . . she pictured his poor crooked nose and wondered if it had ever grown straight again. He was so close, physically. But Jaime too had become someone else. In every sense but that of distance, he was beyond reach. Jaime was gone. So María was gone too.

She lay on, lost to time, place, self, staring into the dark. In some curious way she felt liberated.

She only noticed that a piece of the night had turned to grey when a darker, human form appeared against it and leaned in towards her. She wasn't afraid; pain trumped fear. The figure slowly turned, and left.

Suddenly she knew where she was: in the cave, above the graves. For a moment she thought of all the dead laid out below her. She wasn't afraid of them, either. Perhaps she'd joined them . . . that was it. But no: Ali had once told her that the first thing that happened when they buried you was that two angels came and asked you your name and your religion. 'And what will you tell them?' he had asked. 'Lubna, or María?'

'Both, I suppose,' she said. 'And then I'll tell them I'm a Christian.'

Ali laughed. 'I think the angels are good Muslims. But it's up to you, if you want to make things difficult for yourself.'

The second thing that happened, Ali said, was that you heard the feet of those who'd buried you, tap-tapping as they left.

There had been no angels, no departing footfalls. Only that hunched and soundless figure – the old woman, she remembered now, who lived in the hole next door. Many of the caves up here had occupants, she recalled, poor, mad, reclusive, abandoned. Lubna had sometimes seen their eyes looking at her out of the gloom, like those of frightened animals. The old woman was different. She had always come to the entrance of her lair, and glared like a witch.

And now she remembered why her bloodied feet had brought her here: to ask for help. From whom, she didn't know.

Slowly, the night was greying to dawn. Inside the cave, details began to emerge: rough niches carved in the walls, and a pile of rags that never moved – ever since the Death had come back to the city the year before, people left abandoned clothing well alone. It was rumoured that the Death lurked in it. They said that half the rag-pickers of Granada had died in that last visitation.

Other details were emerging, from her memory. The Death . . . that was why this cave was perfect, Ali had said. Its last occupant had been a victim. No one would come poking round here. 'Just bring what I give you,' he'd told her. 'Take it into the inner chamber' – there was the way in, still dark against the lightening rock –'and put it under the stone that lies in the deepest niche.'

'Why?' she'd asked, knowing she wasn't meant to.

Ali had looked past her and said, 'Someone helps. Don't ask who. Not now.'

And Ali's 'not now' – suddenly the knowledge flash-flooded over her – had turned to never.

She wept at last, sobbed herself to sleep in the cold hard light, and knew nothing more until they came for her.

Chapter 8

'My dear Sinan, I don't deny that thunderstorms are strange things,' Abu Abdallah said. It was the morning after that bolt from the black in al-Bayyazin. 'There are some scholars, for instance, who say that the screw-pine only blooms when lightning strikes near by.'

'Yes, but master . . .'

From his seat on the ambling mule, Abu Abdallah ignored his slave, walking beside the animal. 'And I once heard of the case of a cat in the mountains of the Yemen that was hit by a thunderbolt as it sat on a drum. It was found sealed inside the drum, perfectly unharmed.'

'But master, I swear I saw it.'

'Nonsense, boy. It was a trick of the light, a shadow cast by the flames. When did a thunderbolt ever cut a man's throat?'

'But someone did,' Sinan protested. 'Or some . . . thing.' He pictured that horrible gash, inflicted with subhuman brutality.

'What, you mean that *thing* that jumped across our path? That was a cat, you fool. An ordinary domestic feline. A moggy.'

They fell silent. Both of them thought of that other creature – the man with the green eyes and the look of unalloyed malevolence, scuttling away – what, a minute or two before the bolt struck?

'Master,' Sinan said, 'you told me once about the . . .the *yogis* in India who could change into beasts.'

'You mean the were-tigers of Barwan. Yes, I heard that people had been found dead, killed by them, with all the blood drained from their bodies. God is the most knowing . . . But that was in

45

India – in the East, where the Almighty created nine tenths of the world's wonders. We, Sinan, are in the West – almost as far west as you can go without falling off the edge of the world into the Encompassing Ocean. We are on the solid ground of clear empirical fact.'

Abu Abdallah, however, didn't sound entirely convinced by what he said, Sinan thought. If things seemed solid in the light of day, the events of the previous night seemed to belong to a dream – not to the clear dream-visions that came from God, but to the confusions inspired by Satan. Sinan wanted to blank them out of his memory. He tried to let his senses dwell in the present moment, on this path that wound around the contour of the valley through the rain-washed morning air, taking them from al-Bayyazin to the Alhambra.

But there was no hiding the truth in the clear light of this day. Up above them, sharp against the tawny hillside, a small cortege was picking its way between the terraced graves below the city wall, following a lurching bier. 'Look, master,' Sinan said. 'That must be him they're burying.'

'Not much left to bury, poor bugger . . .' Abu Abdallah said, shaking his head.

They continued in silence, both reliving the nightmare they had gone through only hours before: the pale shocked faces of the neighbours, the chain-gang that had formed, too late, to bring water from the cistern of the local mosque – even Abu Abdallah had lent a hand with the pots – the sweet-acrid stink of water on carbonized human flesh. The corpse, when they got to it, had been so badly burned that it wasn't clear it had ever been human.

Eventually Abu Abdallah spoke again, as they entered the cleft that separated the Alhambra from the sultan's garden-palace of Jannat al-Arif. 'Whatever else they're blessed with here in Granada,' he said, 'it's not charity. What was it that neighbour of his said last night, just as we were dousing the corpse? "Hah! Marinated in wine – then carbonadoed by a thunderbolt! *That's* divine justice for you."'

'That's what he said, master. But I tell you, the man was dead *before* he was burned. I saw ...'

'Enough! Do I have to remind an ass like you that I am the former Malikite Judge of the Sultanate of Delhi? And the former Chief Justice of the Sultanate of the Maldivian Archipelago? Do I have to remind you that you are a slave? That your value as a witness is only equal to that of a woman?'

'Then I'm worth *half* a free man ...'

'*Silence!* When I send you for the chop and the dogs are gobbling up your giblets you won't be a man at all. You'll be worth a pretty penny as a ball-less harem guard – and bugger all in the witness-box.' This time, Sinan refused the bait. Abu Abdallah looked down at him, unable to hide the smile beneath the pretended fury. 'Come to think of it, what *is* the witness-value of a eunuch slave? Hmm ... must be getting rusty ... have to look it up in the *Muwatta* ...'

Sinan kept his counsel until his master's ramblings had ceased and they turned the corner to follow the long, bastion-studded southern wall of the Alhambra. 'She'll back me up, master,' he said. 'About the man being dead before the bolt struck. I mean that slave-woman we saw running from the house.'

'Huh, some witnesses: two slaves, one a woman and the other a black soon-to-be eunuch. But, yes, we should try and find that woman. Apart from anything else, she looked ... highly *promising*.' Abu Abdallah stroked his jutting beard.

For the first time since the events of the previous night, Sinan smiled. His master was getting back to his old self.

'Come on, man. Out with it.'

'Out with what?' Abu Abdallah looked ingenuously at his friend Lisan al-Din.

'My dear sir, you know perfectly well, or I'm not the Grand Vizier of Granada.'

Sinan glanced from his master, who wore the look, too innocent to be true, of a boy caught scrumping figs, to the crumpled and gloomy features of Lisan al-Din.

If he had made it home last night to his palace at the Spring of Tears, the Grand Vizier had not called in on his guest. But Sinan had heard from Lisan al-Din's slaves that the great man often worked late and then stayed on in his office, awake into the small hours, simultaneously compiling several large works of history. That was why they called him, in court circles, the Man of Two Lives. He burned the candle at both ends and left a mere stub of sleep, an hour or two snatched before the dawn call to prayer. Now, set against the light of the lattice in his shadowed cabinet of an office, its ceiling of dark wood picked out in dull and rufous gold, he looked even more umbrageous than usual.

'If you wish, then, I shall spell it out.' The Grand Vizier jutted his lower lip. 'Not long ago, I received letters from a number of our mutual friends – Ibn Khaldun and Ibn Marzuq, to mention but two – informing me of *your death*.' A functionary brought in a paper. Sinan saw Lisan al-Din write a word on it – 'Refused' – without apparently taking his eyes off Abu Abdallah. 'And here you are, sitting before me, to all appearances alive and well. Looking, indeed, as chipper as a man half your age.'

'Ah, yes, my death . . . I can explain everything,' Abu Abdallah said, shifting in his seat and moistening his lips with his tongue. Sinan had never seen his master look so uncomfortable.

'Pray do, dear friend,' Lisan al-Din said. 'I *assume* you haven't been granted earthly immortality.'

'Immortal? *Me*? I'd sooner die! It's . . . as if to say . . . I mean, when my travels, my earlier travels, came to an end, and I was welcomed home as a celebrity, feted by the late sultan in Fez, elevated to his

48

circle of intimates . . . and I'd like to point out here that, to my knowledge, no single person has seen as much of God's created world as I have. Once, in Anatolia, I met an Egyptian traveller who claimed –'

'Oh, get to the point, man!' the Grand Vizier barked. 'You're meant to be dead, for Heaven's sake!'

'Well, after our own former sultan was assassinated – strangled, if you recall, by his, um . . .'

'By his Grand Vizier. My counterpart. I do know the story.'

Until now, Sinan had never seen his master blush.

'The thing is,' Abu Abdallah continued, 'after that sad incident, I lost all influence at court and ended up with a bum posting in the sticks. It's no fun being a provincial judge, I can tell you, stuck in a one-camel town between the Atlas and the Ocean. I stagnated. You know what the poet says: "Only streams that flow are fit to drink, for water that stagnates is sure to stink." Well, I was beginning to stink, metaphorically speaking of course. I was rotting away from the brain down. It got to the stage where if I'd heard yet another idiotic land dispute or yet another scrofulous peasant divorcing his clapped-out wife, I'd have thrown off my turban, stood on my head and screamed, right there in the court room. And there were certain other . . . what-you–might-call predisposing factors.'

Lisan al-Din's basset-hound gaze studied his friend's eyes as they darted about the room. ' "*Predisposing factors*"? Would you care to elucidate?'

Abu Abdallah swallowed audibly. 'Well, financial obligations – debts, to put it bluntly – in Fez. I knew I'd never be able to pay them off on a provincial judge's salary. My only chance was by taking off and seeking God's bounty on the road. At the same time, I knew that if I did that, my creditors in the capital would think I was bolting. So I wrote to a trusted friend and got him to spread the rumour round Fez, that . . . that I'd died.'

Sinan saw the Grand Vizier's jowls quiver, whether in shock or amusement he couldn't tell.

'Well, they were hardly going to come out to the Back of the Back of Beyond Beyond to check up, were they? Oh, that's what I called that miserable place – not bad is it? The Back of the Back of . . .' Lisan al-Din tapped his writing-desk impatiently. 'Well, anyway, one day, before dawn, I took to the road with nothing but the last of my cash. And Sinan, my faithful slave.'

'*And* your irrepressible optimism.' Lisan al-Din shook his head, very slowly. 'Suicide, Abu Abdallah, is a mortal sin. So, I should imagine, is simulated suicide, but we would have to get a *fatwa* on that from someone better qualified than I. Be that as it may: the fact is, here you are, wandering about like a sufi student, off to find your fortune at an age when most men of your station have retired, to be supported and cherished by loving wives and children.'

Abu Abdallah looked down for a moment, then back at his friend. 'I found fame, as you know. Or it found me. The fortune came and went.'

'What about the third *f* ?' Lisan al-Din asked.

'What, "frolicking" . . . ?' Abu Abdallah said with a grin. 'Or to put it plainly, "fu–"'

A stentorian clearing of the Grand Vizieral throat just covered the shameless word; this time, Sinan blushed, on his master's behalf. 'I was thinking of something a *trifle* more delicate,' Lisan al-Din said. ' "Family", as it happens.'

'Oh,' Abu Abdallah said, his smile now a picture of innocence. '*As it happens*, Lisan, I was going to say "fun" if you hadn't interrupted me . . . Well, I admit that women have been one of the joys of my travelling life.' *Have been*, he thought, wondering about his choice of tense. The smile slipped from his face as that haunting woman of the night before flitted across his mind.

'I don't know how you keep it up, at your age,' Lisan al-Din sighed. Clearly he thought of Abu Abdallah's powers as present, and active.

50

'Oh, I suppose it's to do with the humours. I tend towards the sanguine, myself. I take it you're more the atrabilious or melancholy type? With more than a touch of the phlegmatic?'

'So I am informed by my physician,' the Grand Vizier said. 'Which reminds me: can you . . . recommend anything, from your vast experience? Something to, er, rejuvenate the member concerned?'

'What, your old Mamluk's not standing to attention, is he? Like jousting with a rope, is it?'

Sinan's eyes took refuge in a recess of the coffered ceiling.

The Grand Vizier of Granada cleared his throat. 'Well, yes, one could say that, I suppose, in a manner of speaking.'

'Iron filings,' Abu Abdallah said, tapping his nose. 'Guaranteed to stiffen your, um, resolve. Taken internally, of course, with a little crocodile-suet. But, hang on, that's what did for my brother-in-law in India, the sultan of Coromandel. Caused a nasty accident, it did . . .' Sinan held his breath; he had heard the details. To his relief, Abu Abdallah refrained from describing them. 'Hmm,' he went on, stroking his beard, 'there's that funny fish from the Aral Sea. But you've got to eat it fresh – raw, in fact. Ah, I know! Skinks' kidneys. Just the job.'

'*Skinks' kidneys*?' Lisan al-Din exclaimed. Abu Abdallah nodded vigorously. The Grand Vizier threw his head back and emitted a creaking sound that Sinan realized was an expression of amusement. 'Oh, Abu Abdallah,' he wheezed, 'God be praised that you're not dead!'

Sinan saw a figure standing in the door. It was Zayd the Clerk, his fair Berber features trying hard to look unsurprised by the extraordinary phenomenon of the Grand Vizier laughing. 'Yes?' Lisan al-Din said, pulling himself together. 'What is it?'

'With your permission, sir, the latest batch of invoices, for your esteemed signature.'

'God in Heaven . . . I won't even think about how much this is costing,' Lisan al-Din said with a groan as his reed-pen scratched on the papers.

51

'I've had the artisans and the mechanics follow the instructions in al-Jazari's book, to the letter,' Zayd said. 'That's why the . . . the sums are mounting.'

'Take the damned things to Accounts and never let me see them again,' the Grand Vizier said, holding out the papers as though they stank. Zayd the Clerk took them, bowed and hurried out of the room in one elegant movement. 'Do you know al-Jazari's book?' Lisan al-Din asked Abu Abdallah.

'Not as such . . .'

'With your permission, sir, I think you mean his *Book of Ingenious Devices*,' Sinan said.

'*Ma sha Allah!*' the Grand Vizier whispered. 'I keep telling you this boy of yours is a prodigy . . . Where did you light upon al-Jazari's work, Sinan?'

'In the library of the Qarawiyyin Mosque in Fez, sir.' Sinan remembered back to the time when his master had been researching the account of his travels, and he, still a small boy, had surreptitiously explored the Illustrated Books section of that famous library. One of al-Jazari's vivid diagrams came to mind – the water-clock in the form of an elephant.

'In the library of the Qarawiyyin Mosque . . .' Lisan al-Din repeated, smiling at Sinan and shaking his head in disbelief as he recalled his own visits to the greatest centre of learning in the Western world. 'Abu Abdallah, are you sure I can't persuade you to part with Sinan, this marvel of creation?'

'The answer's no, Lisan. But, look now, fair's fair. I've spilled my beans. What about yours? Are you going to tell me about this . . . *ingenious device* that you're knocking up for the sultan?'

'My answer also remains in the negative, my dear friend.' For a moment, the Grand Vizier's features softened; Sinan wondered if he was going to laugh again. 'But since you have been so admirably frank with me about your own . . . ingenious *demise*, then I will impart a little more of the background to my sultanic surprise. Take a pen and paper, Sinan,' he said, motioning towards an alcove in the wall. 'You may use my ink. That's it. Now, write at the top, in the middle, "Isma'il". Ah! As you said, Abu Abdallah, the boy's a calligrapher! "Isma'il I", to be precise. Then the dates of his reign, "713-25".* And now a vertical line down . . .'

Gradually, in Sinan's fine hand, the more recent part of the family tree of the Nasrid dynasty grew down the paper:

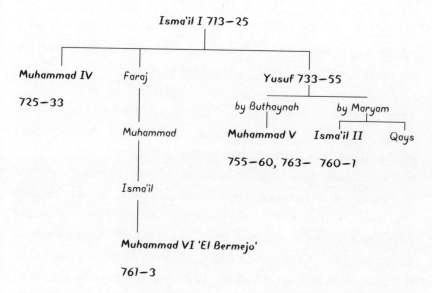

'El Bermejo, as you saw yesterday,' Lisan al-Din said, sitting back, 'is the foul usurper whose head now forms the chief ornament to the gate of this illustrious fortress. It pains me to include him, and that epicene specimen Isma'il II, among the sultans of this noble dynasty. But there you are, all trees bear rotten as well as wholesome fruit.'

'But I don't get it,' Abu Abdallah said. 'I mean, how does all this fit in with your mysterious surprise for the sultan?'

'You will recall,' Lisan al-Din said, 'that the late and blessed Sultan Yusuf died at the hand of a slave – you see, Sinan, black slaves or

*AH 713-25 corresponds to AD1314-25. The dates in the dynastic tree below can also be converted approximately to AD by adding 600.

53

grand viziers, we're all potential regicides – to be succeeded by his son, our own beloved sultan, Muhammad V.' Abu Abdallah nodded impatiently. 'Now, after the first five glorious years of our sultan's reign, his step-mother, Maryam – ex-Christian, ex-concubine, like most Sultana Mothers – hatched a plot with El Bermejo. In short, they toppled our blessed sultan from the throne and installed in his place that miserable half-brother of his, Isma'il, a fat fairy who plaited his hair with silk ribbons . . .' Lisan al-Din shuddered. 'I must admit the coup was deftly planned. The sultan only got away by the skin of his teeth. I followed him, and after many adventures we made it to Morocco, as your master knows.'

'As I know too, by your grace's permission,' Sinan said. 'I remember seeing you in Fez, sir. Three times.' Perhaps Lisan al-Din did recall the slave, then little more than a boy . . . Yes, he could picture those eyes, studying him from the shadows.

'Look, Lisan,' Abu Abdallah broke in. 'I know all this already . . .'

The Grand Vizier held up a hand. 'Constructing history, my dear Abu Abdallah, is like constructing a building. It will not stand unless you lay the foundation first. Where was I? Ah, yes. Then, as the saying goes, God caused Maryam to choke on her own plot: the coarse and behennaed cousin El Bermejo seized the throne in turn, less than eight months later, killing Isma'il and his brother Qays in the process.' A minor functionary appeared with a bunch of papers. 'Oh, these tiresome things,' the Grand Vizier said with a groan.

But the narrative hardly faltered. Sinan marvelled as the Grand Vizier simultaneously scanned the papers, annotated them, and continued his account – of Muhammad V's clandestine return to Spain, his campaign against the usurping El Bermejo, the winning back of his land, city by city, castle by castle. 'Until at last the usurper fled to our neighbour . . . Don Pedro, king of Castile . . . surnamed by his detractors "the Cruel" . . .' a final signature ' . . . and Pedro, in his wisdom, put El Bermejo out of his misery. It is said he dealt

54

the first blow with his own lance. Soon after, a kingly gift arrived in Granada: the traitor's head, and those of his lackeys up there with him on the parapet. Misguided worshipper of the Cross he may be, but Don Pedro is a true friend to the Muslims.'

Sinan looked perplexed. 'But I thought we were supposed to be enemies, sir, and especially here in al-Andalus. The barbaric Christian hordes, I mean, depriving us Muslims of our rightful land.'

Lisan al-Din smiled. 'Oh, we are enemies, at heart. And from time to time on the field of battle. In theory – on paper – we are allies. In practice we are . . . let us say, *friendly* enemies.'

'I don't understand, sir. That is a paradox.'

'So it is, Master Sinan. Welcome to the world of politics.' The Grand Vizier looked at Abu Abdallah, who was staring at the gilding on the ceiling. 'Are you taking this all in, my old friend?'

'Look, Lisan, I'm not gaga yet,' Abu Abdallah said tetchily. 'I've heard it all before. Just tell me what all this has got to do with that thing you're keeping under wraps in the new courtyard.'

'Patience, my friend,' Lisan al-Din said. 'We are on the very verge of the dénouement. Now, Pedro had his own spot of bother with a half-brother – "Henry the Bastard of Trastámara" as the Castilians so infelicitously refer to him.' Abu Abdallah laughed; the Grand Vizier raised a hand. 'As you well know, with our Christian neighbours being limited to one wife, rather a lot of offspring are born out of wedlock.'

'What you save on the mothers-in-law,' Abu Abdallah said, twinkling, 'you lose on the bastards.'

'Oh, very droll,' Lisan al-Din said wearily. 'Whatever, the said Bastard of Trastámara seized the throne of Castile in his own coup, but Pedro regained it with a little help from, of all people, the son of the king of England – "the Black Prince", I believe they call him . . . Strange, is it not? Our beloved sultan and the infidel Don Pedro both succeeded to the throne within four years of each other, both at the tender age of sixteen. Both were temporarily unseated by unscrupulous half-brothers. Both returned in triumph to their thrones. This is why they feel a particular affinity for each other, even if one is a tyrant and misguided Cross-worshipper.'

'So where's the . . . the dénoue-thingie, Lisan? You *still* haven't told me what this has got to do with that sultanic mystery of yours. Or pudding, or whatever it is.'

'Ah, if you ask for an account from the foremost historian of our times, you get the full background, my dear Abu Abdallah. Willy-nilly.'

'The full background to *what*, Lisan, for Heaven's sake?'

'Very well, my impatient friend, I will come to the point. Now that Pedro is safely back on his throne, the sultan has sent him a request – a demand, one might say. You see, when El Bermejo fled to Seville, he took with him the most precious jewels from the treasury of the Alhambra. And when Don Pedro killed El Bermejo he, in turn, took the jewels – "into safe-keeping", as he put it. Some of these jewels are very precious indeed; the lamented Sultan Yusuf, in particular, was a great connoisseur of gems. And one of them, the Great Ruby, is precious above all.' He paused, and folded his brocaded arms.

'The Great Ruby?' Sinan said. 'You mentioned it before, sir.'

'So I did.' The Grand Vizier paused again. Then he held out the empty palm of his hand and gazed at it, as if to materialize the stone. 'It is an enormous balas ruby, peerless in size and clarity, unmatched in the intense redness of its hue – the deep, saturated crimson of gazelle's blood. Its origin is in the distant mountains of Badakhshan, where the lands of the Turkmen and the Tajiks, the Afghans and the Chinese, the Kashmiris and the Khotanis march, where the valleys soar, higher and higher, until they are lost in the margins of the sky.' Lisan al-Din looked at his friend. 'Even you, Abu Abdallah, have never penetrated those regions. Not even in your dreams.'

The old traveller had no response. He and Sinan stared at the Grand Vizier, entranced. 'Now, some of the more imaginative but ignorant of our people here in Granada have put it about that the Ruby is cursed,' Lisan al-Din continued. 'You see, the late Sultan Yusuf acquired it shortly before his dreadful end. The usurper Isma'il was also murdered not long after he claimed ownership of the stone. The next usurper, El Bermejo, actually had it on his unspeakable person when he was killed. Its earlier history is obscured by the mists of Middle Asia, but it is said that it once belonged to the Khwarizm Shah, that unfortunate monarch who met his own end at the hands of the Mongol hordes of Genghis Khan. The Ruby, in short, according to vulgar rumour, is soaked in blood. It is the material embodiment of *al-mawt al-ahmar*.'

'Forgive me sir . . . *red death*?' Sinan said.

'An idiomatic expression for a violent and unnatural demise,' Lisan al-Din explained. 'Be that as it may, our beloved sultan, while he is graciously willing to concede Pedro the other jewels – in return for very welcome services rendered – has requested the return of the Ruby. He argues, with his accustomed cogency, that he himself owned the stone for five years with no untoward effects. Moreover, in his most orthodox wisdom he wishes to impress the ignorant with a truth self-evident to all whom God has enlightened – namely, that no inanimate object can ever have an influence on our destinies. In a word, that all our fates are in the hand of Almighty God, Great and Powerful is He, and that to invest a mere lump of mineral with fateful properties is a species of polytheism.'

A bird swooped down past the lattice behind the Grand Vizier – a falcon, Sinan knew from its desolate cry as it stooped on some small creature down on the hillside below.

'I, of course, drafted the request for the Ruby's return,' Lisan al-Din went on. *'Be mindful, esteemed neighbour of ours*, it concludes, *that kings have gone to war for less* . . . Not bad, eh? Many a true word, as they say, is spoken in jest, and even in diplomacy. Pedro has naturally conceded to this gentle demand. His ambassadors will bring the Ruby and restore it to the sultan, amid suitable pomp, at the opening ceremony for the new court, coinciding with the Prophet's birthday. The whole occasion will be a tangible expression of the ties of neighbourly and mutual interest that bind Don Pedro, may God guide him to the true religion, with our own beloved sultan.' Lisan al-Din looked hard at Abu Abdallah. 'Now, my friend, keep all of this under your turban. The restoration of the Ruby is all part of the surprise. Not even the Sultanic Secretary knows about it. You see, we find these gestures have more effect on the populace when they are unexpected . . . As for the nature of the courtyard's centrepiece, you will have, my dear Abu Abdallah, to possess your pertinacious soul in patience. It is only another two weeks and two days until the ceremony. Assuming,' Lisan al-Din said with a frown, 'that Zayd the Clerk can finish the work on time.'

Abu Abdallah opened his mouth to protest; the Grand Vizier silenced him with a look. 'And on a completely different matter,' he said, firmly, 'I hear you and this marvellous slave of yours were at the site of last night's incident in al-Bayyazin. It would be interesting to hear your eye-witness accounts.'

The wraith-like figure of the fleeing slave-woman crossed Abu Abdallah's memory once more; not that she had ever been entirely absent from it.

Chapter 9

'*Kings have gone to war for less . . . kings have gone to war for less . . .*'
Don Pedro, king of Castile, paced the long reflective pool of his
palace in Seville, the Alcázar, in a swish of Moorish silk, repeating
the words through clenched teeth. The calm water mirrored arcades
where doves crooned and soaring Arabic script declared him
'Sultan Don Pedro'. It had all been done by artisans from Granada –
a mirror-image of his own Castilian painters working now at
the Alhambra for his old friend and enemy, Sultan Muhammad.
And in this looking-glass courtyard, Pedro even had Muhammad's
family motto on the plasterwork beneath the arches: *No one wins
but Allah.*

Pedro thought of the motto now, and substituted it for that other,
infuriating phrase. The throaty Arabic sounds calmed him, like a
mantra – '*Wa-la ghaliba illa 'llah . . . wa-la ghaliba illa'llah . . .*' For a
while, they made the squabbles of earthly kings seem insignificant.
But, as always, the words soon brought back that spring morning six
years before, when he'd had the pleasure of pigsticking El Bermejo.
He saw himself, holding up the dripping Ruby – and the other
phrase came back, with a vengeance: '*Bloody kings have gone to bloody
war for less . . .*'

'Sire,' a soft, panting voice said at his heels. 'I don't know . . .
why your highness . . . is so exercised by the words.' Abraham Ibn
Zarzar was having to trot to keep up with the tall blond king.
Pedro had given the Jewish physician a job when Muhammad lost
his throne nine years before. Since then he had become a fixture –

fixer as well as physician, occasional envoy, constant ear. 'It was a mere pleasantry . . . of Lisan al-Din's . . . And if it was intended as a threat . . . then I assure your highness that it is an empty one.'

Pedro stopped abruptly and swung round to face Abraham. 'But we *have* gone to war for less! Much less. More times than I can remember.'

'Sire, as your noble highness knows, that is all in the nature of a tournament, a great game of chess, played out upon the broad board of Iberia. You lose a few dozen foot-soldiers, maybe a knight or two; you win a castle. Sultan Muhammad does the same.'

'While, off the board,' Pedro said, looking into the pool, willing its calmness to soothe him, 'we swap physicians and interior decorators.'

'As ever, the sharp lance of your highness's jest pierces the target,' Abraham said, with courtierly unction. 'It's all a pastime, sire, between friends. And it's been stalemate ever since the demise of the late and much lamented King Alfonso.'

'*Requiescat in pace*,' Pedro said, crossing himself. His father had been the only crowned head so far to die of the Death. It had happened while he was besieging the Moors on Gibraltar in 1350, on that apocalyptic Good Friday of the pestilence. Pedro remembered the mute, bowed ranks of Muslims and Christians lining the royal corpse's route back to Seville, honouring the catafalque in that strange silent truce. Despite intermittent border skirmishes, the truce still lingered on. The will of God, it seemed, had stayed the worst of war.

The worst of war with the Moors, that was. On other fronts things were bad and getting worse. 'Abraham,' Pedro said, 'I'll tell you the truth.' He looked into his physician's eyes. 'What I fear is Muhammad *not* going to war with me.' The king began to pace again.

'Forgive me, sire . . . . My understanding falls far short of the loftiness of your highness's paradoxical wisdom.'

'The news came last week,' Pedro said flatly. 'We've been keeping a lid on it, so as not to . . . *alarm* the populace.' 'Alarm' was a euphemism: 'reignite' was its plain equivalent. For years, Henry the Bastard's propagandists had been busy informing the Castilians that Pedro their king was a lover of Moors, Jews and other infidels and heretics; that Henry of Trastámara would be their true and Christian monarch. Pedro might have ejected his half-brother from the throne a year before, but the usurper was waiting to pounce again.

'What news, sire?' Abraham said, not wishing to hear it.

'The Bastard's back. His forces have infiltrated our borders . . . with the connivance of those accursed Aragonese.' He grimaced at the thought of his namesake, neighbour and enemy, King Pedro of Aragón.

Abraham was silent. In the current round of the great Iberian game, the real danger wasn't from the black pieces, from the Moors. It was from kings and would-be kings of their own colour.

Pedro halted, turned and stared at his confidant. 'And I'm sure it hasn't escaped your notice that I no longer have the Black Prince up my sleeve to bail me out.'

Abraham nodded slowly. He remembered the terrible falling out between Pedro and his English ally, after they had repulsed Henry the previous year. True to his epithet and his attire, Abraham reflected, the prince from the sunless north in his black helm and breastplate had been no knight in shining armour. In fact, he had behaved more like a common mercenary, digging in his black-spurred heels over payment. It had all been less princely than, well, blackguardly. And as the coffers of Seville were more than usually empty at the time, it had been to no avail. In the end, the prince had left, angry and underpaid, taking his roving army back to France. Moreover, despite his own less than knightly conduct, he had also sworn never to fight again for Pedro – a man whose methods of warfare were, as he put it, so far beyond the pale of Christian chivalry; but then, there had been good reason for that revulsion . . . Frozen now by the cold blue ferocity of his king's gaze, Abraham thought of what they were calling him these days – Pedro the Cruel.

'Without the Englishmen, I need Muhammad and his Granadans even more. If I don't have them, Abraham, the Bastard'll shaft us. We've *got* to keep Muhammad sweet.'

'Then, sire,' Abraham said as gently as possible, 'may it not be prudent to concede Sultan Muhammad's request? If the choice is so clear – a stone, or a throne – then the answer is equally obvious. With respect, I urge your highness to return the Ruby. Besides, you have already told Muhammad that you will do so.'

'Abraham, I am an anointed king. I say what I want; I do what I want. But, in any case, even if I wanted to give it back, I couldn't . . .'

Pedro said the words quietly, but Abraham could see an eruption coming. They were happening more often, these days. The physician looked into the cracking ice of the royal eyes. 'Why not, your high– '

'Because I haven't got the ruddy Ruby!' The doves exploded skyward. *'I gave it to the bloody Black Prince!'*

Then silence, but for the water whispering through the pool.

Abraham laid a hand on his master's brocaded arm. 'His highness should spare a thought for the level of his noble bile.'

'It was the only way to get him to shut up,' Pedro said, almost inaudible now. 'And, to be honest, Abraham, I never liked the damned thing. There was something about it . . .'

It was an old woman's delusion – wasn't it? But the memory had never left him. He saw himself, the proud young king, fresh from killing the enemy with his own hand, planning to celebrate with a new and splendid crown to replace the simple gold diadem of his forebears. He had gone through El Bermejo's gems with his beloved old nurse, God rest her . . . 'And as the centrepiece, Mistress Margarita, what do you think of this?' He'd held the Ruby to the light. The old woman had given it one look: 'No, Pedrillo my prince. Not that one. It has blood.'

'Abraham,' the king said now, 'what are we going to do?'

'Sire, I suppose we could fake it . . .' Abraham cursed the words even as they were leaving his lips. He knew Don Pedro would jump at the idea. And he knew exactly who would be in charge of the deception, and – worse, much worse – who would be responsible for passing the fake off on Sultan Muhammad: he, himself, Abraham Ibn Zarzar.

Pedro's ice melted into a sudden smile. '¡Madre de dios! You brilliant Jew!'

'But, I hasten to add, sire, there may be insuperable technical problems . . .'

'No buts, Abraham. No problems. Get to work. Now. There's no time to lose.'

Chapter 10

'Aah . . . such a lovely, white throat . . .'

The voice came soft, slow and soothing. It made the terror worse. The only way she could resist was by telling herself again that it was a nightmare.

Lubna had been gagged, hooded, dragged from the cave above the graveyard to – where? Somewhere else subterranean, but much deeper. She could tell from the temperature, from the way sounds echoed and from the dead smell of the air. Whether it was day or night she had no idea. So she told herself her soul had left her body in sleep and entered the confused margins of the sphere of dreams. Yes: the hum of voices must be the sound of other sleepers' nightmares. *It must be*, she told herself. Or else . . .

The hood was ripped from her head. Green eyes studied her from between the folds of a turban-cloth. She wanted to cry out. But she didn't. *Go along with it. You'll soon wake up in Ali's arms.*

Something began to stroke her throat, gently, rhythmically. It was harder and colder and more real than the stuff of dreams: a blade. The voice came again: 'Yes . . . such a lovely, white throat . . . such songs came from it . . . such poetry . . . such. . . a *pity*,' the green eyes smiled; the invisible lips whispered, colder than steel '. . . *to slice it open.*'

She dragged her eyes away from his and saw other eyes looking at her, dim in the smoky torchlight. *He wants my fear. He wants my death. But I will not be his victim.*

Lubna saw the glint of the blade withdrawn. 'Tell me what happened yesterday,' the voice said, suddenly conversational, almost banal. There was something in it now that she recognized. Lubna never forgot poetry, and she never forgot a voice. But where had she heard this one? *Where?*

'They came . . . the guests.' Her own voice surprised her: its balance. But then, she thought, *I speak from my own free will. Not because he wants me to.*

'What guests?'

She told him the names.

He nodded, knowing. 'Who else?'

'No one. No . . . someone did come. I don't know who. I heard their voices. His and . . . Ali's . . . Ali had gone back to his laboratory.'

'Yes?'

'Something about money. There was shouting. And I heard the street door slam.'

'What was Ali doing in his laboratory?' The green eyes narrowed, drilled into hers.

'Work.'

'Work . . .' She felt the blade at her throat again, pressing now. '*What work?*'

The words rang from the rock walls like an anvil's clang. *Go along with it*, said the still small voice that fought against her terror.

But she couldn't. She didn't know the answer.

'Shaykh Layth,' another voice said. It was an older man's tone, a scholar's voice. 'The woman is a slave. A *qaynah*. How could she know anything?'

'Just tell me what you saw, the last time you went into the laboratory,' her interrogator said, almost reasonable once more.

'I saw . . . my couscous sieve,' Lubna said. There was something ridiculous in the intrusion of such a prosaic object into the nightmare.

'*Your couscous sieve?*'

'Ali had ruined it.' She almost let herself smile. 'The holes were blocked with . . . stuff.'

'What "stuff"?'

'Oh, Ali's stuff . . . The Elixir of Life for all I know!'

The green eyes opened wide and mad. But the voice was still cold, controlled: 'Do not mock me.' The blade pressed, so hard it numbed the pain it caused. Then she heard a whisper, audible only to her: '*I want the Elixir of Death.*'

This was the end, she knew. A little movement from his hand and the blood would spring, her soul would fly. But she had triumphed. She would die, but not as his sacrifice. And she would be out of the nightmare, with Ali.

But she heard that other, scholarly voice again: 'Shaykh Layth, she knows nothing.'

The blade, the eyes, were downcast. 'Tell me about the thunderbolt,' he asked, without looking up.

Released from the gaze, Lubna now saw that vision of Ali on the floor, his eyes beseeching, his lips trying to shape her name. She didn't want to share that. But, again, she told herself to go along with the nightmare, to get it over. Then they would be in each other's embrace again; awake, or dead, it didn't matter. 'I was in the kitchen when it struck,' she said, neither fear nor sorrow in her voice. 'I ran into the laboratory. I saw him: his throat – *you know, don't you?* – his throat had been cut.'

He didn't know. The green eyes stared, startled.

Something had changed, fallen apart. Lubna heard fragments of speech, other voices breaking the silence – ' . . . he was careless . . . must have talked . . . agents of the Secretariat . . .' There was one louder voice, angry and deranged: 'Shaykh Layth, you haven't got it in you. Let *me* kill her . . . *now!*'

Her interrogator turned: 'Silence!' The other voices ceased. He could control them, if not her. Then he looked back at her and spoke, gently, softly, lulling. 'There is something you have not told me.'

He was right. It came back, sudden, entire, and she knew that if she didn't say now it would be gone for ever. She had to turn those words into sounds, to fix them in her memory, even if that memory had only moments left to live. 'That afternoon,' she said, 'Ali was working on a poem.' His last and most precious poem. She recited it, and the words spooled out like a spell:

> 'Black as the night that fires the heat of lust in early dawn,
> And yellow as the forenoon fire that sears the summer morn,
> And white, pure white's the flame from which the remedy is drawn.
> Black is a castle in Toledo – ask no more, I warn –
> Yellow is the mount of Cádiz, white the graves of Aragón.
> The final, fatal fire is lightning in the rain-cloud born,
> He'll know, who grinds the finest flour, then turns it back to corn.'

Silence. Then Lubna heard a young man speak: 'It's nonsense!'

'The whore's making fun of us!' another voice shouted – that same crazed voice as before. 'Let's kill her, *now*!'

They all joined in and vault became a babel. Then Lubna heard her interrogator – a few quiet words and the clamour ceased. 'Let Sarim speak.'

'Shaykh Layth,' the scholarly older man said, 'we all know what the colours signify. As for the rest, I confess I am at a loss. The ending in particular seems meaningless . . . unless, that is, it refers to the saying, proverbial for wasted effort, "Whatever we ground turned back to grain." Yes: it is almost as if whoever composed this . . . this *doggerel*, was telling us that, however hard we may try, we will not be able to make sense of it. Or perhaps the slave-woman herself can enlighten us?'

Lubna stared, defiant, in Sarim's direction. 'It is not "doggerel". It is my Ali's poem. It means . . . what it says, and a lot more besides.'

'So would you care to share with us the fertile subtext of *your Ali's* poem? Your own amusing achievements as a versifier have not

escaped our notice. Even down here, in the bowels of the earth.'
Sarim permitted himself a dry laugh.

Lubna was silent.

The lunatic spoke, or spat: 'Shaykh Layth, let me persuade her.
I'll get the whore to talk.'

'Hattam,' Sarim said, 'there is no need for you to expend
your energy, much as you would like to. Look at her. She is a
qaynah, a singing slave-woman – a gaudy, squawking parrot. She
understands nothing of what she says. But if you wish to hear my
considered opinion, Shaykh Layth, I believe the Alchemist left a
sign. Whatever else one may think about his poetical abilities, or
lack of them, he was not ignorant of the metrical requirements of
Arabic prosody. And yet he introduced an extra syllable into the
line ending with "Aragón". I believe that some message may be
hidden there.'

'I agree with Master Sarim.' Lubna heard a new voice, precise
and fussy. 'Those three features – the castle in Toledo, the mount
of Cádiz, the graves of Aragón – are more than just similes for the
colours. I suggest that the Alchemist was referring to the *sources* of
his materials.'

'Haydar,' Sarim said, 'I never knew your talents lay in the poetical
direction. You have taken the words from my mouth. I too believe
that the *zindiq* Alchemist was engaging in what is vulgarly called
"a double bluff" – to be precise, he was concealing the concrete
within the metaphorical. The question remains as to the identity of
the places referred to. The castle and the mountain should pose no
problems. As for "the *graves* of Aragon", I am a little perplexed . . .
The word used, *rujam*, is unusual. *Rujam*, to be exact, are the stones
placed upon a grave, in the form of a cairn, to form a convex or
gibbous heap. This may suggest that the sepultures in question are
of a pre-Visigothic, even pre-Roman origin . . .'

'Enough speculation, Sarim,' Layth said firmly. 'Take the verse
down from the woman. We'll consult our Cross-worshipping

correspondents in Seville about those places, since all of them are in infidel lands – may God return them to Islam!'

There was a loud *Amen*, then Hattam's voice. 'Can I do her in now, Shaykh Layth?'

Layth ignored him and waited while Sarim wrote the verse out. When his pen became silent, Layth addressed Lubna. 'Woman, we know how to find you. Speak to anyone, and you suffer.'

'Then kill me now!' Lubna said, challenging.

Layth's eyes smiled, but not his voice. 'Your foul blood would pollute our purity. Besides, you may be of use to us. Until then . . . take her away.' They hooded and gagged her again. 'And remember,' Layth called after her as they led her up the tunnel, '*you* are not worth killing. But a single word to anyone else, and we dig up your filthy lover's corpse and burn what's left of it. We will make ashes of his ashes. *We will make him die a second death.*'

'*Black as the night that fires the heat of lust . . .*'

Layth read the words and the old pain came back, sharp as the agony of an amputated limb. Not that the ache was ever absent – the ache for Mabruk, the black cupbearer with the glittering glance, pouring the starry wine that night twenty years ago in al-Bayyazin, till dawn and drunkenness drowned the other drinkers and he'd taken the slave to his bed, to himself. Now the memory pulsed with the poem, in his veins, like alcohol. They'd both been young. It was just a moment.

The moment lasted seven years. Layth had shut his ears to the slow engulfing tide of whispers.

But he couldn't shut out the deathbed whisper of his father: 'Repent, my son, before you are lost for eternity.' The old man had known, of course . . . And so – how? – had the wandering preacher who slipped into the old man's dawn funeral procession and softly recited God's words into Layth's ear, '*By your life, in their wild intoxication they were blindly wandering . . .'* Who? Layth wondered for a moment. Then he remembered: the men of Sodom . . .'*And then the terrible scream overtook them as the sun came up.'*

In that cold dawning Layth saw Mabruk in a new and lurid light: not lover, but seducer. He sought salvation in the cleansing flames of holy war – and turned Mabruk into his tool, not for pleasure, but for murder. Brainwashed, used, discarded . . . he pictured the young man, the blood of the infidel-loving Sultan Yusuf still on his hands, as they ripped his beautiful black limbs apart and burned them in the fire.

For the windblown dust and ashes that were now Mabruk, the centuries till Doomsday would pass in a blink. Then he would be a martyr in heaven, his sins purged by the sacrifice of a fallen sultan. But what of himself: could he perform his own sacrifice and join Mabruk again – in eternal bliss, pleasure beyond earthly imagination?

Not when his mind was mired in this lower world, in an alley in al-Bayyazin and the glance of another slave, black as the night.

The pain of the path beneath her feet was nothing now. For Lubna knew the nightmare had no end. There would be no dawn and no death; only death in life. Ali her lover was gone. Jaime her brother had been as good as gone these sixteen years past. And she was now just a chattel, a clapped-out second-hand *qaynah*, the property of Ali's heir – his long-estranged brother. She shivered at the thought of the man. He was as frighteningly pious as Ali had been lax, and she knew he saw her as the source of Ali's laxity, the Cross-worshipping contamination whose verses had heaped scandal on the family.

Instinct took her from where they had dumped her, through the dark, back to the ruined shell of memories that had been home. The door still lay wide open. She picked her way over the debris in the entrance passage and into the courtyard. There was a

71

movement against the starlight: the cat? She opened her mouth to call its name . . .

Arms grabbed her. A shape came at her from the front. She kicked out, connected with the soft-hard angle of a crotch – heard a sharp indrawn breath of pain and a curse. Then something hit her and the stars reeled.

Chapter 11

Sergeant Hamid of the Mamluk guard checked the knots that held fast his sultan's proud red standard. This was his favourite time of day, up here on the Watchtower on his early morning round.

And this was a day among days. Ever since the storm of two nights before, a perfect clarity had filled the air of Granada. Down on the plain, villas and farmsteads seemed close enough to touch. Even the distant look-out towers on the mountains stood sharp, guarding the marches of the state with Allah's unfailing aid. Could there be a finer land, a nobler sultan, a more beneficent deity?

Sergeant Hamid knew there could not. And he knew from experience. He wasn't even middle-aged – not yet thirty, perhaps – but he had seen the world. Not just the bits that any soldier saw in border skirmishes and raids into infidel territory. For he had crossed the Strait to guard his sultan in exile in Fez. His mind went back to that hemmed-in, po-faced city that paled beside Granada the great, the glorious. Then, as always, it slipped back further still, to the harsh sierras of his birth, a land haunted by poverty and ravaged by the Death. He tried to recall the faces of his infidel parents, and they wouldn't come. They never did.

But María's face was with him all the time.

He heard a drumming of wings and turned. A pigeon had landed on the eastern parapet. It preened its slate-blue breast for a moment, spread its wings to take flight again – then fell to the floor in a flurry of feathers.

Hamid ran to the spot, looked over the parapet and saw a small figure staring up from the walkway on the wall below, a limp slingshot in his hand and a look of disbelief on his face. 'Hey! You! What do you think –' Hamid stopped himself as the boy ran. It was his sultan's eldest, Prince Yusuf, the heir to the throne of Granada.

Stroking his crooked nose, broken by his own fall from a wall as a child, Hamid watched the prince until he disappeared down a turret-stair. He gently picked the bird up. It was alive, but dazed. Then he froze: attached to one of its legs, like an amulet, was a tiny copper cylinder.

'What I cannot understand, sir,' the young functionary said, knotting and unknotting his fingers, 'is that there has been no authorization for the use of birds. Not for several days. The last entry in the ledger is the bird sent to the governor in Málaga, with your respected order concerning imposts payable by the Genoese merchants.'

'And no one else has access to the pigeon post,' the Grand Vizier said, turning the cylinder over in his palm. The little wax seal was smooth, he noticed: no impression of the tiny eight-pointed star which was the stamp of the Department of Posts. 'No one but yourself, those of vizieral rank, and the few other high office-holders on your list . . .'

'Absolutely no one, sir.'

'Then,' Lisan al-Din said, 'let us see what tidings your dove was bearing.' He nipped the seal off with a thumbnail – the wax fragmented – and tapped the cylinder. A little tube of oiled silk fell out, wound with a fine silk thread. Inside – he marvelled, as ever, at the extraordinary lightness of the 'bird-paper' made by the those devilish-clever Venetians – was the usual double roll, the outer sheet inscribed with the recipient's name . . . Fernando de Guzmán.

It was written in decent Latin script, and it rang a bell: yes, Guzmán was a middle-ranking courtier of Don Pedro, if he remembered right. Interesting; but not astonishing, given the traffic between the courts of Granada and Seville, the Alhambra and the Alcázar. He carefully unrolled the inner sheet, and peered closely at the web of minute characters.

The Overseer of Birds saw a shadow cloud his superior's face. For a long moment Lisan al-Din was motionless. Then the shadow was dispelled by that rarity – less rare these days, they were saying, since the Grand Vizier's old friend had turned up from Morocco – a smile. The Grand Vizier looked up at a glimmer of gold in the coffered ceiling and spoke: 'Summon the Sultanic Secretary.'

Abraham Ibn Zarzar, the king's physician, walked away from the Alcázar, unaware of the market crowd that pressed from all sides. Behind him loomed the great minaret of Seville – or rather ex-minaret, now bell-tower . . . and in the foreground of his mind, a problem loomed – had been towering there, in fact, ever since his conversation with Don Pedro. He was a physician, a man of science, the royal confidant, possessed of power and knowledge. But how to fake a ruby?

And not any ruby. *The* Ruby. All he knew was that it was red, and big – 'Oh, for heaven's sake, Abraham,' the king had said. 'How should *I* remember how big it was? It was . . . *king-sized*, ha ha!' Nor had he done any better with the palace officials. Only the Master of the Treasury claimed to have any distinct memory of the stone. He thought it was round, and an inch across; but then again, on reflection, perhaps it was oval and two inches long. Worse than all this, the fake had to pass muster with its original owner, Sultan Muhammad, his old boss. Abraham knew all too well that the sultan was, like his late father, a connoisseur of gems. And worst of all, he knew who would have to take the fake to Granada: Abraham

Ibn Zarzar. With every step, Abraham cursed himself for his stupid bright idea.

It was a problem that needed the wisdom of Solomon . . .

Solomon! He stopped so suddenly that he caused a pile-up of porters and shoppers on the narrow street. '*Bloody Jews,*' someone was saying. 'Think they own the place, don't they.' Abraham paid no attention. He had lit upon the one man who could help him: his fellow Jew, Solomon of Seville, trader in gems; and, they said, in cabbalistic secrets. And in what else? Abraham had spotted his co-religionist at the Alcázar only the other day, deep in talk with Guzmán. There was something going on there, and, unusually, Abraham had no idea what it was. That was the trouble with Solomon. He let nothing out. Not even his identity: Solomon of Seville was what they called him, even here in Seville.

The crowd had elbowed him aside before Abraham realized where he was. Subconsciously, it seemed, his footsteps had already taken him almost to the jeweller's house. He walked the few remaining steps up a side-alley, found the door, knocked – then jumped as the door flew open even before the echo within had died away. There stood Solomon, in his greasy gabardine and forked beard. If he had servants or household, no one had ever seen them. Abraham stepped into the dark lobby and gagged on the reek of piss and neglect.

'What can I do you for, brother?' Solomon asked, raising a shaggy eyebrow. Abraham shrank from the man's stinking breath. 'A pocketful of diamonds? Small, they are, but of the first water, and with the bloom of Golconda's dust still fresh upon them. Or what about a purse of yellow sapphires from Serendib? Or if you're short of the readies but looking for something a bit *exceptional*, I've just had a small but choice consignment of coral come in. Not any old coral, mind you. Not that pink stuff they give to teething babes to suck on. No; *black* coral, black as my beard, brother, from the island of Socotra. Plucked from the sea-cliffs, from the nests of the bird called *Phoenix*. Or so' – he spat on the filthy floor – 'they say.'

Abraham flinched. 'Actually, I'm after a ruby.'

Solomon stroked his beard, liberating from it the fragments of meals past; its blackness was clearly due to art, not nature. 'Serendib ruby? Star ruby? Or balas?'

'Balas. And a particular one. The one his highness Don Pedro took . . . into safe-keeping . . . when he, ah, put El Bermejo out of his misery.'

'*A particular one* . . . You are speaking of the ruby to eclipse all rubies! I held it! Here, in my hand! But not for long. It had blood. The *first* blood. And so much of it . . .' His voice had trailed away.

'What do you mean?'

'Diamonds have water, brother. Rubies have blood. Or some of them do. As for *this* one . . . It was the most magnificent gem I've ever held, or beheld. And, brother, the most *malevolent*.' He spat again. 'You see, great gems are like great men. You'll find in them the good and the evil that are in us all; only more so, according as to their greatness. Much more so. Good and evil rise by ascending powers, you know, just like price: one carat, five dinars; two carats, twenty dinars; three carats, two hundred. And so on. It is all, as the mathematicks say, *exponential*.' The jeweller paused and shrugged. 'But I was merely asked to advise. Don Pedro wanted it in a new crown. It wasn't for me to put him off it. I even came up with an idea for the setting. Very elegant it was too, though I say so myself . . .'

'Describe the Ruby to me, Solomon.'

'I've told you, brother. It had blood. It was a great gout. A clot. A welling-up and a wallowing, transformed into mineral by Him who made the heavens and the earth, may His Name be for ever blessed . . .'

'I mean its physical appearance.'

'If you are interested in matters merely *exoterical*, I can give you chapter and verse. The Ruby is 170 carats' weight, if it's a carat. That's the size of a chicken's egg to you, brother. And roughly the shape too, though somewhat irregular and inclining to the *rhomboidal*. Picture that in a ring on the dainty finger of your lady-love! The poor digit would shrivel and drop off with the weight of it. And on its face it has an *excrescence*, a drop like a tear, as if it was weeping for its own wickedness . . .' Solomon looked closely at the physician, as if at a dubious stone. 'But why are you asking me this, brother? You who are the eyes and the ears of him who owns the Ruby?'

Abraham ignored the question. 'You said you designed a setting. Did you do a sketch?'

'Of course. But it went, with the stone. To Cristóbal the Moor. The goldsmith of that name. What happened then is not my place to know . . . Ah. Blood. "Like blood from a stone," they say – *but that stone was full of it* . . .'

Abraham breathed a long sigh of relief as the door shut behind him.

It was no distance to the goldsmiths' alley and the workshop of Cristóbal. But the way was fraught with nuisances – heavily-laden mules flattening him against the wall, slippery dung underfoot and, worst, a gang of lay-brothers in the trademark cowls and scowls of El Silencio. Abraham kept as far from them as possible. The members of the religious confraternity known as The Silence hated Jews as well as Moors. And it didn't help to be the king's Jew, either: they hated the king most of all, it was said, for his love of infidels. Their mute and violent stares spooked him.

Cristóbal did nothing to put him at his ease. At the sight of the Jew, he crossed himself elaborately and mouthed a prayer. Above him, looming from the wall, an oaken Christ wearing a gold crown writhed on a large dark crucifix. Abraham looked at Cristóbal's sharp, dark Arab features, and wondered why these converts had to go quite so far to advertise their new faith. Then he thought of El Silencio, and knew the reason.

'I come from Solomon of Seville,' Abraham said. Cristóbal's eyes narrowed. 'And before that, from his highness Don Pedro.'

The goldsmith's expression changed as he recognized the king's Jew. 'How may I serve ... *your honour?*'

'You recall the Great Ruby his highness considered setting in his new crown?'

The Moor's eyes now grew wide. 'Who could forget it?'

Oh, plenty of people, thought Abraham. 'Don Pedro, may the Almighty preserve him, wishes to create a facsimile to . . . to adorn . . . a new battle helmet.' He realized he should have thought this out better. 'I am commanded to instruct you to supply us with the dimensions and other details of the setting you were to execute from Solomon's designs. I assume you kept a record?'

Cristóbal was smiling now. 'Sir, I kept more than a record.'

'So what do you make of it?'

The Grand Vizier studied Ibn Zamrak, the Sultanic Secretary, as he angled the transcript of the pigeon-post message to the light from the window of his chamber in the Alhambra. The manner of the message's interception had been strange enough; the words themselves were stranger still. There was a movement, a quiver, in the man's prominent and glistening Adam's apple. Ibn Zamrak moistened his thin lips and formed them round the words: '*We send our friends, our foes, the following pleasant conundrum . . .*'

The Sultanic Secretary might be a thoroughly disagreeable creature, Lisan al-Din reflected, but he did have a talent for verse. How did that couplet of his go, the one from the ode they were – right now – inscribing on the centrepiece of the sultan's new court?

> *Pure white pearlescent veil of light, strewn with a scattered hoard*
> *Of jewels, liquescent silver pools shot through with gems outpoured . . .*

Yes, he had a way with verse, Ibn Zamrak.

Ibn Zamrak finished reading. The Grand Vizier saw him swallow again, then wrinkle his nostrils into a sneer – a *studied* sneer? 'It's nonsense. It means nothing. And there is one syllable too many in the second hemistich of the fifth line.'

'My dear fellow, I am not ignorant of the rules of Arabic prosody.'

'I did not intend, sir . . .'

Lisan al-Din raised his hand. 'And as you well know, a lot of Arabic verse *is* nonsense. Particularly these days. The metaphors have strayed too far from their referents. In order to make sense of them, one has to be . . . *in the know.*' He stared hard at the Sultanic Secretary: Ibn Zamrak was one of the few with unfettered access to the bird post.

Ibn Zamrak met the stare with raised chin. His unpleasant features might have been cast from wax. But despite the cool of the season, the wax was melting: Lisan al-Din watched a fat bead of sweat leave a trail down the man's temple. 'I should inform you,' the Grand Vizier said, 'that the "pleasant conundrum" was discovered, by God's will, on one of His Presence's postal pigeons. It was bound for Seville. Without the official seal.'

The Sultanic Secretary closed his eyes briefly. 'Then may it not be one of our respected colleagues doing, say, a little cross–border trading? Stealing a march on the suq? The "conundrum" could plausibly refer to . . . to various commodities and their provenances.'

'An admirable idea. But do the likes of –' Lisan al-Din cleared his throat ' – of *Fernando de Guzmán* sully their noble hands in the import–export trade? That gentleman, by the way, is the addressee.' Ibn Zamrak didn't reply. 'You know what these *hidalgos* are like . . . No; the trade, I suspect, is of a different nature. Different, and more dangerous.'

'So, what do you intend to do?'

'I shall let the bird fly on. I shall put out . . . my tentacles, in Seville. And I shall wait and see.' At these words Ibn Zamrak relaxed, slightly. 'And in the mean time, in order to add his well-known powers of observation to mine of deduction – to conjoin, as it were, his eyes with my intellect – I shall call in Abu Abdallah.'

'*Abu Abdallah!* The man's a fool!' Ibn Zamrak hissed. 'And you know as well as I that he is a suspected spy for the sultan of Fez! A suspected *failed* spy, I should say. And besides, that Black of his –'

The Grand Vizier had risen from his seat. He looked straight at Ibn Zamrak and spoke softly: '*Abu Abdallah is my friend.*'

Abraham still felt uneasy in the twilight of the goldsmith's shop. It was that crucifix: the eyes – inset, he noticed, with small red gems – seemed to follow his movements, accusing.

Cristóbal emerged from the darkness of his inner cubby-hole. In his hands was a casket. 'Look,' he said, opening it reverently, like a priest with a holy relic.

Inside was a shapeless brown lump, like a small turd. *Uggh,* Abraham thought; perhaps it *was* a relic, The Holy Stool of San Somebody. He wouldn't put it past them. 'I wanted to get it right, didn't I?' the goldsmith was saying. 'I mean, you don't get orders like that every day, do you? Then I held on to it. As a keepsake. And you never know, do you, maybe the royal mind'll change.'

'What is it?' Abraham asked.

'*What is it?* It's the Great Ruby!' Cristóbal whispered. 'Cast in wax.'

Abraham smiled and offered up a silent prayer of thanks. He'd never thought it would be this easy.

In the Grand Vizier's chamber, Abu Abdallah read the words yet again. Ideas, images flitted across his mind. As for meaning, there was none. But he didn't want to fail his friend Lisan al-Din. Besides, if he could crack this, it might be one step closer to his own vizierate . . . *I wish I hadn't let Sinan go*, he thought. If anyone could see through these thickets of metaphor, it would be his brilliant slave, who was off browsing in the Booksellers' Suq, and no doubt astonishing the natives with his blackness, as well as his brilliance . . .

'Yes? What now?' Abu Abdallah heard Lisan al-Din's voice, speaking tetchily to a clerk.

'Sir,' the clerk said, 'there's been a development. In the case of the al-Bayyazin thunderbolt.'

Abu Abdallah's ears pricked up.

'They brought in the dead man's slave-woman earlier today, sir.'

Abu Abdallah felt his heart quicken. He looked up. For a moment, his glance caught Lisan al-Din's. Quickly, he looked back at the conundrum on the paper: *Black as the night that fires the heat of lust in early dawn* . . .

Yes. There was meaning there. But it was still beyond his grasp.

Chapter 12

'So, woman,' the Chief of the Night said, 'tell us: where *were* you all that time?'

Sinan looked round the crowded *majlis*. When he had first entered the room with Abu Abdallah, it had fallen silent – suddenly, deadly silent, as several dozen pairs of eyes turned to glare at him, the black intruder. Now it was silent once more. But this time the gaze of the room was on the slave-woman, and the silence was that of a held breath.

The woman's outer robe was dusty and dishevelled, but she was decently veiled. And her head, covered by an elegant striped *mandil*, was high. She might have been a slave, but she held herself like a sultan's consort. Sinan glanced at Abu Abdallah, sitting beside him. His master was staring at the woman, his mouth slightly open.

The lips moved beneath the veil. 'I . . .'

A reed pen scratched the surface of the silence, and halted. The crowd was in suspense. Sinan looked round them again: all men, of course, most of them dressed in the wide-sleeved robes and subdued colours of the Granadan middle classes. Two night watchmen standing next to their seated chief had matching tunics of crimson. All the spectators wore the red or green woollen caps that he and Abu Abdallah had adopted, except for the turbaned scribe who sat behind a writing-slope beside the Chief of the Night.

'Twenty-four hours is a long time to disappear. Come on, woman, speak.' For a man whose main job was running the night watch – hence his title – and catching drunkards and other miscreants, the burly Chief of the Night could turn on a surprisingly gentle manner. Sinan, when he and Abu Abdallah had given the man their witness statements earlier on, had found him curt, almost brutal. Then again, perhaps Granada's top policeman had – like everyone else, it seemed – been bewitched by the slave-woman.

She remained silent. The eyes above the veil looked over the heads in the room.

'We are here, woman, to inquire into the death of your master,' the Chief of the Night went on, more firmly, but still with an underlying softness. 'It was assumed that you, too, were a victim of the incident that killed him. My men were looking for your remains in the rubble – and then you walk into their arms, alive and kicking ... *literally* kicking, I'm told. Resisting arrest.'

Sinan saw one of the night watchmen grin and dig his comrade in the ribs. The other man glared back.

'You must admit it is more than a little strange. After all, you may be a woman and a slave, but you are known to be hardly lacking in wits ...'

'*Beware ... her poems have a prick!*' Heads swivelled round, and a nervous titter passed through the *majlis*. Everyone knew the slave-woman's poetical retort to her blind groper. Sinan couldn't tell where the voice had come from.

'*Silence!*' the Chief of the Night shouted. 'Any heckling and you'll be out, the lot of you! Now speak, woman.' His patience was beginning to fray. Sinan could feel an almost physical emanation from Abu Abdallah, willing the woman to talk.

And at last she did, letting her gaze fall for the first time. 'Sir, I do not know where I was. I was wandering. My memory is ... clouded.' She spoke softly but clearly – in an educated voice, Sinan noted, but with a breathy, slightly rasping edge that betrayed her foreign origin.

The reed-pen stopped scratching, and the turbaned scribe whispered to the Chief of the Night. 'Well then,' the big man said, 'would you care to tell us what you do remember? Go back to the beginning of the day your master was killed.'

She inhaled deeply. 'Ali . . . my master . . . was working in his laboratory.'

'Working on what?'

'How should I know? I'm only a woman and a slave.'

The room took an indrawn breath – but a frown from the Chief of the Night silenced it. 'Don't be pert with me, woman,' he said, but without real anger.

Sinan saw that a man had risen from his place on the floor. 'As a neighbour of the deceased Alchemist, may I cast some light on the matter, sir?' The Chief nodded. 'A neighbour but, I hasten to add, *not* a friend.' Sinan recognized him from the night of the disaster, peering at the Alchemist's corpse . . . *Carbonadoed by a thunderbolt –* that's what he'd said. 'As we all know, the slave-woman's master was a notorious wine-swiller. Well, one day, when I, er, chanced to see through the lattice on his street window, I noticed a . . . a what-do-you-call-it . . . an *aspiratus* . . . anyway, a contraction composed of unnatural-shaped vessels furnished with cocks and spouts, such as are used in the instilling of rosewater. And on subsequent occasions I happened to sniff a smell coming from the said lattice. Now, sir, if wine is the mother of mortal sins then, I tell you, this was the stink of their great-grandmother.' The Shaykh's glare staunched an outbreak of laughter. 'Sir, I am not a scientific man myself, but it is my convention that the Alchemist was engaged in extracting *al-kuhl,* the very essence and spirit of wine, in order to make it even more delectatious to men's health and morals.'

The man sat down and another stood up. Again, the Shaykh nodded permission. 'You want to know what he was up to?' Sinan recognized another face from the night of the disaster, an older man with a fleshy 'raisin' on his forehead like a blind third eye – clearly an assiduous performer of prayers. 'Undermining the natural order, that's what!' There was a general tut-tutting.

85

'Like the rest of his deluded kind, the Alchemist was trying to change base metals into gold. Now, just think what effect that would have on the Exchequer of our beloved Sultan!' He paused, enjoying the ripple his words had set off. 'And I have it on good authority that he was also trying to compound *al-Iksir* – the so-called Elixir of Life – in a vain attempt to subvert the will of Him Who alone allots the lengths of His creatures' sojourns in this lower world.'

More shock-waves passed through the room. Sinan turned to Abu Abdallah. His master's eyes were still on the slave-woman, standing proud but momentarily forgotten in the thrill of scandal.

'*Please sir* . . .' A youth had risen and was trying to speak.

'Shut up and let the boy talk!' the Chief of the Night barked at the onlookers.

'I saw Ali the Alchemist hanging around the lavatories at the mosque, sir, with a leather bag and a trowel, collecting . . .' the youth blushed, '*stuff.*'

There were several calls of 'Me too!'

'What "stuff"?' the Chief of the Night asked. 'Was he a gardener?'

'*No, he was looking for the Elixir of Life!*' It was the same voice that had quoted the slave-woman's poetic put-down. There were a few raucous laughs.

'*SILENCE!*' The Chief of the Night's bellow cut the laughter dead. 'One more interruption and I'll have the lot of you belled about town!' Sinan was puzzled – then remembered seeing a man in the Granada suq, a merchant who'd given false measure, they said, mounted back-to-front on a donkey wearing a bonnet topped by a tinkling bell. 'This is getting us nowhere. Let us get back to the facts of the day in question.' He turned a now purple face to the slave-woman. 'So, your master was in his laboratory. What were you doing?'

'I was preparing lunch,' the woman said. 'We were having guests.'

'Tell me their names.'

Before the slave-woman had finished recounting the guest-list, the wit's voice cut in again: '*The Wine Appreciation Society of Granada . . .*'

This time the Chief of the Night spotted him. 'Chuck him out,' he commanded. The watchmen obliged. 'Now, woman, did anyone else come that day?'

'No, sir . . . I mean, Yes, sir. I heard a knock at the door in the afternoon, but I was busy with the guests so I couldn't go. Then I heard raised voices in the laboratory – Ali, and whoever the other man was. As soon as I could get away, I went in to check everything was alright. Ali seemed angry. He said he had to get away, to the farm. He's got . . . he had a small vineyard on the far edge of the plain, below Jabal Shulayr . . .'

'Hah, "a small vineyard" . . . and I bet he was going to take that *aspiratus* of his so he could go and instil his spirits –'

'No speaking out of turn!' the Chief of the Night bawled. 'Now, woman,' he went on, his voice gentle once more, 'let us go to the heart of the matter. When did you last see your master?'

The slave-woman looked down for a long instant, then raised her head and spoke as if to the ceiling. Sinan noticed that Abu Abdallah's fingers were interlocked, his knuckles pale. 'The guests had gone, sir. I went into the laboratory. Ali had taken something from the kitchen, something I needed. While I was with him, he said . . .' For the first time, her voice faltered. Sinan watched the lips moving beneath the veil – moving rhythmically, as if shaping a prayer, or a poem. Then her head fell, and her voice returned, much smaller. ' . . . It was the last thing he said.'

'What did he say, woman?' The Chief of the Night's voice was soft, coaxing.

Suddenly she raised her head again, and shook it slowly. Below the line of the *mandil* her brow was furrowed by the effort of remembrance. 'But, no . . . it wasn't that. There *was* something else. The last thing he said was . . . "We'll be needing a good long length of wick, for the lamps. This is all we've got left." He had this bit of wick in front of him, you see, and a big new copper lamp, a sort of lamp I'd never seen before. Big, it was, and marked with . . . with grooves. Then he said, "The evenings are drawing in." 'There was a catch in her voice now. 'Yes. That was the very last thing he ever said to me. "*The evenings are drawing in.*" '

Hardly anything but the ghost of the words came out. From the corner of his eye, Sinan saw his master mouth that whispered last phrase, as if repeating a spell.

When she spoke again she had regained her voice: 'And then the bolt struck. I ran back in. And there he was. Ali. On the ground. Looking up at me. With his throat cut.'

She said it so quietly, so matter-of-factly that for a moment no one realized what it implied. And then – Sinan realized Abu Abdallah's hand was gripping his arm – a tremor seemed to shake the room and the onlookers looked about in disbelief. Sinan tried to stand, but Abu Abdallah's hold – and his look – silenced him and pinned him to the floor.

The slave-woman was still speaking. 'You see, sir . . . someone had . . . cut his throat . . . There was blood . . . so much blood . . . he died . . . And the fire was so hot . . . and I . . . ran out . . . and . . . and . . .' But no one was listening to her in the wave of shock that had swamped the room and struck even the Chief of the Night dumb.

No one but Sinan.

She knew. She was staring through the crowd, at him. She knew he knew.

The shock-wave swelled, broke, became a surge of voices, and then the watchmen were among them, sticks whirling. Slowly a bruised and ragged sort of order returned.

The Chief of the Night had risen, his face as dark as his title. '*This inquest is at an end!*' He turned to face the slave-woman. 'It is clear to any man of reason that the allegation we have just heard is nothing but the hysterical delusion of a woman and a slave . . .'

'*No!*' she said, squaring up to him.

' . . . a woman and a slave . . .'

Again, Sinan tried to stand. Again, Abu Abdallah stopped him. 'Sinan, forget it!' he growled. 'They'll never believe you. You know they hate Blacks.'

'Sir,' Lubna was saying, her voice crescendoing in ardour, 'you only saw my Ali's body after it had been burned. I tell you again, *someone had cut his —*'

' . . . *a woman and a slave*, I repeat, whose wits,' the Chief of the Night was saying, his own voice growing louder, 'have been addled . . .'

'Master,' Sinan said, hurt, 'what you mean is *you* don't believe me!'

'Sinan, I believe you now.' And with that Abu Abdallah himself stood up to speak.

'Sit down, that man!' the Chief of the Night thundered at Abu Abdallah. 'A woman and a slave, I say, whose wits have been addled by the death — the death *by divine intervention* — of her master, the agents of which, namely thunderbolt and fire, are all too clearly the sign of God's implacable wrath.' He looked with grim satisfaction at the roomful of nodding heads. 'Wrath directed against a notorious wine-bibber, free-thinker and sorcerer. As you all know, the penalty for such *zindiqs* is death by fire. God Almighty has dealt this one his just deserts in this world, and He will hold him to account on the Last Day.'

'But my master was a good man!' the slave-woman cut in.

'Woman, the only good thing about your master was the manner of his death. Now be gone. The *zindiq*'s heirs will decide your fate.'

'*And I will find out who killed my Ali!*'

'Be silent or you'll find out what's inside the dungeons of the Alhambra! Take her away.'

The two watchmen propelled the woman at arm's length through the crowd, who were now all standing and watching her, half appalled, half fascinated. As she passed him, Abu Abdallah spoke, quietly but audibly: 'I'll see you vindicated, my dear!'

But she didn't hear him. Her eyes were on the black man by his side.

Sinan, too, was on the point of speaking, but her look made him falter: a swift look, but so penetrating that it seemed to linger inside his eyes after she was gone. He couldn't make it out. But he knew that there was disbelief in it. Disbelief . . . and need.

And it was only when she was gone that Sinan realized *she* had spoken to *him* — had whispered words so clear, even in the clamour of the dissolving crowd, but so strange that he wasn't sure he'd heard them right.

Chapter 13

'*I seek refuge with God,*' Haydar said through clenched teeth, looking from the lumpy mess in the mortar to the youth's equally lumpen features, '*from worthless work*. Pulverize, boy! Pulverize! You're not making porridge . . .'

'Please, sir,' Dirgham said, 'what does "pulverize" mean?'

Haydar rolled his eyes and aimed a silent prayer through the rock ceiling of the underground chamber. He snatched the pestle from the boy's meaty hand.

'Here I am,' he said, methodically pummelling the moistened willow ashes, 'at the cutting edge of science, the meeting-place of the technologies of the East and the North, and they give me you for an assistant.'

'But, sir, Shaykh Layth said you needed help, sir, so we can make the Remedy quicker.'

'Yes, *help*, not hindrance . . . Look, you must make more of an effort or you'll be back on bag-duty.'

A well-timed leather bag appeared in the entrance of the chamber, deposited by the unseen hands of a fellow Lion. Layth was right, of course: they had to increase their rate of production. Of the contents of the line of unprocessed bags, their vital ingredient constituted one part in two hundred at best. One part of pure and unadulterated 'snow' in two hundred of dross.

'But, sir . . . *why* does the ash have to be so fine?'

Haydar almost snapped. Instead, he took a deep breath. Maybe if the boy could understand the importance of his task, he would approach it with a better attitude. He looked at Dirgham in the candlelight from the glass-covered sconces – an extravagance, but a necessary one, here in this chamber – and thought there might perhaps have been some faint glimmer of intelligence animating those gormless features.

'Look,' Haydar said, wearily, 'the unrefined matter comes in and undergoes the first stage, the crude separation.' He indicated the two fellow Lions sitting on the ground over the large tray, carefully using small brushes to remove the grosser impurities from the contents of the bags. He saw Dirgham gawping at the men, as if he'd only just noticed they were there. 'The next stage is our first new piece of technology, the Syrian process. This is where you come in.'

Dirgham nodded slowly. For the first time, he looked faintly interested. 'Why is it called "Syrian", sir?'

'Because it was developed by a Syrian, Hasan the Lancer, a native of Damascus. Many years ago, admittedly. But it was kept secret by the regime there, and only leaked to us recently.'

' "Leaked"?'

'Yes, by an operative in the Egyptian Sultan's assassination squad.' They might have degenerated into mere hired killers, Haydar reflected, but the so-called Hashshashin, who had given their name to the art of political murder, still had their uses . . . 'Anyway, until we knew about the Syrian process, the snow was purified by simple crystallization – heating in water, skimming off the scum, then allowing the clarified solution to solidify slowly. Now we know that by treating the snow with willow ashes, we can cause precipitation of the liquescent matter prior to crystallization.'

The boy had glazed over. 'In simple terms,' Haydar went on, '*suitable for dunderheads*, when we mix the untreated snow with ashes and water then heat the mixture very gently, the ashes carry away the dirt and leave the snow much cleaner. This makes the Remedy much more effective. But – and this is your job – the ashes must be as fine as possible.' Dirgham was nodding again. Something had sunk in. 'And then there's the other new piece of technology . . .'

But Haydar stopped himself. He handed the pestle back and watched Dirgham wield it, more deftly now, mouthing, '. . . *pulverize . . . pulverize . . .*'

Haydar went back to the mixture simmering in the brass vessel, and to pondering that other new technique, the northern one. Again, the idea for it went back a long time. But no one had ever put it into practice. Until now.

And yet he didn't know exactly what it was. He had his suspicions; but all he knew for certain was what the English monk had written, the line of Latin that their Cross-worshipping correspondents in Seville had passed on: *Si fieret instrumentum de solidis corporibus, tunc longe major fieret violentia.*

He had wrestled with that text. Sarim, the learned Lion, had translated it immediately: 'If the instrument were of solid materials, then the violence would be far greater.'

A big bubble rose in the bowl and burst.

It was the nature of the instrument that he didn't know. He suspected only two people did: Layth, and the shadowy Asad – the Lion in the palace who, but for his *nom de guerre*, had remained a secret to the rest of them.

For a while Haydar's thoughts simmered with the liquid. But soon his mind was lulled to near-blankness by the rhythmic sounds in the chamber – the soft laborious brushing, the breathy burst of bubbles, Dirgham's now rhythmic pummelling and whispered ' . . . *pulverize . . . pulverize . . .*'

Something went *snap!* And brought him back to the moment: low-grade charcoal in the fire-box beneath the brass bowl. He must speak to Layth. They really couldn't afford to economize. The risks were too great . . .

The risks would – *should* – be even greater. For there was that third new piece of technology, neither of the East nor the North, but home-grown, here in Granada, by Ali the Alchemist. On it hung the whole success of the Lion's venture; without it, all their labours, their years of planning to get the Red One, would be wasted. But no one knew what it was — not Layth, not even the mysterious Asad. Its meaning was locked in that maddening verse, and the key had been lost with the death of its author.

Yet again, Haydar peered in the candlelight at his copy of the transcript:

> *Black as the night that fires the heat of lust in early dawn,*
> *And yellow as the forenoon fire that sears the summer morn,*
> *And white, pure white's the flame from which the Remedy is drawn.*
> *Black is a castle in Toledo — ask no more, I warn —*
> *Yellow is the mount of Cádiz, white the graves of Aragón.*
> *The final, fatal fire is lightning in the rain-cloud born,*
> *He'll know, who grinds the finest flour, then turns it back to corn.*

The difference in the light. It was one of the things that always took Sinan back to his other life.

In that other existence, the afternoons used to end with no ado. He could still picture the dousing of the red-hot sun in the shuddering horizon, the sudden descent of night. In the years that followed, the ones he'd spent with Abu Abdallah in Morocco — in the Maghrib, the Land of the Setting Sun — afternoons seemed stretched, or squeezed, according to the season. Here across the Strait the effect was even greater. And the sun never rose as high as it had in the land of his childhood, where it burned the wide grasslands yellow and left the flocks panting in the shadow of baobabs. Instead it seemed weary, sloping away across the sky. Sinan thought back too to his first look inside the Alhambra, where the light seemed different again, touched by darkness even in daytime.

Here in the library of the Grand Vizier's palace by the Fountain of Tears, the light had yet another quality, filtered by lattices and speckled with book-motes and with the sounds of rippling water from the garden below. Sinan longed to be let loose on the piles of manuscripts that tottered in labelled alcoves: it all reminded him of those early days in the great mosque-library of Fez, before his master's fall from grace. But he squatted dutifully by the door, lulled by the library hush, watching Abu Abdallah holding the paper to the declining sun.

'Lisan,' the old man said, breaking the rippled silence, 'I've looked at it every which way, and to be honest with you I can't make head or tail of it. Not yet, at least.' A late fly buzzed drowsily; Sinan's eyelids drooped. ' "*Black as the night that fires the heat of lust in early dawn* –" '

Her eyes. Even before the sound had reached his brain Sinan saw them again, and their look of disbelief and need. *These were the words she'd spoken.* 'Master!' he shouted, springing up.

Lisan al-Din turned his heavy head at the outburst, and glowered over his jowls.

'*Sinan!*' Abu Abdallah hissed. 'I do apologise for my slave. Sometimes I think I can't take him anywhere. But you see, among his many other qualities, he's a great fan of poetry. It does over-excite him at times, though. It's all to do with the excessive natural hotness of his humours, coming as he does from the Negrolands.'

'The line is hardly *that* inspiring,' the Grand Vizier said, taking the transcript from Abu Abdallah's hand.

'But master . . .' Sinan cut in.

'Oh I know, you're dying to recite something yourself, aren't you my boy. Well, you'll just have to possess your soul . . .'

'*Master . . .*'

' . . . in patience, Sinan!' Abu Abdallah glared at his slave then glanced at the Grand Vizier, who seemed absorbed in the poem once more. Then he looked back at Sinan and slowly mouthed two words: *Think 'vizierate'*.

'Oh, please listen to me, master!' Sinan whispered back.

Lisan al-Din looked up, frowned at the slave, and spoke. 'If we consider the metaphorical implications of the three colours, the possibilities are countless. At the obvious end of the scale, they can refer to different human races – the black Negro and the white Frank; "the sons of the Yellow One" is an old circumlocution for the Greeks. "White", as you know, often refers in poetry to the flash of weapons. "Yellow" can denote emptiness. A "black one", if we consider more abstruse possibilities, was for the poets of the Age of Ignorance an arrow smeared with blood and considered a fortunate omen. And so on. The potential referents are all but infinite . . .'

Sinan could hardly contain what he knew about the mysterious verse. He wondered how long the Grand Vizier's literary discourse would go on.

' . . . And then there is the added problem that colours are in themselves, so to speak, slippery creatures. "Black" often refers to "green" when seen at a distance: one speaks of the "blackness" of a stand of palms in a far oasis . . .'

'Lisan, there's something important . . .' Abu Abdallah said.

' "Yellow",' the Grand Vizier continued, ignoring him, 'occasionally signifies "black" in the poetry of the ancients, apparently by transference from black camels, which are said invariably to have an admixture of yellow hairs in their coats . . .'

'But you're forgetting,' Abu Abdallah managed to slip in, 'that all the colours in the verse are to do with *fire*.'

'My dear friend, do permit me to approach that point by my own route. Now, the repeated mention of fire in the verse first suggested to me a connection with the heavenly bodies, which are fiery in nature and differentiated by colour – in fact, the verse contains that direct allusion to the sun, "yellow as the forenoon fire". The fact, however, that the phrase is an overt simile – "yellow *as*" – tends to nullify my hypothesis. One does not describe a cup, for instance, by saying it is like a cup. So, on balance, I am leaning towards the supposition that the verse may conceal something of –' he looked portentously at Abu Abdallah ' – *of alchemical import.*'

Sinan was almost beside himself: he had heard that first line of the verse from the slave-woman of the Alchemist! Abu Abdallah, he noticed, seemed equally excited. 'Just what I'd thought!' his master exclaimed, clapping his hands. ' "Black" stands for lead, "yellow" for gold, "white" for silver. Great minds, you see, Lisan . . .'

'I dare say,' the Grand Vizier replied, 'even if some of us arrive at our conclusions by luck, and others by logic. Be that as it may, let us proceed for the moment upon the basis of this assumption. Now, the first three lines of the verse list metals. I propose that lines four and five take us from the metaphorical to the concrete, to literally solid ground – namely, the provenances of the minerals in question.'

'You took the very words from my mouth, Lisan.'

'The final couplet, however, is highly obscure. Its significance escapes me – unless that last line refers to the proverb, "Whatever we ground turned back to grain." Which implies that the versifier is telling us indirectly that our efforts to understand his message have all been in vain.'

' "*And verily,*" 'Abu Abdallah recited, ' "*you have been granted of knowledge but a little.*' "

'How true the words of the Almighty are,' the Grand Vizier said, 'and especially of some of us, my dear friend. Still, the beginning of wisdom is to know that we do not know. Let us return to the relative *terra firma* of the couplet that might be described as "topographical". Now, Cádiz, as is well known, occupies a low-lying spit of land.'

Sinan felt a chill at the name. His master had mentioned Cádiz, that nest of Nazarene pirates, on their crossing of the Strait.

'There is nothing there that could even remotely be described as a "mount". But there are mountains inland, belonging to the province of Cádiz. The rocks there, if they are anything like those of our blessed Granada, might appear yellow in certain lights. As for the castle of Tulaytulah – "Toledo", as its infidel occupiers call it – being black, I believe this is contrary to the truth. And "the graves of Aragón" . . . "*Rujam*" are tombs covered by stones piled up in a rounded form. I have observed structures that might be described by the term, dating from the era of the most ancient Iberians. But precisely where such sepultures might be located in the kingdom of Aragón I do not know. Hah! Let us consult al-Shaqundi's *Treatise on the Superiority of al-Andalus* . . .'

The Grand Vizier rose stiffly and made for an alcove labelled 'Travel and Topography', repeating the three place names from the verse, '*Qadis, Tulaytulah, Araghun* . . . *Qadis, Tulaytulah, Araghun* . . .' He found the manuscript and was lost in its pages, peering closely at them in the failing light.

Sinan saw his chance. He was up and in three strides over whispering in his master's ear.

Abu Abdallah cleared his throat. 'Lisan,' he said, smiling, 'I think I *can* help you. My slave, I mean my powers of deduction, have opened a new line of inquiry.' The Grand Vizier looked up from the manuscript. 'But I need to spend some time, with . . . with . . . I mean, you know the man who was killed by the al-Bayyazin thunderbolt? I need to spend some time alone with his, er, *qaynah*.'

'*The Alchemist's slave-woman?*' Lisan al-Din's sagging features suddenly plumped and coloured like dough in a bread-oven. 'Well, well, my friend . . . Seeing as you're into clever and poetical slaves –' he nodded towards Sinan '– she'd be the perfect complement. You could run them against each other, male versus female, black versus white! And,' the features had become what Sinan could only think of as a smirk, 'I hear she's a bit long in the tooth, but still what is vulgarly called *a looker*. Come to think of it, should *I* make an offer for the woman to the Alchemist's heirs, before you get your paws on her?'

The Grand Vizier's creaking laugh echoed round the library.

Chapter 14

'You've told me a thousand times how it happened. What I want to know is *why* she said it. And to *you*, Sinan, of all God's creatures!'

Sinan didn't answer. They turned a corner and descended a steep stepped alley. A boy drove a laden donkey past them, pressing them against the wall. At this time of the morning, the alleyways of al-Bayyazin were full of people and animals. Sinan thought how different it all looked from the last time they came this way, by lamplight and lightning, the night of the thunderbolt.

' "The heat of lust in early dawn . . . " Honestly,' Abu Abdallah said, smiling mischievously at his slave, 'anyone would think she . . .'

'Think what, master?'

'That she fancied you.' Abu Abdallah was still looking at him, but the smile had gone.

Sinan felt himself blush. For a time they walked on in silence, hearing only the echo of their own footsteps and those of passers-by bouncing off the long blank walls of the houses. At last, Sinan spoke. 'What *I* want to know, master, is how the Grand Vizier got hold of the poem. And why he's so interested in it.'

'I don't know, Sinan. I just don't know. All I know is that he gave it to me and asked if it rang any bells. The problem is, it doesn't. Not yet. But I feel – I'm sure – there's more to it than meets the eye.' They turned into a narrow passage, a deep slot between high houses. 'Much more,' Abu Abdallah added, as if to himself.

Sinan felt a sudden chill, and realized where they were. The dimensions looked different in the daytime; but there was that same sense of entrapment, of buildings leaning towards each other to block out the sky. Even the shadows seemed deeper and darker than they should have been. And Sinan saw in his memory's eye the shadow that had moved, here, and turned into a man, and that green gaze of loathing and lust.

The trap opened, and he breathed again. But both he and Abu Abdallah were silent again now, reliving that night of half a week ago, here on the Alchemist's street. The debris outside the house had been cleared away, Sinan saw, but the window opening where the lattice had been was still uncovered and framed by scorch marks: it stared across the street like a sightless eye roughly rimmed with kohl. Nor had anyone tried to block the street doorway, although the door itself, hanging out of its frame, had been propped against the wall. They crossed the threshold of the hole and picked their way through the semi-darkness of the entrance passage, calling out, '*Allah! Allah! O Protector! O Coverer!*' to announce their presence to the woman they hoped to find within.

She was there. Abu Abdallah emerged into the central courtyard, and Sinan saw the alarm in the eyes above the veil. Then, when he himself stepped over the shadow-line into the light, her alarm changed to incredulity: framed by the rectangular darkness of a doorway, she looked at him and the frown around her eyes relaxed. Abu Abdallah introduced himself. 'Forgive me,' he added, 'for coming unannounced like this. But be assured that I am here to help you.'

The woman looked from master to slave then back again. 'No, sir,' she said, finding words, 'you . . . you must forgive me. I am not able to receive you in a fitting way.' Her speech – clear, correct, but with that foreign edge to it, a roughness of aspiration that fascinated him – took Sinan back to the morning before and the *majlis* of the Chief of the Night. 'As you can see,' she went on, hesitantly, opening the folding leaves of a broad five-panelled door and leading them into a shadowed reception room, 'there has been a . . . an accident.'

'I know,' Abu Abdallah said. 'It is the accident that has brought me here. Or should one say, "the incident"?'

Sinan saw the woman's step falter at the word. 'Please,' she said, indicating a cushioned divan, 'make yourself as comfortable as you can, sir. And pray forgive me for the state of the room. The circumstances . . .'

Abu Abdallah inclined his head and an awkward silence settled on them. Sinan sat cross-legged on the floor inside the entrance. He looked round. Although dishevelled, the room suggested a certain prosperity, if not luxury. There was some good stuccowork on the walls and decent carpets on the floor, but everything was covered with thick black dust – blown in, no doubt, by the wind that had accompanied the thunderbolt. The slave-woman had tried to tidy up, Sinan noticed. She had also gathered various objects on a brass tray in the centre of the room: a small casket; a carnelian rosary; a dagger in a silver sheath, freshly polished; some slim volumes, finely bound but scorched; and, incongruously, he thought, a couscous sieve. He sensed these were physical remnants of a life lived together. Keepsakes – that she couldn't keep, Sinan reflected. A slave like him, she owned nothing. Not even herself. He felt her eyes fall sidelong on him, and looked down.

'May God have mercy on your master's soul,' Abu Abdallah said gently, 'and may He comfort you in your loss.'

'God bless you, sir,' the woman said. 'To hear your prayers is in itself a comfort. No one else has extended the hand of condolence to me since my master was . . . since my master died.'

'I also wish to express my sympathy in a practical way,' Abu Abdallah went on. 'I'm here, as I said, to help.'

'But sir, I am not worthy . . .'

'And in order to help,' the old man continued, ignoring her in his kindliest tone, 'I will ask for your assistance.' Sinan saw his master withdraw a roll of paper from his sleeve. 'Do you read?'

'Of course, sir,' she said. Lines appeared around her eyes – the outer margin of the smile beneath the veil. 'Ali, my master, taught me.' She took the paper and unrolled it.

A veil may hide features, Sinan thought, but it cannot hide feelings. He saw the woman's eyes, wide with shock, staring at his master, then at himself.

'I'm sorry. I didn't mean to disturb you,' Abu Abdallah said. 'All I wish to know is what the poem means.'

'Forgive me, sir, but I cannot understand such things. I am a woman and a slave.'

'But a highly ... accomplished woman, as I'm told,' Abu Abdallah said.

'Sir, all I know is that it means what it says, and a lot more besides.' Her eyes seemed to search the room before coming to rest again on Abu Abdallah. He was watching her, head to one side, smiling encouragement. Sinan studied his master's features – gallnut face, squirrel-bright eyes, jutting beard – and thought, not for the first time, how they never appeared to age. Also not for the first time, the same thought crossed his mind that had occurred to Lisan al-Din: Abu Abdallah, like the fabled ageless wanderer, al-Khadir, had come to an arrangement with Time.

Abu Abdallah nodded almost imperceptibly. 'Sir,' the woman said softly, 'Ali composed the verse that afternoon, the day he died.'

Sinan saw his master's head straighten, his eyebrows rise slightly – then remembered, with a shock, the line near the end of the transcript. How did it go? 'The final, fatal fire is lightning from the rain-cloud born . . .' That most perplexing part of the poem had gained sudden, frightful meaning.

'So,' Abu Abdallah said, grave now, 'it is as if your master predicted the thunderbolt . . . as if he foresaw his own death.'

'Sir, Ali was a brilliant man, gifted in more respects than I can enumerate. But he had never before revealed a gift of prophecy. And in any case, he was not killed by the thunderbolt. He . . . he . . . but *you* know, don't you.' She had turned to Sinan. For a long moment, everything disappeared but those eyes, looking at him. Then she turned back to his master and the rest of existence flooded back. 'God may have been angry with him, sir,' she was saying, that alien edge to her speech further roughened now by ardour. 'Ali did things that you Muslims should not do. But his heart was good. And does your holy book not say, sir, that "God forgives *all* sins"?' Her breast heaved, she drew her *mandil* down and wept silently beneath it.

'I . . . I . . .' For the second time since they had come to Granada, Sinan saw Abu Abdallah lost for words. 'My . . . dear woman,' he said eventually, 'whether your master's death was caused by a thunderbolt or through human agency, its time was fixed, before Time itself began, by Him Who alone apportions the length of our lives. That said, when you told the Chief of the Night that he . . . came to his allotted period by the hand of a murderer, I believed you.' The slave woman looked up, startled through her tears. 'I believed you *from the bottom of my heart.* And I mean to discover who his killer was.'

Sinan looked at his master: he was smiling again, his head raised, but even the half-light in the room could not hide the fact that the usual brightness of his eyes was accentuated by a film of his own tears.

'And now,' Abu Abdallah continued, gathering himself and his robe as he rose from the mattress, 'I will, with your permission, go and investigate your master's laboratory. No, no, there is no need for you to come. I know where it is.'

'The house is yours, sir. But, with respect, I urge you to be quick. My master's heirs may come at any moment, and if they find you here it . . . it will be inconvenient.'

Sinan stood. 'No. Stay, Sinan,' Abu Abdallah said over his shoulder. 'I'll call you if I need you.'

Sinan sat again and fixed his eyes on the pattern in a dusty carpet. He wondered why his master wanted to investigate the laboratory alone. Over the years, Abu Abdallah, although himself an acute observer with an almost miraculously retentive memory, had come to rely on his slave's insights. 'I mine the gems and hoard them,' he'd once said, 'but I need you to arrange them on the string, my boy.' Perhaps he wanted to form his own insights first, Sinan thought.

A sound cut into his reflections: beads clicking, and a string of other sounds, rhythmic but meaningless – *avemariagratiaplenadominuste . . .* He glanced up. She was looking at him, light and dark, the shadowline of her hair obtruding from beneath the *mandil*, cutting into the milk-white brow. Her fingers became still for a moment, then began again. '*Subhan Allah subhan Allah . . .*' she said now, in Arabic, still looking at him. The movement of the beads ceased. 'I was saying a rosary, for Ali's soul,' she said. 'Before they take it all away from me. Before they take me away.'

'Did your master not free you?' Sinan said.

She stared at him, surprised by his perfect grammar. 'You can speak . . . I was beginning to think you were nothing but your master's shadow.'

He shrugged, suddenly not knowing what else to say.

'No,' she went on, 'Ali did not free me. He would have done so straight away, of course, had I borne him a child; but . . . And he did not write a will. So I am now the property of his heirs. And they hate me!' She laughed.

'How could they hate *you*?' The words came out more forcefully than he might have wished.

'Ali's brother is . . . excessively pious. He believes I led him astray, that I . . . contaminated him with my Christian ways. You see, I never converted.'

Sinan stared at her: this was the first avowed Nazarene he had ever met.

She shook her head. 'Don't look so shocked! You're as bad as they are. And I should tell you, I've never been this . . . this close before. I mean, to a Black.'

Sinan smiled at her candour. She laughed, then stopped herself. There was that look again in her eyes. Need. He cast his own eyes down.

'And then there are some verses . . . of mine,' she went on. 'Ali's brother thinks they have brought notoriety to the family.'

'You are a poetess!'

She laughed again. 'It might be more correct to call me a versifier.'

'But then, why are you so concerned about your master's brother? You are no kitchen-slave,' Sinan said. 'Surely he will respect your learning.'

'On the contrary. He will punish me for it. He will make me his skivvy. And . . .worse than that. And however learned I may be, however well-versed in Arabic prosody and playing the lute and entertaining guests and all the other arts of the *qaynah*, who wants a *qaynah* as old as me?' Sinan almost spoke, but cut himself short – without even knowing what he'd meant to say. 'The best I could hope for would be to become a trainer of singing slaves. But Ali's brother would never let that happen. No; the arts of poetry and song are anathema to him. He wishes to make me suffer.'

'Is there no one else, no one you could turn to?' Sinan said.

She smiled sadly. 'I myself had a brother – *have*, if God, by His grace, has preserved his life. The Death was very bad in Granada a year ago. So many perished. My master tried to find out, but it was impossible to get news. You see, after we were captured, Jaime – my brother – was taken into the Mamluks.' Sinan pictured the elite, aloof soldiers of the Sultanic guard, across the valley at the Alhambra, ready to die for their ruler and their Muslim faith. 'They converted him, of course. So, even if he's still alive, he's as good as dead to me. And I to him . . .' She hung her head for a second, then raised it. 'But what of your own history? Forgive my curiosity, but I never expected a . . . one of your race to . . . to . . .' her words failed, but her eyes were eloquent, regarding him with

105

that same look of disbelief and need, ' . . . to be able to express himself so . . . beautifully.'

◈

I could buy her, Abu Abdallah thought.

The laboratory still stank of hellfire and, faintly but unmistakeably, of the sweet rank smell of roasted flesh. But Abu Abdallah's mind was in the room across the courtyard, contemplating the slave-woman. Tragedy had made her even lovelier, lent her a deeper darkness to set off her radiance. Light and dark . . . the houris – those incomparable women of Paradise – were named, he reflected, for their *houar*, the contrast of light and darkness in their eyes.

I could buy her, if I had the money . . .

The new thought sobered him and brought him back to where he was. In the half-light he could see no sense in the wreckage, only the inchoate aftermath of the lightning-strike.

Lisan al-Din would lend me the cash . . .

He took another step in and something crunched beneath his foot – something made of glass.

Illusion shattered: it would be like all those other times, all those other concubines. He wanted something more: *I want her to want me.* He knew she never would. Not in the way he meant.

His eyes were adjusting after the brightness of the courtyard, and he began to make out dull gleams: something beaklike, glass again, broken off a larger vessel of the sort he imagined alchemists would use; what looked liked a twisted copper hook, projecting from the scorched plaster of the wall – he touched it and it drew blood from his finger; a heavy mortar of brass upturned in a corner. He didn't know what he was looking for, and wondered whether to call Sinan: if there was a thread to be followed through this darkness, Sinan would find it . . .

Sinan. She wants Sinan. He knew it from her looks, even if she in her loss would never have admitted it to herself. Even if Sinan had no idea of it. *God*, he thought, *he's so bright in some ways, that boy of mine, and so ignorant in others . . . I could buy her for him! And it would be torture for me.*

Something else caught his eye, a steely glint half hidden in the thick black dust on the ground: a scalpel. He picked it up, blew it clean, admired its balance.

I must go back to them, he thought. *There's another question I must ask. And even if I want to be alone, I don't want them to be alone. God*, he almost said aloud, *I'm jealous of my slave.*

Still holding the scalpel, he made for the door, turned to have a last look – and saw a pair of eyes looking up at him, saw a swift upward movement, heard a stifled cry – his own . . . and laughed: the cat glared at him for a moment from the window-ledge, then dropped soundlessly to the street below.

'My master taught me what I know,' Sinan told her. 'My master, and the library of the Qarawiyyin Mosque in Fez.'

'The Qarawiyyin! The greatest centre of learning in the West!'

He nodded. 'I was lucky, you see. I was captured young. I must have been about nine years old. I had time to learn.' There was, of course, that other, deeper layer of learning, acquired in his other life. But he never spoke of it. Who would want to know?

She did. 'Tell me,' she said, 'about your life before. I know so little of the . . . the Negrolands.'

Sinan smiled. 'I too know little, now. It seems so long ago, so far away. My father was a chief among our people, and a famous hunter. We used to spend days, weeks away, tracking game. Sometimes it was just the two of us. Sometimes we went with my father's men and hunted lion . . . Do you know, when you hear a lion growling at you from inside a thicket, there's no more terrifying sound on earth. Or more thrilling!'

She stared at him, excited and alarmed.

Something appeared in the doorway. Sinan's head jerked round: he saw a long grey body slinking in. 'Away with you, Jinni!' Lubna said to it. 'There's nothing for you now.' She shook her head at the disappearing cat. 'Poor Jinni. Ali always said he was possessed by the *jinn*. But tell me, if your father was a nobleman among the blacks, then how, if I may ask, did you come to be a slave?'

'They came down the Great River, to take our land – the army of the emperor of Mali. My father led the resistance. They killed him.'

The scene came back as it always did, clear as a miniature in a book: the riverbank, the blur of the wielded war-club, his father gazing at him through a veil of blood, the spear slipping from his grasp, his own world slipping away.

Then the page turned to the next miniature. There he was, a small boy stunned, holding on to the hand of a small girl, all he had left of his world, while she looked at him with infinite compassion. He loved her so much, even now, that he couldn't bear to –but the page turned again, and they had come for them, and were dragging him away, and despite himself he turned his head and saw them holding her against the tree, grinning and panting like dogs.

The next page was blank.

He looked up and saw that she was looking at him. The incredulity was gone. Instead, there was compassion. ' "*We two are strangers here,*" ' she said, then stopped.

' "*And strangers,*" ' he said, eventually, completing the line of the ancient poet known as the Wandering King, ' "*are to one another kin.*" '

'That being so,' she said, 'then we had better know each other's names.'

'Sinan,' he said.

A heartbeat's hesitation. 'Lubna.'

They both looked up at the doorway. Abu Abdallah was there, looking at them – but as if seen through a lens, at a great distance.

'I will bring you water, sir,' Lubna said at last, breaking the lens, 'and dried fruit. I am sorry. It is all I have.'

'There is no need,' he said. The was a hollowness in his voice that Sinan had never heard before. 'And besides, you said your master's heirs are due. But I do have one more question. It is a question of great importance . . .' Abu Abdallah's voice was whole again. He was looking directly at her, once more the investigating judge. '*Who else heard your master's verse?*'

Sinan saw fear and confusion in Lubna's eyes. 'Sir, I . . . do not know. As I told you, Ali only composed the verse that afternoon. Someone did come. I heard an argument in the laboratory. But I don't know who it was.'

'You must try to think,' Abu Abdallah said softly.

'I swear to God, sir, that I don't know.'

Sinan looked at her, and thought: *Veils can't hide feelings, and they can't hide lies.* This was no lie. But *she* was hiding something. There was still that fear in her eyes.

Abu Abdallah gave her a long look, his head cocked slightly, but Lubna remained silent. 'What about this?' his master said, holding up a small bright knife – a scalpel, Sinan realized. 'Have you seen it before?'

'Sir, I . . . Ali . . . I don't know.' Suddenly her eyes widened in panic and turned towards the door. Sinan heard it, too – a low hum of voices, out in the courtyard, moving nearer; but – thank God – slowly. They sounded as if they were looking round. Lubna was on her feet. 'I'll get them into another room,' she whispered. 'Distract them. You slip out. Quick as you can. They won't see you, by God's grace.' She was almost at the door, looking out. 'Ah, they've gone into the laboratory. And . . . and . . . sir, there *was* someone . . . somewhere else. I'll take you there. I don't know when. It may be some time. They'll take me with them,' she said, hardly audible, glancing out of the door again. 'How can I send you word?' she whispered.

'I'm staying at the Fountain of Tears,' Abu Abdallah whispered back. 'At the Grand Vizier's.'

Lubna stared at him.

'Don't worry, my dear,' Abu Abdallah went on. 'Your secret is safe with me. You have my word as the former Malikite Judge of Delhi and Ambassador Plenipotentiary to China . . .' Outside, the voices were back and getting closer.' . . . the sometime Chief Justice of the Maldivian Archipelago . . .'

'*Master!*' Sinan hissed.

Lubna was smiling. 'Sir,' she mouthed, 'I trust you!' Then, with a last look at Sinan she stepped into the light and welcomed her unwelcome guests.

Sinan and Abu Abdallah peered out from the shadows behind the door-jamb and saw her shepherd a tall man and a dumpy woman into another room. Then they tiptoed out through the courtyard.

Sinan felt his heart thumping at his ribs, and he knew it wasn't just from fear of getting caught.

Chapter 15

'Two weeks and two days,' the Grand Vizier said in his gloomiest voice, 'and the birthday of the Seal of the Prophets will be upon us.' He looked up at the sky, the only untroubled surface in the silent turmoil of the new court. ' "*God is my Sufficiency, and the best of protectors.*" '

Sinan could see little difference in the court since their first visit, four days before. The four porticoes were still filled with scaffolding and plaster dust and the ceaseless, almost soundless activity of dozens of tilers, plasterers, calligraphers, painters and carvers, all slowly encrusting the shadowed recesses with geometry and arabesque and poetry and the word of God.

'But I still don't get it,' Abu Abdallah said. 'Why the hurry? Our old Sultan in Fez, God have mercy on him, postponed the opening of his great college, oh, half a dozen times, and it's none the worse for it.'

Lisan al-Din groaned. 'My dear Abu Abdallah, our own Sultan has decided in his blessed wisdom that the Prophet's birthday is the most – the *only* – auspicious day for the inauguration. Besides,' he glanced around and lowered his voice, 'don't forget we've got those confounded ambassadors from Don Pedro, bringing the Ruby.'

'Make them wait, for heavens' sake!'

'Oh, I wish I could . . . But we *cannot* be seen to be disorganized. You see, we may be allies on paper, but the alliance is unequal. We, Abu Abdallah, are in effect Pedro's vassals. Between ourselves – though of course the whole of al-Andalus knows it – we Muslims are here on sufferance. Pedro may be sympathetic to our blessed Sultan. But God save us,' Lisan al-Din added in an undertone, 'if Henry the Bastard ever gets his usurping posterior back on the throne of Castile. I've just had a report . . .' He stopped himself and cleared his throat. 'But that's as may be. In short, my friend, this glorious Alhambra is the Sultanate of Granada in miniature – a microcosm, so to speak, of seven centuries of Islam in al-Andalus, and the only safeguard for its future here. Any signs of weakness on our part, and the Cross-worshippers will be on us like vultures.'

The declining sun burnished the ivory, ochre and lapis lazuli of the court and threw its carvings into deepening relief. To Sinan, the marble columns seemed to dance, the stucco arabesque to ramify endlessly, intimating infinity. How could anything so complex and so beautiful ever be said to be finished – let alone in sixteen days?

And at the mid-point of it all, that enigmatic tent. Abu Abdallah peered closely at it and opened his mouth to speak.

'Do not even ask,' the Grand Vizier said quietly.

He led them through a doorway on the north side of the court. Sinan remembered wondering, on their first visit, what lay beyond it. 'At least we have one hall finished,' Lisan al-Din said.

Sinan shivered – they seemed to have walked into a cavern made of frozen light. The dense stalactite carving set off a play of brightness and darkness that made the whole chamber appear to be in motion, turning on the axis of a dome that hovered above them. It was all both insubstantial and oppressive. Sinan's eye came to rest on the nearest piece of stucco calligraphy. It was a poem. "Behold," he recited in an undertone,

> ' "the cupola is lost to sight, it soars so high,
> Its beauty visible – but also hidden from the eye.
> The stars extend their spangled hands to it from Gemini
> While, whispering secret blandishments from heaven,
> the moon draws nigh . . ." '

112

Sinan was disconcerted to see that Lisan al-Din was listening to him. 'So, what do you think of those lines, Master Sinan?' the Grand Vizier asked. 'The Nazarenes put paintings on their walls. We put poems on them. Come on, boy, your considered opinion, if you please!'

Sinan gulped. 'You . . . you wish to hear *my* opinion, sir?'

'Of course I do! Why do you think I asked you? You are what I'm always searching for – the unsophisticated and impartial critic. You see, we don't know what's good any more, because we're so far up our own poetic backsides.'

Sinan was stunned by such a phrase coming from so dignified a mouth.

'Come on, Sinan. You know what they say, "There's nothing to be embarrassed about in the world of learning." '

Abu Abdallah was grinning encouragement. 'Well,' Sinan said, 'the . . . the contrast, sir, between visible and invisible beauty, I find striking. But the lines are perhaps a little spoiled by the references to heavenly bodies. It is a . . . an overused metaphor.' Sinan saw the Grand Vizier smiling at him and suddenly felt his mouth go desert-dry: had he just criticized the poem to its author?

'Spot on, you ebony prodigy, spot on!' Lisan al-Din's dry laugh echoed up in the cusped vault of the dome. 'And in case you wonder who the poet is, it is our very own Sultanic Secretary, Ibn Zamrak. Sometimes, I almost envy him his poetic facility. But yes, he does miss the mark as often as he hits it.'

Silently, Sinan sighed in relief – then pictured Ibn Zamrak, emerging from the shadows of the Audience Hall – the serpentine approach, the sibilant voice – and suddenly felt queasy, overwhelmed. They were in a flawed paradise, a beautiful cage built on dungeons.

'Of course,' the Grand Vizier went on, 'poetry apart, we do have our own bit of Nazarene-style interior decoration . . . Come and see the progress in the eastern hall.'

They crossed the court and entered the painted chamber. Much of the scaffolding was left, and the Christian painters were still at

113

work, even in the failing light. One more ceiling painting, however, was now completely revealed.

'Well I never, Sinan,' Abu Abdallah exclaimed. 'They're playing chess up there on the ceiling, those Nazarenes, just like civilized people do!'

Sinan looked closely at the fresco. 'And look, master, I think the man dressed in red can win . . . in three moves.'

The Grand Vizier clapped his hands and shook his head in disbelief. 'Oh, Abu Abdallah, your Sinan is beyond all price!'

'Exactly,' Abu Abdallah said. 'That's why he's not for sale.'

One of the Christian painters climbed down the scaffolding and stared at Sinan, who was feeling even more like a performing bear than usual.

'Which reminds me,' Lisan al-Din said, narrowing his eyes at his old friend, 'while we are on the subject of clever slaves . . . What did you get out of the Alchemist's woman?' One eye opened, then closed in a lascivious wink.

'Nothing,' Abu Abdallah said flatly. 'Nothing at all.'

'Come on, man, out with it. You can't hide anything from me. Since you went to see her this morning, you've been looking positively *sanguine* . . . Oh!' Lisan al-Din froze in mid-flow.

'Lisan, are you alright?' Abu Abdallah sounded alarmed. He took hold of the big man's arm. 'You're not having a seizure, are you?'

'*Melancholy* . . .' the Grand Vizier murmured, still immobile, ' . . . *bilious* . . . *phlegmatic* . . .'

'Lisan! Speak to me!'

' . . . *sanguine!* Can't you see? The verse . . . It is another possibility . . . I mean, that the colours in the verse are those of the humours – those bodily dispositions, the balance of which controls the state of health of man, and indeed, through their analogues, the four elements, of the macrocosm of man, of the universe itself! Do you not agree, Sinan?'

Sinan was lost. 'Sir, forgive my ignorance . . .'

'Black is black bile,' Lisan al-Din explained, 'which promotes the melancholy humour. Yellow is yellow bile, which promotes the bilious humour. White is phlegm, the phlegmatic humour . . .'

'So where's the fourth humour?' Abu Abdallah cut in. 'Where's red?'

'Mmm. You are correct, my friend. We are missing the sanguine. Missing blood.'

✧

Like blood from a stone, Abraham recalled, with a shudder of distaste. That was what Solomon the gem-merchant had said.

Abraham Ibn Zarzar was beginning to feel less like Don Pedro's confidant than one of his under-footmen. All this running about Seville . . . But the job could be entrusted to no one else. Secrecy was everything when you were faking a ruby. The Ruby.

He fingered the pouch containing the two shapeless lumps of red glass – one, the glazier had explained, stained with an admixture of copper, the other, of gold. Which was nearer the shade of the genuine stone? Cristóbal the goldsmith hadn't known: 'To be honest, your honour, colour's not my thing. Shape, yes, but not colour. You need to go back to old Solomon.'

The medical side of Abraham's brain had likened the two different hues of red glass to those of blood: venous and arterial. Now, on Solomon's doorstep, the thought crossed his mind once more. *Like blood from a stone,* Solomon had said . . . *and that stone was full of it.*

He reached out for Solomon's door-knocker with a reluctance verging on repugnance. It wasn't just that the man stank rotten and gave him the creeps. He had also spotted him again, the day before, in the Alcázar, in agitated conversation with Fernando de Guzmán. Abraham smiled darkly at the image of the fastidious *hidalgo,* holding himself back from the fog of halitosis that hung about the decayed jeweller. What could possibly bring so ill-matched a pair together? If he broached the matter with either Solomon or

Guzmán, even indirectly, they'd clam up and he'd never know. But there was one thing he was sure of: that he was observing the symptoms of something deep, as yet undiagnosable, and probably malignant.

He shuddered again, then let the heavy knocker fall, bracing himself for the door to fly open even before the echo died.

The echo rang empty: he knew at once that no one was inside.

'If it's him within you're after –' the voice at his side made him jump ' – he's gone.'

Abraham turned and saw a youth, his thin pale face framed by lank Jewish side locks.

'Left before first light, he did. Carrying a travelling-scrip. If you could call it that. Looked more like a shit-picker's sack. Smelt like it, too . . . your honour.'

Damn! Abraham cursed to himself. He dropped a coin into the boy's outstretched palm.

'Obliged, your grace. But I can't tell you no more. Not unless . . .'

Another coin.

'He looked like he was in an 'urry . . . your majesty.'

A third and bigger coin.

'*An un'oly 'urry.*'

Chapter 16

'Oh dear, oh dear,' Ibn Zamrak the Sultanic Secretary said, looking round the new court in the stark morning light. Despite the early hour, the activity of the artisans was quietly frantic. 'A mere . . . *ten* days to go till the birthday of the Seal of the Prophets. And *so* much,' he turned to the Grand Vizier, 'still to do.' He sighed, a hiss between the teeth. 'To report to the blessed Presence of our beloved Sultan on progress made – *or lack of it* – will be a most painful task.' The Sultanic Secretary looked as if he would relish that pain. It was the Grand Vizier who would answer to the Sultan if the deadline was missed.

Lisan al-Din needed no reminders. The time that had elapsed since he last stood here with Abu Abdallah had flashed past. *God, nearly a week . . . Time is a sword,* he thought yet again, loathing the platitude. *If you don't cut it, it'll cut you.* And now, as autumn accelerated, the blade was coming down on him in a headlong fall of shortening days. But the Grand Vizier refused to be provoked. 'On the contrary, dear colleague, you may report to His Presence that we have another of the flanking halls finished. Come and see for yourself,' he said, making for the painted eastern hall; then stopping. 'But I forget. You are averse to polluting your pious eyes with images of living beings.'

Those eyes looked at the Grand Vizier with the piety of a pair of poisoned bodkins; then turned as a figure emerged from inside the central tent. 'Ah,' Ibn Zamrak said, adding oil to poison, 'Zayd the Clerk of Works! Our very own scion of the *ancien régime* of

Granada! The ancient *Berber* regime. Fallen on hard times. Or not, as the case may be . . .' he added in an undertone, rubbing his fingertips together out of sight of his superior, and smiling like a crocodile. 'Did you know, your eminence, that the Nazarenes, in their wisdom, use our Arabic word *barbari*, "Berber", as a term of contempt? As in "barbarian" . . . But I forget: you too are a Latinist.'

Lisan al-Din ignored the Sultanic Secretary. 'Pray tell us of the progress on the Sultan's centrepiece,' he said to Zayd the Clerk.

Zayd addressed the Grand Vizier. 'Sir, we have been putting the finishing touches to his honour the Sultanic Secretary's verses.' A slight nod in Ibn Zamrak's direction, but not a look. 'Only a few more vowel markings need to be gilded.'

'And the technical side?' Lisan al-Din asked.

'We should be ready for a test-run in a week.'

'*A week!*' Ibn Zamrak cut in. 'Do you really think a safety margin of three days is sufficient? As you may have heard, perfection is God's prerogative.'

'And in Him do I put my trust,' Zayd said gently.

A fourth man had appeared beside the Grand Vizier – his confidential clerk. He hovered for a while, then cleared his throat to break the toxic silence. 'Forgive me for interrupting your meeting, sir, but you have a visitor. Under normal circumstances, I would not . . . but you said, sir . . .'

'Who is it?' the Grand Vizier asked curtly.

'*Sulayman al-Ishbili*,' the confidential clerk replied.

'Well, I never. Solomon of Seville . . . Here, no doubt, with more gems for our beloved Sultan's collection. And with not inauspicious timing. Bring him.' The confidential clerk ushered the jeweller to a spot some yards from the Grand Vizier. He looked even more decayed than usual, following a six-day forced march from Seville. The dust of the road had turned his yellow Jew's turban khaki;

indeed, Lisan al-Din thought, he was so dusty and rotten-looking that he resembled a corpse on Doomsday – and one that has missed the last trump.

The Sultanic Secretary stared at the newcomer, his nostrils twitching. 'I will leave you to your *guest*,' he said, in an undertone. 'And with the respectful observation that this blessed spot, which was to have been a college for the teaching of the word of God and the traditions of His Prophet, peace and blessings upon him, has now become not only a pleasure-palace, but also the resort of Hebrew pedlars and Nazarene interior decorators. Not to mention superannuated spies sent by the Sultan of Fez, and their snooping black slaves.'

'I ask you, sir,' Lisan al-Din said, softly but sharply, 'to show more respect to the wishes of your Sultan, the Commander of the Muslims, to whom alone you owe your present station. *And,'* he added, softer still but with even greater vehemence, '*to my friend Abu Abdallah.'*

Ibn Zamrak turned and glided out of the court, leaving behind him a faint disinfectant smell of vinegar and another horrible silence. Slowly, sounds impinged on the Grand Vizier – the creak of wooden scaffolding, knives working damp plaster, muffled taps of tilers' mallets – almost inaudible sounds but, to Lisan al-Din, a noise that grew in a mocking crescendo. What had been his baby had become a ravening parasite, eating up not only the gold in the treasury but also himself. How would it all end – if it ever did? From every side the motto of the Sultans answered him: *La ghaliba illa 'llah*. No one wins but Allah.

At least he had Abu Abdallah to distract him. And, more immediately though less pleasantly, Solomon of Seville. He looked across at the Jew and beckoned him with a shudder. It was not a matter of his faith – 'To you your religion, and to me my religion' was God's own word on the matter, in the Noble Qur'an. It was the man himself – his greasy gabardine and greasier scrip, all covered with a thick scurf of dust; his filthy black forked beard hanging from a half-moon of white roots; the rancid smell that increased as he approached.

At least, the Grand Vizier reflected, it was all an excellent cover – and all the better for being unfeigned – for one of his most useful double agents.

'So, Solomon my friend,' he said, 'what jewels have you brought us this time? Come and lay out your wares – but in the privacy of the belvedere, I think.' They entered the north hall, followed at a distance by the Grand Vizier's confidential clerk, and passed beneath its airy dome. Through another small hall, and they were in the most gorgeous room of the whole new complex. It was a small square chamber, richly decorated within, but whose chief glory was the view from its wide windows – over a leafy pleasance that seemed to hang in the air like a garden of Babylon and, beyond the deep dark valley of the Hadarruh, to al-Bayyazin, glittering on its hillside.

'A fitting casket,' Solomon said, looking round the chamber, 'for the pearls I've brought your eminence.'

'I call this belvedere "the Sultan's Eye",' Lisan al-Din said with undisguised pride. 'May God preserve its owner. But to business. What have you brought me?'

'As usual, my offerings are not of the gemmological variety. This time they are, rather, *epistolary*.' The Grand Vizier nodded. 'I am a mere messenger, charged with delivering the letter concerned to a place of safety. I understand that the bird post, swifter though it is than my arthritic shanks, is currently in a state of . . . *compromise*.' Lisan al-Din tried not to let his dismay at this news show: they must have discovered evidence of his tampering with the catapulted pigeon's message. 'Now,' Solomon continued, 'I hasten to add that the agreement between myself and the letter's consignees did not specifically prevent the possibility of a little, ah, *divagation* on the part of the document, in your eminence's direction.' He drew a small sealed scroll from the crusty folds of his sleeve and held it out.

'What you do with it is your own business. "See no evil," that's my motto. But be careful with it.'

Lisan al-Din took the letter and examined the seal, a coin-sized disc of red wax in which the knots of the letter's double tie-strings were embedded. The ties themselves were threaded through holes that pierced the paper. Like its miniature counterpart that he had removed eight days ago from the bird-post letter, this seal was unmarked – or so it appeared. But Solomon's claim that the pigeon post was compromised had alerted him: he had to be more careful this time. He placed the scroll on a ledge, then clapped three times. The confidential clerk appeared instantly. The Grand Vizier handed the young man the scroll. 'Do not be alarmed,' he said to Solomon. 'He is utterly trustworthy.'

'Sir,' the clerk said, 'the seal is plain. Should I break it, then seal it again?'

'Indeed, the seal appears to be plain. But I suspect some secret mark. Look at it closely. Your eyes are sharper than mine.'

The clerk peered at the seal in the soft north light, then smiled. 'There's a tiny piece of red thread, sir, projecting from the wax. You wouldn't even notice it if you weren't looking. Shall I . . . ?'

'Yes. Perform your surgery.'

The Grand Vizier noticed that Solomon was sweating.

The clerk disappeared for a minute, then returned with a small brazier borrowed from the artisans. He pulled his pen-case from the sash at his waist, and took from it a tiny glittering scalpel with a curiously serrated edge; he buried the blade for a few seconds in the glowing coals of the brazier. Then, with a frown of concentration, he sawed through the thickness of the brittle wax, parallel to the seal's face, praying he'd judged the cut right so as to miss both the knots of the ties and the embedded thread. Solomon watched, holding his breath. If this went wrong . . . it didn't bear thinking about. But it was a gamble where, on balance, he stood to gain – in the form of the Grand Vizier's gold.

The upper face of the seal came off – intact. Solomon took another inward breath. The clerk mopped his brow with his sleeve, and studied the knots, half-exposed within the lower part of the disc. Wielding the tip of the scalpel with a surgeon's care, he now prised the knots out of their waxen matrix, then teased them open, noting the manner of their tying.

Solomon breathed out again.

Lisan al-Din took the scroll, unrolled it – and raised his eyebrows almost imperceptibly. 'Hmm. Transcribe it,' he said, handing it back to the clerk.

The clerk drew a roll of paper from his waist-sash and began copying the characters, Solomon following the transcription with narrowed eyes.

In less than five minutes the copy was done. Lisan al-Din looked at it for a moment, then took the clerk's pen and added at the bottom of the paper: *36:12:5.*

Solomon frowned at the figures. 'We have a new and somewhat complex filing system,' Lisan al-Din told him, while the clerk carefully retied the strings of the letter and replaced them in their wax bed. 'Modern bureaucracy for you! But I like to think it keeps these clerks of mine on the ball ...' The clerk produced a tiny phial from his pencase; from it he let a few minute drops of clear liquid fall on to the lower part of the seal, then gently – very gently – pressed its obverse face back into position. He then returned the scroll to Solomon and left the chamber with the copy, and a slightly puzzled bow to his superior.

Solomon examined the seal. Even to his sharp and suspicious eyes, there was no trace that it had been tampered with. He sighed and offered up a silent prayer of thanks.

'So then, Master Gemmologist,' the Grand Vizier went on, 'tell me the news from Seville.'

❖

In the secretariat attached to the Grand Vizier's office, deaf to the scratching of reed-pens around him, the confidential clerk stared at the figures his boss had written. Lisan al-Din certainly was keeping him on the ball: it looked as if he'd dreamed up a whole new filing system, off the top of his head. Or was the old man beginning to lose it? The figures were meaningless. If they looked like anything, they looked like a Qur'anic reference. . . 'Chapter thirty-six of the Noble Qur'an . . .' the clerk said to himself. Then aloud: 'Of course. The Chapter of Ya-Sin.' The surrounding pens stopped scratching and their owners stared at him. He smiled to himself: given the mysterious nature of the letter before him, it would be just like the old man to go for one of the Qur'anic chapters of the Mystical Letters. He began reciting soundlessly, counting off the verses on his fingers.

'When I left Seville,' Solomon said in the exquisite seclusion of the belvedere, 'the latest whispers were that Henry the Bastard was already regrouping his forces for another go at the throne of Castile.'

'That is hardly news,' the Grand Vizier replied wearily. 'Those whispers have been doing the rounds of al-Andalus for the past week or so. What I want to know is what Pedro's going to do about it.'

'Only the Lord, may His Name be for ever blessed, could plumb the depths of the mind of our most puissant sovereign,' Solomon said, shaking his disreputable turban. Lisan al-Din watched the dust coming off it – and God knew what else. 'But from what my . . . tame *jinn* in the Alcázar tell me, I hear Don Pedro's praying hard for help against his half-brother. Help from Granada. From you, your eminence.'

'Again, that is hardly an enlightening piece of information. Pedro hasn't any English princes up his sleeve this time. We're his only allies.'

'And, your honour, even his own subjects are going against him. Or the Christians, at least. The Bastard's agents are out and about, accusing Don Pedro of *maurofilia*, of being an admirer of Moorish infidels . . . I mean, with respect sir, of you Muslims. And as you know, there's not a little, er, substance to the claim. Many a true word spoken in jest, as they say – and in propaganda!'

'This is all very well, Solomon. But I need hard facts: diamonds . . . rubies . . . The stuff you're hawking is only semi-precious.'

'Well,' the Jew said in an undertone, glancing over his shoulder at the entrance to the chamber, 'there are those in Seville who'd stop at nothing to drive a wedge between Christians and Muslims. Even if it meant whipping up the bloodiest war in the history of our blessed Andalus.' Lisan al-Din nodded gloomily. '*And from what I hear,*' Solomon continued, whispering now, 'there are those here in Granada who want to do the same. Hah! Christian extremists . . . Muslim extremists . . . Look at them on the map and they're poles apart. But in truth they've gone to *such* extremes that they've met on the far side of this round globe we call the earth . . .' They both turned at the cry of a bird swooping past the window. 'Or, to . . . *variegate* my figure of speech,' Solomon continued, 'and resort to common parlance, the zealots of your two respective faiths are two sides of the same coin. The only one who stands to gain from it all is Henry the Bastard. And,' Solomon added with a grim smile, 'heads or tails, it's us Jews that lose.' He cleared his throat, and only just stopped himself spitting on the pristine floor of the Sultan's Eye.

Lisan al-Din gave Solomon a hard look. 'You said that there are those who want to drive a wedge . . . *Who are they?*'

36:12:5. It must be, the confidential clerk said to himself. He checked again. Chapter 36, the Chapter of Ya-Sin. The twelfth verse . . . he recited silently again, now counting the words within the verse: *We revive the dead . . .* beginning at the fifth word: *and write down what they presented, and the footsteps they leave behind, and note every thing in detail in a clear record.*

He tapped his brow. It looked like a sign; an order. But what had anyone presented, except this bit of paper from the Jew? He'd already written that down. As for footsteps . . . whose footsteps? And then laughed out loud and made the scribes jump.

In seconds he was out of the door. In less than a minute he was in the Office of the Chief of Intelligencers. 'Sir,' he panted, 'urgent message from the Grand Vizier. He's got a visitor. A Jew. He wants him followed.'

'Who are they?' Solomon repeated. 'You want to know who it is that plans to undermine the whole status quo of al-Andalus? Your eminence, you wish to add some *significant* jewels to your purchases. To be blunt, they don't come cheap.' The Grand Vizier was growing impatient. With a wave of the hand, he gestured to Solomon to go on. 'Well, sir, in Seville there is an association called, officially, The Brotherhood of Our Father Jesus of Nazareth. Bit of a mouthful, isn't it, so most people call it The Silence, after a particular characteristic of its members. Most of them are what one might call small-time, back-alley *enthusiasts*. But they've got a hard core. And it's them that are wanting to screw up – if you'll pardon the expression – the peaceful cohabitation of our various faiths.'

'Hmm. And here? You said there are Muslim zealots here in Granada who are bent on the same end.' Lisan al-Din could hardly believe that he was asking this creature for information on subversive groups in his own Sultanate. He'd heard rumours – of the existence of a cell of extremist *murabits*, 'fighters of the frontier' bent on launching a jihad that would wreck the delicate equilibrium in which Granada and Castile coexisted; but they had been no more than rumours. Until now. 'Who are *they*?'

Solomon sucked in air between his raddled gums. 'I wish I knew, your eminence. That would be a pearl of great price indeed, for both of us . . . But I don't know. And, as you're well aware, I'm not in the business of fakes. That's why you pay me so . . . *generously*.' He smiled like a fox.

'Solomon, my friend,' the Grand Vizier said amicably, 'I've always appreciated the quality of your goods. And that is why I have a last request. Tell me: who are your . . . suppliers of information – your "tame *jinn*", as you put it, in the Alcázar?'

Solomon was still smiling, but shaking his turban. 'Now, now, your eminence. You know full well that we middlemen can only maintain the impartiality of our positions, vis-à-vis supplier and consumer, by the exercise of total *confidentiality*.' The fox-look stayed, impenetrable now.

The Grand Vizier tried to ignore it. 'I am especially interested in any . . . business that a certain courtier may be conducting. Namely, Fernando de Guzmán.'

◈

'I know the old man's been driving us all mad,' one of the under-scribes murmured to his neighbour in the secretariat. 'But it looks as if His Confidentiality over there has literally lost his mind . . .'

For the second time, the Grand Vizier's confidential clerk was laughing to himself over the same piece of paper. He'd never thought it would be this easy. But, as he'd suspected while he was making the transcript, Solomon's apparently mysterious letter used a substitution cipher. Admittedly, it was a progressive rather than a simple substitution cipher. Still, in cryptographical terms, it was child's play.

TMOISCRFX XFQQOGDC DLXXXHQ IGD

XTX TENQCB MO AELINRPHED ZVHTN BLR OTLHL
EDRIQMSGQ

LF ZESCEV EOLOAZ XDXN DHGC DTCL EZE RFVZS
GGZRAZFXN BLBDCT MEGVOB

QDODHN FNGPSED FHOE HZAM XAFVNCP XCNR
IOVQMXGLTMS AODCXOTTNV

OQ DQOBRHR TXMM FSNTXFPEXPZ RTRREP HVM
FBZGDO GG XCOIFCRD

Since the script was Latin, it was almost inevitable that the
letter was in the Latin language too. And Latin letters almost
inevitably began with the same phrase: _____ _____
SALVTEM DAT, '*So-and-so* *to-So-and-so* GREETINGS GIVES'.
He looked at the third and fourth groups of characters:
DLXXXHQ IGD. The lengths were right . . . He jotted down
the Latin alphabet

ABCDEFGHILMNOPQRSTVXZ

and counted backwards from D, the first character in the group:
C, B, A, back to Z at the end of the alphabet, X, V, T, S. So S was
D minus 8. The next character in the group should be L minus 9.
It was. Then X minus 10 . . . yes, L. With the next X, the number
of letters subtracted was 1. So the progression went from 1 to 10
and then started again at 1. Again, he chuckled to himself at the
naivety of the Nazarenes. They might be proficient with the blunt
instrument of war. In anything more subtle, they had a long way to
go. He continued his decipherment:

$$D - 8 = S$$
$$L - 9 = A$$
$$X - 10 = L$$
$$X - 1 = V$$
$$X - 2 = T$$

127

$$H - 3 = E$$
$$Q - 4 = M$$

$$I - 5 = D$$
$$G - 6 = A$$
$$D - 7 = T$$

So DLXXXHQ IGD, as he had expected, was SALVTEM DAT, 'greetings gives'. It was as clear as a beacon on a mountain-top.

He turned to the first two groups, the ones that would give the names of sender and recipient: TMOISCRFX XFQQOGDC. A quick calculation showed him that the encoder had even been so helpful as to start the progression by the addition of one character. The result, however, was curious in the extreme:

$$T - 1 = S$$
$$M - 2 = I$$
$$O - 3 = L$$
$$I - 4 = E$$
$$S - 5 = N$$
$$C - 6 = T$$
$$R - 7 = I$$
$$F - 8 = V$$
$$X - 9 = M$$

SILENTIVM, 'silence' . . . It was almost the most basic code in the book; but one that hid an unexpected opening. He sucked his reed pen then continued.

The second word was equally strange: LEONIBVS, 'lions'. So,

SILENTIVM LEONIBVS SALVTEM DAT

'The silence gives greetings to the lions.'

The Grand Vizier studied Solomon closely: there might have been the minutest flicker of an eyelid at the mention of Fernando de Guzmán; but nothing more. The fox-grin remained.

Solomon spoke through it. 'You wish to investigate the private affairs of Don Fernando de Guzmán? Then, with respect, your eminence will have to journey to the Alcázar of our noble Seville and interview that gentleman yourself.' Then, sudden as a mask falling away, Solomon's smile disappeared. In its place was a hard gaze, as if at a dubious gemstone. 'My payment.'

The Grand Vizier was about to clap his hands again – then remembered that his confidential clerk was engaged in something infinitely more important. He drew his pencase and a scrap of paper from his own waist-sash and wrote: *To the bearer, Solomon of Seville, the sum of 5 (five) gold dinars only, being payment for a pouch of pearls.*

'You are a hard man,' Solomon said, watching the words spool out.

Lisan al-Din looked at him then added at the end of the order: *(small, fourth quality).* 'Next time,' he said, signing the docket, 'bring me only the best.'

Solomon took the paper and left without another word. The Grand Vizier remained, wondering where the nearest place was where he could wash his hands.

Eventually he rose. At the same moment, his confidential clerk appeared in the doorway of the belvedere. The young man was flushed and excited. 'Sir, we've got someone following him . . . That was what you meant, sir?'

'Yes. Good man. There was no time to be lost. I knew that once he was gone he'd melt away. Don't be misled by appearances: that old Jew's as slippery as a salamander.'

'Here's the deciphered transcript, sir. It was a substitution code. Progressive substitution, but of the most elementary sort, sir.'

Lisan al-Din studied the paper for a moment, then stroked his beard. 'Well, well . . . How strange. But perhaps not. And here, at last, we have our fourth colour. Our fourth humour.' He smiled at the clerk for the first time in the latter's ten years of service. 'We have blood! Go and find Shaykh Abu Abdallah.'

In a gloomy house across the valley of the Hadarruh, Lubna gave the couscous sieve another shake. Then she tipped the oversized grains that remained back into the wooden bowl, and began rubbing them between her hands once more. It had always been an act of love, doing this for Ali: in fact, kneeling on his kitchen floor as she shaped the grains with reverence between pressed palms, it had almost been an act of prayer. For her new master, it was a penance. A torture. She could hardly believe the man was Ali's brother. Of course, they'd been estranged for years; but still. She thought back to her own brother, to Jaime, and wondered whether the years had taken him as far away from her as this; if the Death hadn't taken him away entirely.

She repeated the sieving process and squinted to see if any more grains remained. Even now, mid morning, scarcely any light penetrated this smoke-blackened hole of a kitchen. It was a week since she'd seen the sun. A week since she'd said farewell to that funny old Moroccan gentleman and his black slave – 'Sinan . . .' She whispered the name into the darkness. Ali's name she couldn't bear even to whisper.

A shapeless figure appeared in the doorway. Her new mistress. 'The kitchen boy's not risen from his pallet today,' she said in her shrill unpleasant voice. 'Says he's dying, the lazy brat. Perhaps he is. Been coughing his lungs up these past six months. Hack hack hack, hack hack hack, day and night. Drives you bloody mad.'

Lubna looked at her mistress's baggy silhouette, and wondered if there was any trace of human kindness left in it. Poor woman: it had probably been brutalized out of her long ago, if her husband treated her anything like he treated his new slave-woman . . . Ali's brother – no, she *couldn't* think of him as that, however hard she tried – professed piety; but one recommendation of the Muslims' prophet seemed to have eluded him entirely, the one that said, *Do not come to your women like beasts do to theirs . . .*

'Anyway,' the woman continued, 'you'll have to do the shopping yourself today. Go in the last hour of the forenoon – you'll get the best prices then, even if the good stuff's gone. But mind you're quick about it. And don't forget, I'll be counting every single last copper when I check the change.'

The silhouette went. At last! This was her chance. She went to the tiny lattice, smaller than the window of a prison cell, praying that the usual beggar-boy was there. He was. She poked a piece of stale bread through one of the holes and whispered: 'Do you know the Spring of Tears? Good. Run there, quick as a bird. Ask for the house of the Grand Vizier. Got that? Find a house-slave, tell him to get Sinan the Black. Yes, the *Black* . . . Yes, he really is black, but no, he won't eat you . . . Tell Sinan to come with his master to the market of al-Bayyazin, at the end of the forenoon. Now repeat that to me.' *And next time,* she added to herself, *I'll give you something better than stale bread.*

'Spring of Tears,' the child said. 'House of the Grand Vizier. Sinan the Black. Al-Bayyazin suq, end of the forenoon.'

Abu Abdallah stared at the decoded transcript in the dappled light of the Grand Vizier's office.

SILENTIVM LEONIBVS SALVTEM DAT

NIL SCIMVS DE ORIGINIBVS NIGRI VEL FLAVI CANDIDIVE

ID TANTVM SCIMVS QVOD RVFA APVD VOS FESTO BAPHOMETI VESTRI ADERIT

ITERVM DICIMVS TVNC ESSE OPTIMAM RVFI
ADIPISCENDI OCCASIONEM
DE COLVMBIS ILLI COGNOVERVNT NOLITE VTI
CVRATE VT VALEATIS

He stared, and saw in those alien characters nothing but the trails of insects and the tracks of birds.

Everything was sliding from his grasp: vizierates, time, Lubna . . . At last, word had come from her – and then his hopes had dropped like a stone as, hard on the heels of her message, another had arrived: an urgent summons from Lisan al-Din. Now, the meaningless marks swam before him. Not for the first time in his life, Abu Abdallah cursed his tendency to end up treading in his own bullshit.

'Where was it you used to tell me you'd picked up your flawless Latin?' the Grand Vizier asked.

Abu Abdallah swallowed. 'Um, it must have been Constantinople . . . But, Lisan, it was thirty years ago. It's really rusty now.'

'Oh, nonsense. You can't possibly forget such an elementary language as Latin! And this is so simple, even by the low standards of that tongue, that I feel there must be something more to it. I just thought you might have a few insights, that you might be able to tease out the subtext. Not that there ever is much subtext in Latin. Metaphor, periphrasis, double entendre, paronomasia . . . such ornaments are the preserve of our own divine Arabic speech.'

'To be honest, Lisan, I think it's the result of my having perfected so many other languages in the intervening years,' Abu Abdallah said. 'You know, Turkish, Persian, Dhivehi – that's the language of the Maldivian archipelago where, I don't know if you remember, I served as Chief Justice . . . In short, my Latin's so rusty it's seized up, and on top of that it's been buried under those other languages.'

'Well,' the Grand Vizier said, smiling askance at his friend, 'permit me to oil your highly developed but neglected linguistic faculties.' He took the sheet from Abu Abdallah and translated: '*From the*

Silence – we'll . . . let us say, we might come back to that later – *to the lions* – whatever they may be – *greetings. We know nothing of the provenances of black and yellow and white. All we know is that the red one will reach you from us on the feast-day of your Baphomet* – whatever, or whoever, *that* may be. *We say again that this is your best chance to get the red one. They know about the pigeons. Do not use them. Farewell.*'

Abu Abdallah clapped his brow. 'And there, Lisan, as I was about to say when I first saw the transcript – but, you know, my mind went blank until you so eloquently jogged it – there is the fourth colour, red! The set of humours is complete now. Do you remember my theory about them, you know, that the colours represent the humours?'

'I believe it was *my* theory. But that hardly matters. The thing is that all the elements of the humoral metaphor are now in place. It now remains to exercise our intellects and extract the concrete from the abstract – the mineral, so to speak, from the matrix. Or, if you prefer the vulgar expression, to find the wood among the trees.'

'Absolutely,' Abu Abdallah said. 'And I think I'm already beginning to identify a good quantity of lumber, or timber, or mineral, or whatever it is we're looking for, although I'm coming at it from the angle of the celestial humours. Now, I picked up quite a lot of the ancient astrological lore of the Indians during my time as Malikite Judge of the Sultanate of Delhi – that was before my appointment as Ambassador Pleni–'

' –potentiary to the Emperor of China,' Lisan al-Din cut in. 'We *do* remember.'

'So, as I was saying,' Abu Abdallah continued, 'I think you'll find, if you double-check with your Department of Astrology, that on the feast-day of Baphomet – my theory being that this is the Nazarenes' term for Yahya who baptized Jesus the son of Mary, peace be upon them all: "John the Baphomet" is what they call him you see – the red planet Mars will enter the constellation of, er, the Scorpion, coming from the direction of the north, from the lands of the Nazarenes. This will produce a universal superfluity of the – what's it called? – the *sanguinaraceous* humour, leading to ... to an ... um ...'

'Master,' said a voice – that of Sinan, who was squatting as usual by the doorway, 'don't you remember what his eminence the Grand Vizier told us about the Great Ruby? That they'll bring it from the land of the Nazarenes on the birthday of the Prophet? Don't you think "the red one" in the message could be the Ruby? Which would mean that "Baphomet" is the Nazarenes' name for the Prophet Muhammad, peace and blessings upon him?'

'*Thank* you, Sinan,' Abu Abdallah said. 'I was working round to that point myself, if you hadn't barged in on me like that.'

His master sounded unusually peeved. Sinan knew why. Abu Abdallah would rather be elsewhere. With Lubna. And so, if he admitted it, would he; or part of him.

'Yes, thank you indeed, Sinan!' the Grand Vizier said warmly. 'That is the incontrovertible conclusion to which the application of logic would have led me too, had not your youthful and limber brain beaten my aged and sluggish cerebrum to it. Come to think of it, I believe "Baphomet" is an intentionally blasphemous corruption of the name of the Seal of the Prophets, dating back to the time of the Nazarene occupation of Palestine. And yes, *rufa*, "the red one", could hardly be anything but the Ruby: "Rufa *apud vos ... aderit ... optimam* rufi *adipiscendi occasionem*." '

'*Rufa ... rufi ...* ' Sinan said, repeating the alien words. 'Why are they different, sir?'

'One is nominative, the other genitive,' Lisan al-Din explained. 'Just like Arabic: *ahmaru, ahmara*. But ... bless you, since you mention it, the gender's different too. The first is feminine ... hmm, it probably refers notionally to *gemma*, "gem". The second is masculine, so it must refer to ... what on earth is the Latin for "ruby"? *Rubinus*, I think. But there you are. Latin is such an imprecise and illogical tongue. Not like our divine and immaculate Arabic. Latin, Master

Sinan, is the tongue of Franks and Nazarenes. Arabic is the tongue of angels, and of God Himself.'

'Grammar apart,' Abu Abdallah said, 'the meaning's clear as crystal: these "lions", whatever they are, are going to have a shot at seizing the Ruby. You've got to admit it's a daring plan.'

'And doomed to failure, my dear friend. You can be sure Don Pedro will have the tightest security on his side of the border. He can't afford anything going wrong. He needs us. And on our side of the frontier the ambassadors will have a picked Berber cavalry escort. They'll see the Ruby all the way to the treasury of the Alhambra, which is as impregnable as human ingenuity can make it. So our would-be jewel thieves will fail – unless they can cut their way through a hundred Berber knights.' The Grand Vizier folded his embroidered sleeves. 'Or through a hundred cubits of living rock.'

'So that's that,' Abu Abdallah said. 'And,' he glanced through the lattice at the sun, rapidly approaching its zenith, 'if you don't mind, I'll be on my way.'

'Oh ... I was hoping you would come and see the further progress in the new court. For one thing, the painted hall is completely finished. Perhaps Sinan could provide us with some more of his choice observations on the figurative art of the Nazarenes.'

'I'd love to, Lisan. But I've got a previous engagement. Previous, and pressing.'

'What could possibly be more pressing,' Lisan al-Din said, 'than to indulge the whim of the Grand Vizier of Granada? What – or who?'

Abu Abdallah looked sheepish.

The Grand Vizier's shoulders began to heave, and he emitted his wheezing laugh: 'I know: the Alchemist's slave-woman! Don't tell me you've made a pass . . . I mean, an *offer* for her already!' He winked at Abu Abdallah. 'It's quite all right, my friend. You don't need to feel embarrassed. If it was a choice between me and her, I'd go for her too, any day. Or night . . .'

The confidential clerk had been hovering outside, waiting for the little Moroccan and his slave to leave. He cleared his throat and stepped into the Grand Vizier's office.

'What news?' Lisan al-Din said, no trace of his amusement left.

'Sir, the Jew was followed as you instructed. He's now in his lodging in the New Funduq. But he went there by a very roundabout route – via the cemetery of al-Bayyazin, in fact. And while he was at the cemetery he went into one of those caves in the cliff, sir, the ones that overlook the graves.'

Lisan al-Din looked thoughtful. 'Was the particular cave noted? There are scores of them.' The clerk nodded. 'Then set a watch over it. Quick as you can. Someone utterly reliable and discreet.'

The clerk slipped out, wondering whom to send. One of the Mamluks, perhaps . . . Yes. He knew who.

Chapter 17

Lubna led them higher and higher up the steep alleys of al-Bayyazin. She had waited in the market until the noon prayer-call sounded and she'd known that her lateness would earn her a beating from her new master ... before, or after that other, nightly violation? And then they had come, Sinan and Abu Abdallah, and she hadn't cared any more.

Now they climbed in silence, Abu Abdallah with an agility that belied his age, Sinan with his silent-footed hunter's stride. Eventually the houses thinned and they came to the first graves in the terraced cemetery. Above them, the line of the city wall followed the contour of the hillside. Beneath it was the low escarpment pierced with caves. They might have been the burrows of a colony of rodents; except that the inhabitants were men and women – poor, mad, abandoned, dispossessed, but human. From the cave entrances, eyes stared out at the intruders.

Lubna was aware of the two other pairs of eyes behind her. Again, yet again, she opened her mouth to explain – what? The truth was, she didn't know why she was bringing the two men here. The cave led to her captors, and somehow – she was sure – to Ali's killer. She raged, she blazed to know who they were. But she blazed cold. Those other eyes, glinting green above the veil, had seared themselves into her memory, and that voice: '*We will make him die a second death.*'

She shivered; then thought of the little man climbing the path behind her. At least she felt safe with him, and with Sinan ... The growl of a dog cut into her thoughts.

'Qur'anic reference, Sinan?' Abu Abdallah said. Lubna looked up and saw the dog, sitting at the entrance of a cave.

'*And their dog, with forelegs outstretched, at the entrance.* From the story of the People of the Cave, master. The Chapter of the Cave, verse 18.'

' "Spot on, you ebony prodigy!" ' Abu Abdallah said, imitating the Grand Vizier's orotund tones.

Lubna smiled. Yes, she felt safe in this moment. And more than safe. It wasn't just that she'd been taken unawares by the – what? – the *presence* of the first black man she'd ever looked at, a physicality more powerful than beauty, that despite everything, despite even Ali, had hit her in the pit of her stomach. It wasn't that Sinan alone had believed her that morning in the *majlis* of the Chief of the Night. No: what surprised her – overwhelmed her – was the way *he* looked at her. Not as a commodity, or a distraction, or a utensil, or a receptacle for nightly and brutal insemination; but as a human being. Since the day of her enslavement only one other person had looked at her like that, and he was dead.

That was why she was bringing them here. To be with Sinan. The realization shocked her.

And now – they were at the mouth of the feared familiar cave – that shock stifled even the dread that haunted this spot.

She led them in. 'You may be wondering, sir,' she said, once their eyes had adjusted to the half-light, 'why . . .'

' . . . why you have brought us here,' Abu Abdallah said. 'Yes, I am.' He squinted at the pile of rags on the floor and bent down to inspect them.

'*Don't!*'

Abu Abdallah jerked upright.

'Forgive me, sir. But they belonged to a pauper who lived here and died of the Death, last year,' Lubna explained.

'Master,' Sinan said, 'I believe it is debatable whether the agent causing the Death can remain in something inanimate.'

'We'd have to ask Lisan al-Din about that,' Abu Abdallah said. 'He's written a treatise on the, what's it called? The Contagion Theory, I think. But that's as may be. You were about to tell us, dear lady, why we are here.' He scanned the niches carved into the cave wall, visible now in the gloom.

Lubna was silent for a while. 'You see, sir, I used to . . .I mean Ali, my master, my late master, used to send me here with messages. I think, I *know* there is a connection between the verse he wrote and this place. And with his . . . his death.'

The word lingered.

'Forgive me for pressing,' Abu Abdallah said gently, 'but can you tell us more?'

Lubna led them into the inner chamber. 'I would bring the messages here, and leave them in this niche,' she said, showing them the deep alcove in the back wall. 'Under that stone.'

Sinan lifted the stone and felt beneath it. There was nothing there.

'Can you tell us whom the messages were for?'

In the chamber of her memory, in the dark of another cave, she saw a face half-shrouded by *shash*-cloth and shadow, and green eyes, lit from within, staring into her soul. 'Sir, I do not know.'

Abu Abdallah was smiling at her, encouraging, his head to one side. Lubna could feel the lie written in her own eyes. But no: it wasn't a lie. She didn't know who her captors were. 'I think we will find out in time,' Abu Abdallah said. 'One way or another.'

Silently and methodically, the two men searched the cave, feeling around all its nooks and niches, and found nothing. When at last they made for the cave entrance and the early afternoon sun, Lubna spoke to their backs and broke the silence. 'Sir, I apologise. I have wasted your time.'

Abu Abdallah searched for an answer. It never came.

It was Sinan who saw him first. The man was crouching by a grave, watching him with wide wild eyes. He knew that look, and the crooked angle of that nose. From where?

Then Lubna saw him too. At first the light blinded her after the gloom of the cave, the beard concealed him. But only for an instant – and then the years parted, fell away like a ripped veil.

She stared, stunned, and said – no more than a breath expelled – '*Jaime*.'

His lips moved: '*María*.' Then sound came: '*Jaime está muerto . . . mayyit. MAYYYYIT!*'

A Spanish whisper that ended in an Arabic howl: Jaime is dead.

Sinan, his hunting instinct in control, tensed himself, sprung as the madman lunged . . . and met nothing but air.

The man had dived the other way and was off, bounding over the graves like a beast in flight.

Motionless, they watched him diminishing until at last he disappeared behind a stand of trees below the valley head.

No one, not even sharp-eyed Sinan, noticed the other figure that moved in jerks along the base of the escarpment. It was the figure of an old woman, hobbling with unnatural swiftness.

Sergeant Hamid ran along the track, his beggar's rags flying. He told himself he was doing his duty. But he knew he was running away from his past. Hamid was running away from Jaime.

He *would* do his duty, of course . . . But not all of it. He'd tell them about the little man and the Black; not about María. And then he'd tell them it was a mission he couldn't do any more – that he'd been found out. That, at least, was the truth.

Except that he knew he wouldn't tell them that. He would go back, bravest of the Mamluks, terrified of his own sister, aching to see her again.

Panting, his pace slowing, he reached the great gate of the Alhambra with its cresting of heads. The guards barred his way. Hamid yelled at them: 'Don't you know your own sergeant?'

Slow recognition of the parade-ground voice, then a swift salute. He entered the massive portal followed by grunted apologies. A change of clothes, and his own men hadn't known him. María had known him through the camouflage of years.

But then, she was the only one who had ever truly known him.

At least, here in the doglegged darkness of the empty gateway, no one could see his tears.

At last Lubna said it again, to break the wall of strangeness and silence that had surrounded her since that resurrection of her brother among the tombs. 'Sir, I feel I have wasted your time with empty holes and . . . madmen.' She knew she couldn't tell them about Jaime. Not when she scarcely believed it herself. But how to explain that brief, soft touch of identities – *Jaime . . . María . . .* – a moment of siblinghood salvaged from the years of separation?

'Far from it, dear lady,' Abu Abdallah was saying. 'It was worth it for the pleasure of seeing you, I mean your . . . magnificent city, from a new angle. Such a pleasing prospect of the valley, and the Alhambra, and . . . so on . . .'

Lubna managed to smile to herself. If Abu Abdallah had caught that whisper of recognition between sister and brother, he was too much a gentleman to ask for amplification. But another awkward silence settled on them.

The further they descended among the houses tumbling up the valley-side of al-Bayyazin, the more her thoughts gathered momentum, until they bounded on, unstoppable. In the avalanche of events over the past ten days she'd lost her lover and mentor, been kidnapped, arrested, publicly interrogated, re-enslaved, raped nightly, had found a lost brother – then lost him again, too.

To what? To religion? She had clung to the shreds of the Christian faith that had always clothed her. Jaime was a Mamluk, his fealty to the Sultan only matched by his loyalty to Allah.

Or had she lost him to insanity? There he'd been, lurking among the graves in rags. But that stare of his wasn't that of a madman or a fanatic: it was the look of a man who was terrified.

By what, she couldn't tell.

All she knew was that her more recent past had crumbled about her. And that now even her deepest history, the bedrock of her being, had risen up and cracked apart.

The future was unthinkable.

So Lubna took refuge in the moment, safe between her two unexpected guardians, one of them – despite herself, she smiled again – besotted with her, the other . . . But she didn't know about Sinan, not even she, the *qaynah* trained to know how men feel.

Chapter 18

'*From the Silence to the Lions, greetings,*' Sarim translated, for the third time since the message had arrived.

'Cut the niceties,' Layth growled. Haydar, who had been summoned to give his scientist's opinion on the message, saw his Shaykh's green eyes smouldering in the torchlight. He had never seen Layth looking so angry.

'My apologies, Shaykh Layth . . .' Sarim said.

'Just get on with it!' Layth's yell rang through the tunnels.

'*We know nothing of the, er, provenances of black and yellow and white,*' Sarim continued, his thin scholar's voice shaking. '*All we know is that the red one will reach you from us on the feast-day of your Baphomet,* Muhammad, that is, peace and blessings upon him – '

'And damnation on these Nazarenes for corrupting his glorious name,' Layth spat. 'And on you, Sarim. *Get on with it!*'

'*We say again that this is your best chance to get the Red One. They know about the pigeons. Do not use them. Farewell.*'

'And there you have it,' Layth said to Haydar, now with chilling softness. 'Our most eminent Professor Sarim here can't read anything between the Nazarenes' lines. I assume you cannot do so either, Haydar. So, do we just carry on and hope it works?'

'I don't see what else we can do, Shaykh Layth. The message is clear enough: the Nazarenes cannot help us. At least production of the Remedy remains steady. By God's grace, we are on course to have the necessary quantity ready ahead of time. It's just that we're missing the Alchemist's improvement, hidden in that verse of his . . .'

'You don't have to remind me, fool,' Layth hissed. Then his voice exploded: 'We *must* get the Red One! A chance like this may not come again for years. Decades. *Ever!*'

'And the fact that it is the heretical "feast-day",' Sarim added with quiet malice, when the echo had died, 'of the birthday of the Seal of the Prophets, peace and blessings upon him, means that we will be killing two birds with one shot, by striking on the occasion of that pernicious innovation. Hah! Our infidel Sultan now thinks he has to keep up with the Nazarene neighbours and their *Christmas* . . .'

'If only it was as easy as killing birds,' Layth said, shaking his head. 'So, Haydar, have you nothing at all to contribute?'

Haydar swallowed hard. 'I know it is a strange notion, Shaykh Layth, but it has crossed my mind once or twice before, and I recall the idea now, with Sarim's reference to shots, whether we might not use *firearms.*'

Layth said nothing, but looked at Sarim.

'It may be an option,' Sarim said. 'I remember well the reports of the godless father of the current godless Sultan using the *midfa'*, or "propulsor", in the defence of al-Jazirah some twenty-five years ago. It cast iron balls and flames into the ranks of the Nazarenes.'

Layth licked his lips. 'A foretaste of hellfire for them . . .'

'The Nazarenes themselves have developed their own firearms, Shaykh Layth,' Haydar added. 'They call them *"cannon"* in their language, I believe. And I heard that the King of England's son, the one known as the Black Prince, used them only last year against Henry the Bastard when fighting for Don Pedro.'

Layth looked at Sarim. 'But for us – are they feasible?'

'To be practical, Shaykh Layth, we could not possibly procure even one of those propulsors in the given time. The smallest type of firearm, the so-called "kohl-pot", would be more of a possibility – I mean those iron tubes that are fixed on to pieces of wood and held against the shoulder . . .'

Layth's eyes were glowing. 'Yes, go on.'

'Then again, think how long it would take to have even one of them made, even if we could find someone to do it. The manufacture of firearms is a sultanic monopoly. And then there would have to be training. Intensive training. Time, logistics, everything is against the idea, Shaykh Layth.' He saw the glow leave Layth's eyes. 'And to be honest,' Sarim went on, trying to console his leader, 'firearms are more a matter of shock and awe than of death and destruction. The common soldier may tell horror stories about them, of the wounds they cause never healing and so on, but in reality they are little more than toys. Give me a well-made crossbow any day. Or one of those English longbows. Believe me, Shaykh Layth, firearms are a fad that will soon fizzle out.'

'God,' said Layth, 'is the most knowing . . . But you are right. Time's too short. It's too late to change course now. And besides . . .' he closed his eyes and held his head. '*They know.*'

Sarim and Haydar looked at each other for a long moment. Eventually it was Sarim who spoke. 'What do they know, Shaykh Layth?'

'About us. They're on to us.'

For the second time this day, Umm Ahmad hobbled past the sufi shrine that stood on the south-east slope of the Alhambra hill. Now, in the dead hours of early afternoon, there were no visitants at the small tomb-chamber. Not that anyone would have noticed her, a wrinkled crone of sixty dressed in rusty black; or only one of those do-gooders who hovered round such places. She laughed to herself at the thought of the man who'd come up to her this morning and held out a copper to her, thinking he'd buy his place in Paradise with it. She'd taken it – and thrown it in his fat speechless face. She didn't care about coppers. Only about Green-Eyes' beautiful, shining, clinking silver.

Silver. That was why Umm Ahmad dragged herself all the way here from her cave – twice, today. The first time, with the

message from the Jew, had earned her ten dirhams. This time –
God, her feet ached, her joints throbbed and burned, the Devil
take them – she'd make Green-Eyes pay her more, or she'd curse
him to his face and see him cringe. Besides, she was bringing
news of great value. A good twenty dirhams' worth. Umm
Ahmad moistened her lips at the thought of the coins dropping
through the secret hole and landing, with that satisfying 'plink',
in the buried pot that contained her hoard. She turned off the
track and dragged herself with a groan through the breach in
the high old wall.

Ever more painfully, Umm Ahmad followed the steep track down
through the tangled bushes, avoiding the thorns that tried to grasp her
cloak and the roots that reached up to trip her. This place, they said, had
been the palace garden of a Jewish vizier, back in the days of Berber rule,
before kings built on the Alhambra hill. Now it was an abode of the *jinn*,
a small haunted no-man's-land of ancient olive trees and gnarled holm-
oaks between the bustle of the city below and the grandeur of the
Alhambra. No one dared to cross its boundary, not even by day. Only
Green-Eyes and his men. And Umm Ahmad, in whose opinion all the
jinn and ghouls and *afrits* of al-Andalus could go and screw each other
in hell. She reached the side-track and made for the face of the hill.

The track opened out suddenly into a small clearing on a
collapsing terrace. There, facing her, was the door – a biggish door
of heavy rough planks like the door of a gardener's store. Strangely,
it had no handle and no lock, nor even a key-hole. Even more
strangely, it led into the hillside.

Cursing her joints, Umm Ahmad stooped down, picked up a
stone and rapped.

' "*They're on to us* . . . " What do you mean, Shaykh Layth?' There
was a note of panic in Sarim's voice; but he forced a smile. 'If you
are referring to the warning in the message about not using the

birds, then, with respect, that could hardly mean that we have been found out. It is surely–'

The three men looked up abruptly at the sound of the knocking, distant but clear . . . then relaxed: it was the old woman's signal, three short knocks then a long, three times. Strange, though. She'd already come once today.

Layth still looked worried. Haydar knew he hated the old witch who spied on their drop-off above the graveyard. She was the only person who was not afraid of the Lions' chief. But there was a real edge of fear in Layth's voice when he spoke. 'Sarim, Haydar . . . do not tell the other Lions, but there is more to it than just the matter of the birds. There is news from the Alhambra: Asad reports that the little Moroccan and his Black have been snooping round the new court again.'

'Shaykh Layth, with the greatest respect, I cannot understand why you believe, in your great wisdom, that those two are such a threat . . .'

'Sarim, I do not merely believe they are a threat . . . I *know* it,' Layth said quietly. He wondered whether to tell his two lieutenants about the fateful night of the thunderbolt, the night the Alchemist was lost. About the encounter in the alley with the Moroccan and the Black . . . and then, like scabies, desire came crawling under his skin.

'Shaykh Layth?' Sarim said softly.

Layth didn't hear. If he couldn't have the Black, then the second-best pleasure would be to kill him . . . And was it second-best? That beautiful body would be penetrated, if not by hot flesh then by cold steel.

Someone was speaking to him with great insistence. 'Shaykh Layth . . . *Shaykh Layth* . . . The crone is here. She has urgent news. Most urgent.'

'I could make your master an offer for you,' Abu Abdallah said to Lubna. 'An offer he couldn't refuse.' *I'd have to touch Lisan al-Din for the cash*, he thought.

Only the lazy intermittent splash of water filled the silence. Even the fountain outside the Grand Vizier's guest pavilion seemed to be taking a siesta in these dead afternoon hours.

'Sir,' Lubna said, her eyes downcast, 'I know that he would never agree.'

Abu Abdallah listened for the sadness in her voice, but heard an edge of . . . what? Relief? *All these women I've known, and I still don't really know them.*

'You see,' she went on, 'to punish his dead brother through me is more important to him than money.'

He didn't want to admit it, but he himself was relieved. He'd gone through it all so many times in his head, in the small hours when the fountain slept and only the nightjars broke the silence at the Spring of Tears, and had always arrived at the same unspoken conclusion: he wanted her to possess him, not the other way round. And yet she was possessed in this unaccountable way by Sinan. That much he did know. Even now, she was only partly present with him. The other part was off in the Grand Vizier's kitchens, where Sinan had gone to fetch their lunch. He sighed. 'Then all we can do, dear lady, is to escort you back to your new master and tell him you were wandering up at the graveyard – which, even if it is a little less than the truth, is certainly no *more* than the truth. And we can add that you . . . your mind has been deeply troubled by your recent tribulations.'

Lubna shook her head slowly. 'It won't have any effect on him.'

Abu Abdallah drew himself up and jutted his beard. 'Then *I* shall have an effect on him. I shall tell him who I am: Shams al-Din Abu Abdallah of Tangier, known as Ibn Battutah, former Malikite Qadi of Delhi, former Chief Justice of the Maldivian Archipelago, former . . .' He stopped, seeing Sinan appear in the doorway, seeing the beginning of a smile exchanged with Lubna over the tray of food. 'But . . . that was who I was. And now . . . *what?*' His voice had trailed away to nothing. The two slaves were silent. The fountain faltered.

And then Abu Abdallah cleared his throat abruptly and spoke with his usual jauntiness. 'Lunch. That's what, my dear. God knows, you need it. You look as if this new master of yours is starving you. Come, Sinan, look sharp with that tray!'

❁

'The same slave-woman as before, you say?' Layth was looking askance at the old woman.

Umm Ahmad rubbed her fingertips together, right under his nose. 'Yes. Do you think I'm senile? Give me my money.'

'And the little old foreigner, with the beard that sticks out, and the Black?'

'My money.'

'And a spy, as well, out by the graves? How are you so sure?'

'I've told you. He had a clean shirt under his rags. And he was well-fed. Strong-looking. Nazarene-looking . . . *My money.*'

'Oh, give the hag whatever she wants, Sarim. Haydar, prepare four daggers. Yes, fool, the Hashshashin daggers! And you'd better have enough poison for them. They must be eliminated. *Now.*'

'Shaykh Layth,' Sarim said, 'with the utmost deference . . . is this wise?'

Layth ignored him and strode out into the main chamber, speaking as if to himself. 'Hattam can take the spy . . . Dirgham must be blooded . . . he can take the slave-woman. Maybe Jassas for the old man . . .'

Sarim was behind him. 'B . . . but, Shaykh Layth, it is daytime. Can so many of us risk being seen, out in the open?'

Layth turned the green fire of his gaze on the older man. 'I have told you. They must be eliminated.' The eyes blazed but the voice was ice-cold. Sarim froze, terrified. '*And I,*' Layth continued softly, his eyes closing, '*will take the Black.*'

149

Chapter 19

Outside the gate of the Grand Vizier's palace by the Spring of Tears, Sinan felt the beginning of a chill in the air. He and Abu Abdallah had prayed the mid-afternoon prayer before setting off with Lubna, and now the sun was well into its long autumnal slide down the sky. He wondered if he would ever get used to the strangeness of these northern latitudes; or to the feelings, so long buried, that the woman walking in front of him had awoken.

He tried to shake the feelings off. In no time she would be gone.

Lost in reflection, Sinan paid no attention to the Grand Vizier's guards, or to the row of squatting supplicants across from the gate. He didn't notice the tiny signal made by one of the waiting petitioners, a man wrapped in a *taylasan* against the coming cold. Nor was he aware that, just after Abu Abdallah's small group had passed, this man and two others rose and left the line.

'Sir,' Lubna said when they were round a bend in the track and out of earshot of the people at the gate, 'I must reiterate my apologies to you. I think I will never again have the opportunity to do so. You have been so kind, and I have wasted your time to no purpose by taking you to that empty cave.'

Abu Abdallah laughed. 'And I say, stuff and nonsense my dear! I hardly need to tell you that the company of a civilized woman like yourself is a joy to a clapped-out old greybeard like me.' He raised a hand and waved away Lubna's remonstration. 'And besides, I have always found that caves, even empty ones, are often doorways into regions unknown.'

151

The little group fell silent for a few moments. 'Why is that, sir?' Lubna said. She wanted the silence to fill with talk, not forebodings of the end of this brief reprieve.

'Beware, beware the traveller's tale!' Abu Abdallah said portentously. 'Once you get me going I can't stop.'

'I would not wish you to stop, sir.'

'Very well. But I will give you just one example. When I was staying in the city of China the Great, in the lands of the Great Qan, in what they call the regions beyond the wind, as far east from the central cupola of the Earth as we are west, I went to visit a famous holy man who dwelt in a cave outside the city. He was two hundred years of age, or so they said, but all his faculties were intact – even, forgive me madam, his procreative ones, though how they knew that beats me. On seeing me he took my hand, sniffed it, and said, "You are from one end of the world, and we are from the other." He then entered his cave, I followed . . . and found no trace of him within.'

'How could that be? Surely there was some secret hiding place.'

'God is the most knowing. I didn't find one. What I do know is that the emptiness of the cave was an illusion. So too is the emptiness of your cave, dear lady. What we need to know is not only where to look, but *how*.'

Their footfalls sounded loud. None of them, not even Sinan, was aware of the softly following figures, always keeping out of sight around the bends in the track, waiting until their victims reached the crowded market streets of al-Bayyazin. That was the place, Layth had told them, the place to strike: like lightning, without warning, where even if you couldn't land a proper blow the poison would run its agonizing course.

'Haven't you always said that everything in China is wonderful, master?' Sinan said.

'As I've told you, my boy, the Almighty created nine-tenths of His wonders in the East. Take that reception I was invited to in al-

Khansa in the furthest east of China. The biggest city in the world, it is – three day's travel just to cross it! Of course, they may have put on a special show because of my visit – by the way, I don't think I've told you, my dear,' Abu Abdallah said, turning to Lubna, 'that I was visiting China in my capacity as Ambassador Extraordinary and Plenipotentiary from the Sultan of Hind. Anyway, they had these great gilded barges on the lake, in the forms of dragons and serpents and phoenixes and the like, and they staged a mock battle in which the ammunition was oranges and lemons. And the fireworks!'

'*Fireworks*, sir?' Lubna said.

'Things like arrows that shoot into the air, without the aid of bows, or run about the surface of the lake like starfish gone mad, or revolve with the utmost speed, and burst into fiery colours – "*Qahhhh!!!*" – ' and Abu Abdallah jumped into the air, spreading his arms to the sky, his robe flying, making the two slaves laugh out loud ' – yellow, white, red, every colour but black! And they probably *could* do black as well, only you'd need sharp eyes to see it against the night sky.'

Lubna was still laughing; saving up the laughter, if she knew, to see her through the rest of her life. But behind her, Sinan was deep in thought again. The image of black fire at night . . . it had summoned up that line of verse – *Black as the night that fires the heat of lust in early dawn* – and those other colours, yellow, white, now red as well. 'Master,' he said, 'what makes these fireworks fly and swim and so on? You've never told me.'

'Heaven knows, my boy. But I think it's the fire itself. Something to do with alchemy. Come to think of it, I did happen to ask at the time. Or rather, it was later on, when I was aboard a Chinese ship that had a device for throwing these bowless fire-arrows at pirates. As far as I remember, they work by a mixture of sulphur and charcoal, all ground up together. That's it . . . and there was something else too. Some special ingredient. I can't for the life of me remember.'

They rounded a corner. The declining sun lit the patches of white that, even this late in the year, still topped Jabal Shulayr. Abruptly, Abu Abdallah turned, making the two slaves stop in their tracks. 'That's it!' he said. Much further back, a figure wrapped in a *taylasan* darted for a gap in a wall; Abu Abdallah didn't notice him. '*Snow!*' he exclaimed. 'Chinese snow!'

A man coming up the track with a laden donkey faltered in his step and stared at the little foreigner uttering strange words, and the Black.

They walked on. 'But sir,' Lubna said, 'how can something cold like snow generate heat and fire?'

'Oh it's not your actual snow. It's metaphorical snow. The substance in question is white and light and – that's it, I knew there was something funny about it – they find it in nasty fetid places. It's all coming back to me now . . .' They had to edge to the side of the track as a group of porters came past with bulging sacks on their backs. 'You see,' Abu Abdallah continued, 'I stayed in China the Great with a merchant who exported the stuff. It's that sort of white bloom that grows on the walls of cellars and stables and latrines and so on.'

They were now in the warren of al-Bayyazin, its alleys busiest of all at this hour, and were nearing the small thronged marketplace. But the minds of all three of them were elsewhere: Abu Abdallah's was on the far coasts of China; Lubna's back in her cell in the approaching house, dark and narrow as the grave, waiting for the footfall and the breathing that began her nightly rape; Sinan's mind was hunting for some trace, some half-remembered sign that would make sense of it all and put them on the trail. None of them was aware of the swelling hubbub of hawking and hustling about them, of the sleeve-twitching beggars, or the apothecary with his rack of dried roots and lizards, or the man who sat soliciting for alms and displaying what might have been a ripe pumpkin but was in fact his own distended scrotum; nor of the professional farter with his giggling audience and his patter – 'Hark to the art of the fart! The bigger the tips, the louder it rips!'; nor of the street preacher who in a thin reedy tenor reminded slave and sultan, prince and pauper, whoremonger and holy man that they could hope for nothing more than the grave and the mercy of God. Nor were Sinan and his companions aware of three figures threading their way through the crowd, all with hands gripping hilts beneath their robes, bearing down on them.

Suddenly Sinan found what he was looking for. '*Master!*' he called over the heads of the market-goers. 'I've remembered!' He pushed forward, past Lubna – he just caught the musk of her clothes, her body – and reached Abu Abdallah's side. 'You know you said this "Chinese snow" comes from latrines and so on, and that it's all something alchemical? Well, that morning when we were in the *majlis* of the Chief of the Night, there was a boy who said he'd seen Ali the Alchemist in the mosque lavatories with a bag, collecting some—'

Just in time he caught the glint of steel aimed at Abu Abdallah's neck, caught the arm that held the dagger and wrenched it as hard as he could. He didn't hear the clatter of the dagger on the cobbles, but he felt the tearing of twisted gristle and muscle and the pop of bone torn from socket, heard the shriek of pain that silenced the market square and turned a hundred heads towards him. The torque of his parry had spun him round – and he saw another glint, a blade quivering for an instant in the grip of a gawping youth, and yelled at Lubna, '*RUN!*' – and then, too late, the flash of yet another blade, aimed at his own breast, and the fire of green eyes, and the flame of loathing . . .

. . . and lust. The eyes closed and the blade hesitated, a mere sliver of a moment.

The dagger flew at his heart, but that fraction of time was enough for Sinan to dive.

He hit the cobbles, waited for the blow.

It didn't come.

The sound of feet running away. The crowd's held breath escaping in unison, a drawn-out '*Aaaah*'.

Sinan sprang up, saw Abu Abdallah standing surprised but composed – 'Very good of you to ask,' he was saying to the crowd, 'never felt better, obviously wasn't my appointed hour . . .' – saw over the heads a figure in a *taylasan* dodging and weaving through the onlookers with the agility of a polecat, just enough ahead of the spreading ripple of realization to get away.

Sinan was after him. The crowd parted like a bow-wave before the charging Black. The attacker disappeared into the mouth of an alley.

It was a blind alley. He had him! But where was he? An image flashed – the Chinese cave of disappearance – as Sinan's momentum took him crashing into the dead end.

It wasn't a dead end. It was a T-junction where both turnings looked hardly wide enough to admit a cat, let alone a man. Sinan scanned the dust for a sign. *Which way?* For a moment, it was so deathly silent that he wondered if in fact he hadn't got away. If he was really dead, and this place was his grave. And in the silence he pictured those green eyes, drawing him down into the deepest layers of his past, beyond memory.

But he heard the knocking of his heart, felt the swish of his blood around his limbs, and knew he was alive. Then another sound, behind him – a breath, *a footstep*.

He spun round, but this time it was too late to evade the blow.

Chapter 20

This time Lubna had known where she was running.

She fondled the rough masonry. It still had some warmth left in it. But the sun had left the valley, and the line of the Alhambra's bastions that marched and beetled along the wooded slope was darkening to the shade of bruised flesh. Light lingered only on Jabal Shulayr, turning the scant snowfields lilac.

The scene had inspired a hundred odes, a thousand stanzas, myriad verses, a few of them by Lubna. But now she knew the beauty of it was a lie.

She looked up at the holes that pierced the escarpment above the graveyard, and remembered what Abu Abdallah had said about the cave: that its emptiness was an illusion. She shook her head. The old man had meant well, but he was wrong. Emptiness, nothingness, death were the only realities. Everything else in this world of creation and extinction, coming-to-be and passing-away, was fleeting, insubstantial, illusory.

The thought took her back to a night several Ramadans ago, when she and Ali had watched the show the wandering puppeteers put on in the marketplace of al-Bayyazin. *Khayal al-zill*, they called it, 'shadow-fantasy'. The puppet-masters knew the truth: that the world was a pantomime, and that the parts we play in it have no more substance than the shadows of their pasteboard mannikins, lurching behind their backlit sheet. Those puppets were the reality, their audience the illusion. She remembered how they'd watched them packing the figures away after the show, tenderly wrapping them up one after another in the linen sheet that had borne their fleeting forms. Without warning, the chief puppeteer had turned to her and smiled: ' 'Tis their winding-cloth, my lady,' he said softly. 'And when I'm a shadow too, it'll be my shroud.'

She shivered now as she had shivered then. This time Ali didn't squeeze her hand although he was so near, just a fathom down in the ground. She realized she was still stroking the stones that covered his grave, but the warmth of the day had gone from them too.

And what of her living companions – if they were still living? Abu Abdallah might have got away. But Sinan . . .

She snatched her hand from the cold stone – it felt like adultery to think of Ali and him at the same time – and that final split-second scene played once again. Sinan's yell. A flash of steel quivering in the corner of her eye. The other flash as she wheeled around to run, aimed like a lightning-bolt at her black saviour's heart.

That ancient line of verse came back, the one she'd shared with him the time they'd been alone: ' "*We two are strangers here . . .*" ' Now she remembered who it was that the poet had been addressing: a stranger in a tomb.

They were all shadows now.

There was one flicker of life: Jaime. Or rather, she thought, if her brother had committed suicide against his – their – own past, the man who used to be Jaime.

'In one important respect,' Layth said quietly, pacing back and forth in the flickering torchlight of the underground chamber, 'this afternoon's mission was a success. All four of us are back and, as far as we know, undetected. In other respects . . .' he halted, looked from Lion to Lion, then roared, '*it was a total failure!*'

The echo died. A moan rose from Jassas, lying on a straw mattress in a corner.

'Indeed, Jassas,' Layth continued. 'You may have some excuse for failing to eliminate the old man. He was an easy target, but well guarded. I admit the fault was partly mine. I should have disposed of the Black first. As for you, Dirgham . . .' The youth shook visibly. 'What can I say? You may be hardly out of nappies, but to kill a slave-woman is child's play. Especially when you have a dagger poisoned with a compound of wolfsbane and strychnine. All you had to do was prick her flesh. I wasn't asking you to disembowel her in the middle of the suq.' They all stared at the boy, his shapeless face crimson in the torchlight.

'So,' Layth went on, still pacing. 'Now we come to our brother Hattam, noted for the vehemence – I almost said the violence – of his enthusiasm for our holy cause. Hence my assigning him the spy as his victim . . .'

'Shaykh Layth,' Hattam shouted, 'I did what –'

'Shut up!' Layth studied Hattam's mask of anger then spoke quietly, shaking his head. 'You failed me, too, Hattam.'

That was why Lubna's feet had known where to take her this time. To be with Ali, yes. But also because this place was the only link with her living brother.

Then she realized the dark reality on which that straw of hope floated, remembered Jaime's rags, his look of inexpressible fear – and knew her brother was as good as dead too. She lay her head on Ali's grave and wondered what she'd do if Jaime's angry spectre really did come back to haunt her.

The corpse of her lover; the living ghost of her brother . . . in other circumstances Lubna might have smiled at the company she sought.

She didn't know just how close Jaime was to her – a bare furlong away, in a clump of bushes by the path that led from the Alhambra; or that his last thought had been of her, his sister; or of how he was now lying with his head all but severed from his body.

⊙

Layth confronted Hattam. The man's hands and face were still crusted with the spy's gore. 'I explained to you in the clearest possible words, Hattam.' He spoke slowly. 'Stab him, I said. The poison numbs the region of the wound, almost instantly. That numbness terrifies and incapacitates the bravest man. Swiftly, it spreads. And in its wake comes a burning, a fire that will make him beg for mercy. When he does, hold out the little empty flask that Haydar gave you. Tell him it's an antidote. Tell him you'll give it to him if he tells you who sent him; they always do tell. And, after he's told you, *then* you finish him off. Or you watch him die. I thought you might enjoy that . . . That's what I told you, Hattam. You don't have to have a brain like Haydar's or Sarim's to understand those instructions.' A torch crackled. '*I didn't tell you to rip his head off!*'

Hattam was grimacing silently at the floor of the cave. Abruptly his own head jerked up. 'And what about *you*, Shaykh Layth? *What about your Black?*'

The other Lions stared at Hattam, shocked by the malice in his voice.

Layth tried to fix him with a level green gaze. 'The Black . . . overcame me.'

Hattam smiled.

'You don't know what Blacks are like,' Layth said. '*You don't know their power.*' He looked from Lion to Lion, and knew for the first time that he was in danger of losing them. 'See what he did to Jassas over there! He almost tore his arm out of its socket, with his bare hands . . .'

The Lions didn't look at Jassas. They looked at him, Layth. Everything was falling apart.

And then Layth heard a voice, from the entrance to the side-chamber that housed the laboratory. It was the only Lion, other than the injured Jassas, who had not taken part in this nightmare of a meeting: Haydar.

'Shaykh Layth! *Shaykh Layth!*' The scientist almost danced into the main chamber. 'I've cracked it!' They all stared at Haydar now. 'Those lines in the Alchemist's verse – *I know what they mean!*'

Chapter 21

'Ah, the Jewish gent . . .'

Abraham Ibn Zarzar heard the voice sounding from the fiery interior of the workshop.

' . . . come for his, ahem, *ruby*.' The glazier's round and glistening face appeared in the doorway. 'I've cracked it, your honour,' he said mournfully.

Abraham stared at him.

The glazier grinned. 'Don't worry sir, not literally, ha ha! Just a little in-joke in the glass trade . . . Hang on, your excellency, and I'll get it in a tick. *Cracked it* . . .' he repeated to himself, disappearing into the inner room. 'Always gets them.'

Abraham turned away from the heat emanating from the half-seen workshop, and studied the samples of stained glass that were set into high openings above the street door. The panels were artfully done, but what with Cristóbal the goldsmith's crucifix and now this, he'd had his fill of creepy Christian iconography over the past week. The late-afternoon light of Seville seemed to give a horrid life to the scenes – blood spurting from the neck of a decapitated martyr; a fork-bearded king labelled 'Herodes', supervising the skewering of Innocents (Herod might have been based on Solomon the gem merchant, Abraham thought with a grim smile); naked sinners herded into hellfire; a horned and laughing imp. Abraham looked away in distaste. It may all have been skilful in execution, but compared with the cool aniconic spaces of Don Pedro's Moorish Alcázar, it was crude and barbarous in taste.

He heard the glazier come back, turned – and saw a blaze of red held up in his fingers, caught between the firelight from within and the sunlight from the street. An intense and saturated red, neither the plangent red of copper nor the dusky red of gold, it was of a richer hue than either, and it seemed to spark and pulse with an inner fire. He remembered Solomon's comment on its original: '*Blood* . . . That stone was full of it.'

'As you can see, my lord,' the glazier said, 'I've been experimenting. And I think I've got it. Since your grace couldn't quite recall the precise shade, I've achieved an intermediate one between copper-red and gold-red. A new shade, one with depths to it, though I say it myself. Now, sir,' he raised a hand, 'don't ask me how! Tricks of the trade . . . '

Abraham had had no intention of asking. 'And the shape?'

The glazier took Cristóbal the goldsmith's box off a shelf, opened it and set the fake beside the wax cast of the real Ruby. 'I think you'll concur, sir, that it's as near perfect a replica as it is possible for human hands to make. And, by the way, sir,' he added in a sly undertone, 'have no fears . . . I mean, *No questions asked* . . . '

Abraham ignored him and examined the two versions, looking at them from every angle. They were to all appearances identical in form, down to the distinctive teardrop-shaped excrescence on the face of each one. Again he remembered Solomon's words – ' . . . as if it was weeping for its own wickedness . . . '

He looked up at the glazier's expectant face, and nodded. To himself, he admitted that the fake was better than he could have ever hoped for – and ready with time to spare. His departure for Granada, accompanied by the lesser members of the ambassadorial suite and escorted by a squadron of cavalry, was set for the morning after next. A week's travel would take them to his old home, Granada, and they would have a day to wash off the dust of the road before the presentation ceremony on the birthday of the Muslims' Prophet.

Ever since he had suggested the deception to Don Pedro, Abraham had been cursing his stupid tongue. Even his sleep had been haunted by dreadful nightmares about the day he'd have to hand the fake to his old master, Sultan Muhammad. Now he looked at it, and pictured it against black Egyptian velvet in the elegant – and unimpeachably genuine – silver-gilt casket chased with Arabic professions of friendship between the two sovereigns that Cristóbal said would be ready on the morrow. He saw himself bowing to kiss the Sultan's hand, and then humbly presenting him with this earnest of eternal amity between Alcázar and Alhambra. And he saw this glorified glittering lump of glass as the talisman that would safeguard Don Pedro's throne and, ultimately, the whole Muslim presence in al-Andalus.

'Smashing, isn't it, your eminence – as we say in the trade! *Smashing*, ha ha . . . '

Abraham looked into the glazier's grinning face. He reached out for the Ruby – yes, he thought of it as that, now – and thrilled at the magnificence of the deception he had wrought.

Then he picked it up and his guts plunged.

It wouldn't deceive anyone. Let alone a connoisseur of gems like Sultan Muhammad. There was a warmth to it in the palm, a clamminess, almost a sugar-candy stickiness. And worse, the weight . . . Abraham didn't know precisely what 170 carats felt like. He knew though that it would be – what? – half as heavy again as this.

No: except to look at, this bauble, this gewgaw wouldn't fool a child. And it was too late to do anything about it.

The glazier watched, eyebrows raised, mouth set in a quivering grin, waiting for his client's final word of approval.

Abraham turned away and looked up at the laughing imp and the scenes of decapitation and hellfire, and wondered how his journey to Granada would end.

Chapter 22

'Come on, Sinan,' Abu Abdallah said. 'Always look on the bright side.'

Sinan almost allowed himself to snap at his master. Instead, he bore the thudding pain in silence and went on staring through the barred window, across the valley and its welling shadows at the Alhambra, bone-white in the dying light. The scene quivered and swam. The blow had affected his sight.

'Look, we may be in gaol,' Abu Abdallah went on, 'but at least it's a gaol with a view. Besides, you know what God Almighty says in the Qur'an, "*It may be that you dislike something . . .*"'

'"*. . . when in fact it is for your own good,*"' Sinan said. 'The Chapter of the Cow, verse 216.' He turned to his master and looked at him from his own far continent, the dark diagonals of his face darker still in the twilight.

'I do believe you're spot-on with the reference, my boy. And by the way, you look quite fetching in that bandage, even with the bloodstain . . . Strange to say,' he added in a flat tone, 'I'm not surprised she liked you.'

Sinan turned and looked at the last dim outline of battlements. From somewhere nearby, a long scream pierced the silence. Nausea joined pain: this was a place not just of confinement, but of torture.

'You know,' his master said, ignoring the sound, 'I'd never thought of you as an object of attraction for the fair sex. Perhaps I'd better put Plan B into action . . .'

167

Sinan looked round and raised his eyebrows. *God, even doing that was painful.*

' . . . or should I say, into *operation* – that little bit of cosmetic surgery I may have suggested before. You see, I found out the going rate for eunuchs. Your scribal abilities might just about make up for your unfashionable shade.' He raised a hand. 'Don't take it personally, dear boy. It's just that, you know, since the Sultan's father was murdered, black hasn't been the in colour for slaves here in Granada.'

Sinan watched his master chuckling silently.

Another cry rang out, like the mewing of a peacock. It ended in a strangled gurgle.

The smile melted from Abu Abdallah's face. 'Oh Sinan, you know I'd die before I sold you. And when I do die, you're freed in my will. It's just that . . . what will happen between now and then God alone knows. That is, if *either* of us gets out of here alive.'

'Come on, master,' Sinan said flatly. 'Look on the bright side.'

Abu Abdallah smiled. 'Alright. Let's assume we do get out of here, minus a few fingernails or whatever. There's still that other little problem . . . You know as well as I do how the finances stand. At zero. Oh, why did those damned clever Indians have to invent that accursed number? And I don't have to tell you that my vizierate's up in smoke. And your secret secretaryship with it. I mean, there's only one person who could have had us banged up like this. His eminence, the great patron on whom our futures used to depend, my old friend Lisan –'

A bolt shot back. The door creaked open. An oil lamp came out of the gloom, in the hand of a large figure in a grand vizieral robe.

' – al-Din! By God, Lisan, you're going to have a long life, if that old superstition's true! You came dead on cue!'

'My dear Abu Abdallah . . .' the Grand Vizier said gently, putting a large hand on the little man's shoulder. 'I beg your forgiveness. And yours too, Sinan. I did not intend them to use force. But the Chief of the Night's men are not known for their subtlety and, confronted by your unwonted appearance, they took fright and struck pre-emptively, as they saw it. I can only hope that both of you are as comfortable as possible in the circumstances.' He put the lamp in the window embrasure.

'I was just saying to Sinan,' Abu Abdallah said, 'that at least it's a cell with a view. And even its own latrine. No complaints in that quarter ...' The air was rent by another nearby shriek, the laugh of a half-human hyena. 'The other prisoners are a bit high-spirited, though.'

Lisan al-Din smiled. 'You are not in prison, my friend. You are in the *maristan* of al-Bayyazin.'

'The *maristan*, sir?' Sinan said. 'The hospital?'

'Precisely. It has not long been open. It is another of my babies. You are in the secure psychiatric wing – in one of the superior chambers, I should add, reserved for distinguished inmates. It was the least I could do. And you'll even have an ensemble of musicians performing for you down in the courtyard *iwan* tomorrow. Some relaxing little numbers for lute, rebec and tambour. Nothing too exciting of course.'

'*Musicians*, sir, in a hospital?'

'Of course, Sinan. It is all part of the treatment. Galen, al-Farabi, Ibn Sina, all the great philosophers and physicians have stressed the importance of music in restoring equilibrium to the unbalanced humours.'

'I don't wish to sound ungrateful,' Abu Abdallah said, 'but my humours are in perfect equilibrium and always have been. As for Sinan, he might be prone to the odd bout of excessive excitability – it comes from being born in the Horrid, or should I say Torrid Zone, you know – but that knock on the head seems to have put it right for the moment. What I mean is, Lisan, we're not lunatics. Not even distinguished or superior lunatics. So, *why are we here?*'

The Grand Vizier folded his embroidered arms. 'I do not know quite how to put this ... Let us say, I had to have you removed from the scene, at least temporarily. Until after the birthday of the Prophet.'

'But *why?* What are we meant to have done? For God's sake, we were the victims of attempted murder! You do know about that, don't you?'

'My dear Abu Abdallah, I am the Grand Vizier of Granada. I know everything.' He looked down into his friend's eyes. 'And I thank God for your escape from death. But there is another matter . . . Let me not beat about the bush: you have been observed visiting the secret rendezvous of plotters bent on stealing sultanic treasure.'

Abu Abdallah stared at his friend. '*What?*'

'That cave above the cemetery of al-Bayyazin . . . It was under surveillance. You and Sinan were seen not only entering it but also, apparently, investigating it with great thoroughness.'

'But, Lisan, I can explain, I was trying to . . . to help . . . someone . . .' Abu Abdallah's voice had dried up in his mouth.

Again the Grand Vizier laid a heavy hand on his friend's shoulder.

'You do not have to explain, my friend. *I* know that you are innocent – innocent, at least, of any wrongdoing; whatever else you are guilty of. But that is not the belief in some quarters. Indeed – and I do not wish to have to tell you this, but I fear I must – the ear of His Presence has been poisoned against you.'

'*The Sultan?*' Abu Abdallah's eyes were wide with disbelief. Lisan al-Din nodded. 'Bloody hell, Sinan. We're in the shit.'

'And deeper in it than you imagine,' Lisan al-Din said softly. 'You see, the agent who reported your visit to the cave was found shortly after his return there. Murdered.'

This time Abu Abdallah laughed. 'Come on, Lisan! The joke's gone far enough. You want me to believe we're under suspicion of killing an agent of the sultan? Pull the other one!'

The Grand Vizier shook his ponderous head. 'I am afraid that you are very much under suspicion. If you will allow me to play the role of what the Nazarenes call *advocatus diaboli*, the Devil's advocate, I will say that you are the prime suspect. You are thought to have had a motive, connected with your visit to the cave. You

170

were in the right place at the right time. And, my dear friend, you most certainly have the weapon.'

'Sinan,' Abu Abdallah said, turning to his slave, 'please tell me this is all a nightmare.'

'You have the weapon,' the Grand Vizier repeated, levelly. 'You have the weapon with you here, now. As I speak to you. You are as good as red-handed.'

Abu Abdallah had lost the power of words.

Sinan asked on his behalf. 'What weapon, sir?'

'You, Sinan.'

A long animal whimper slid into the silence through the window, a sound of inexpressible human anguish.

Lisan al-Din closed his eyes. 'There are several dozen people who are prepared to bear witness to your extraordinary strength, Sinan. They saw you all but tear a man's arm out of its socket. Indeed, some have said that you *did* tear it off, and brandished it like a club, and munched on the flesh, and other such nonsense. The point is, the murdered agent was killed by someone possessed of similarly extraordinary strength. Someone endowed with almost bestial violence.'

Sinan looked at the Grand Vizier in the lamplight.

'I repeat, *I* know you are innocent. Both of you. But many others do not think so. Including, as I said, the Sultan, whom God keep and preserve . . . And there is more that you should be appraised of. With the coming ceremony on the birthday of the Prophet, tensions in the Alhambra are winding up to fever-pitch. Between ourselves,' Lisan al-Din went on in an undertone, 'certain people would be delighted were the ceremony to be a failure. And in particular, a certain person with designs upon the office of Grand Vizier.'

'The Sultanic Secretary – Ibn Zamrak?' Abu Abdallah whispered.

Lisan al-Din looked grim. 'If those designs were realized, your lives would be in mortal danger. You will be safe . . .' he raised his chin, 'as long as I remain Grand Vizier – as I shall, by the grace of God.' For once, Sinan thought, Lisan al-Din's voice lacked total conviction. 'Pray for that grace, my friend – my *friends*,' he added, his own voice now a whisper, looking at Sinan. 'God knows, a slave's prayers may be answered when the pleas of free men go unheard.'

Another tortured cry came from a neighbouring cell. A gloomy smile spread over the Grand Vizier's face. 'For the time being, think of it as a rest-cure, if that is the phrase.' He clapped his hands.

Two Spanish slaves came in bearing a chest. 'Your personal effects,' Lisan al-Din explained. 'And . . .' a third slave entered with a chess board, a box of chessmen and another lamp ' . . . something to help you wile away your involuntary holiday. I hope the food will be to your liking. The recipes, indeed the entire schedule of menus, are planned according to the strictest principles of Galenic dietetics, as expounded by al-Razi. And now,' he rose, 'I beg your leave. I do not expect to see you until after the birthday of the Prophet and the return of the Ruby.' He smothered Abu Abdallah in a brief brocaded embrace, then inclined his head to Sinan. The Grand Vizier's eyes were unnaturally bright in the lamplight – bright, Sinan saw, and moist.

The bulky figure paused in the doorway, then turned back. 'Again I ask you, pray for me. Pray that all will go as it should. It is not only my future – and yours – that hangs upon the coming week and its momentous culmination. It is also the future of thrones . . . Perhaps even the fate of Islam in al-Andalus.'

The door closed and the bolt slid shut. Sinan and Abu Abdallah sat in silence. All was dark now beyond the puddle of lamplight that lapped feebly at the shadows. Each man willed himself not to speak about their predicament.

'Well go on then, boy,' Abu Abdallah said at last. 'Set the board up.'

Slowly – any sudden movement made the blood surge like molten fire through his temples – Sinan took the chessmen from

172

their box. He began with the two kings, then placed a vizier beside each one. 'Isn't it strange, master,' he said through his pain, 'how closely the game reflects life. The king hardly moves. It is his vizier who is the active one, going in all directions. And even the lowliest of the men, if he exerts himself, can make himself vizier.'

'*Ibn Zamrak* . . .' Abu Abdallah said with a grim smile.

Sinan pictured the Sultanic Secretary looming out of the shadows, and shuddered at the image, cadaverous and greasy. A sudden memory struck him, of reading somewhere about buried corpses exuding fat: grave-wax, it was called.

'Let us indeed pray that Lisan al-Din doesn't fall,' Abu Abdallah continued as Sinan arranged the rest of the pieces. 'But come on, look sharp. I might even beat you for once, with your brains scrambled by that knock.' He moved an ivory foot-soldier forward. 'So watch it, Master ebony prodigy.'

Abu Abdallah went straight at him. Sinan responded with desultory defensive moves, black and white shimmering and swapping colour in the fitful flicker of the lamp. He really wasn't in the mood. It was not only that his brain was scrambled. Rather, his whole mind seemed to be elsewhere.

'Hah!' Abu Abdallah took the first black foot-soldier. 'Makes a change to do battle on a level field.'

Sinan sent one of his elephants across on a rash sortie – and saw the piece felled by his master's knight. He then lost two more foot-soldiers in rapid succession.

'Goodness, you really are out of it,' Abu Abdallah said gleefully, rubbing his hands together. 'Anyone would think you'd changed sides. In case you've forgotten, you're black, Sinan, and I'm white, just like we've always been, ever since you were knee-high . . .'

'That's it, master!' Sinan exclaimed. 'Black and white – and yellow!'

Abu Abdallah looked puzzled.

'Don't you remember, just before they attacked us in the suq, you were talking about China, and those fire-arrows, and how they're made?'

'I do indeed remember, Sinan. But I wasn't born yesterday, and if you think you can put me off my game with idle chit-chat, then tell me . . .' he moved a castle up the flank of the board and planted it with a triumphant *clack!* ' . . . what you're going to do about *that*.'

Sinan ignored him. 'You see, master, it's not where you look that matters, but how.' *Look, son,* his dead father said to him from far off in that other life, that other tongue. *Look from every angle till the light strikes the traces.*

'Oh, cut the philosophizing, boy, and make your move.'

'But it's your philosophy, master. You said it in the cave.'

'Bless me, so I did. And never a truer word spoken. Come on! You're meant to move in the time it takes to recite a *fatihah*.'

Sinan ignored him again. 'An alchemical mixture, you said, black charcoal, yellow sulphur and the white stuff you called "snow", the substance you said comes from cellars and lavatories. And then, just before they attacked us, I remembered about Ali the Alchemist collecting something from mosque lavatories.'

Abu Abdallah was staring at Sinan. 'Go on then, boy. Don't keep me on tenterhooks just because of a piffling game of chess.'

'Think, master. The Alchemist collecting something in lavatories . . . The three colours in the Alchemist's verse . . . All the references in the verse to fire . . . I believe – no, I'm *sure*, master – that the verse tells you how to make it. I mean, that it's a recipe, for . . .'

'*Al-Dawa* . . . the Remedy . . . That's in the poem too – and, of course, that's what some people call it, that stuff they put in those tubes that go *qahhhh!* I remember seeing some of them back in the year 'fifty-one in the fort on Jabal Tariq – you know, that big mountain where we landed, next to al-Jazirah, the one that sticks into the Strait. "Come and see this, old chap," the

174

commandant says. "Latest technology. Very hush-hush. We call it the *propulsor*." I just twiddle my thumbs while he explains about it, then I say, "Oh, that's old hat. Saw those things years ago, I did, when I was the Sultan of Hind's Ambassador Plenipotentiary to the Great Qan of China and Cathay." That took the wind out of his sail, I can tell you. Or should I say, the *Remedy* out of his *propulsor*, ha ha.'

Abu Abdallah chortled to himself in the flickering lamplight. A sudden gibbon-like cry from one of the lunatics brought them back to the moment.

'Master,' Sinan said, 'assuming we're right about all this, what I don't understand is why the Alchemist decided to hide the recipe in a verse – I mean, if everyone already knows about it. You said you heard about the Remedy back in 'fifty-one. That's nineteen years ago. It could hardly be a secret any more.'

'You're right there, Sinan . . . But maybe the Alchemist came up with some sort of improved recipe. I reckon the secret's in that second part of the poem, the bit that mentions those place-names. Those three places here in Spain. Goodness me, what were they? My memory must be going.'

Sinan closed his eyes and tried to drag the names up from his own muddied memory, from that afternoon a week ago in the Grand Vizier's library. They wouldn't come. Bars of pain blocked his brain.

He opened his eyes – and his gaze fell on the untouched corner of his side of the chess board. 'Black . . . castle . . . That's it, master!

> "Black is a castle in Toledo – ask no more, I warn –
> Yellow is the mount of Cádiz, white the graves of Aragón."

Tulaytulah . . . Qadis . . . Araghun . . .'

A week ago. It suddenly seemed an immense span, an abyss of time. The effort of recollection had exhausted him. The unfocused pain in his head now became a rhythmic throb that seemed to beat to those alien syllables.

Tulaytulah . . . Qadis . . . Araghun . . .

The lamplight had long ago consumed itself. But those place-names pulsed on, conspiring with the thrumming ache in Sinan's head, the thin mat and the hard floor to repel all hope of sleep. He could tell from Abu Abdallah's shallow breathing that his master was awake too, up on his superior mattress on its built-in dais. Tulaytulah, Qadis and Araghun beat on in counterpoint with the nocturnal cries of their fellow-inmates.

It's how you look.

He'd looked so long, so hard that he could see nothing any more. *Look from every angle.*

Tulaytulah . . . Qadis . . . Araghun . . . For a moment his mind wandered, inconsequentially, to breakfast. He wondered what they'd give them, if morning ever came; what Galenic recipe—

The answer struck him pure and clear as the moonbeam slanting through the bars. '*Master!*' he called, sitting up.

'Who? What? Dawn? Already?' Abu Abdallah mumbled groggily. 'For heaven's sake, boy, look at the moon. It's still the middle of the night.'

'But the verse, master. The *recipe*. For the Remedy.'

'Sinan, stop rambling.' Then Abu Abdallah continued to himself, 'Poor fellow, I shouldn't be too hard on him. It must be that bang on the head.'

'But can't you see, master? If it is a recipe, then there's one thing recipes always need.'

'Come on, then.' Abu Abdallah said, sounding lucid now. 'Out with it.'

'Master, don't you remember teaching me the *abjad*?'

176

Chapter 23

'It's the *abjad!*'

The Lions stared at Haydar. Here was the man who measured out his words and his feelings like his powders, in precise little amounts – crowing with delight and jigging on the spot.

'Shaykh Layth, I said, the Alchemist's verse – I know what it means! Don't you know the *abjad?*'

Silence and puzzlement. Then Sarim spoke, strange rhythmic works like an incantation: '*Abjad hawwaz ḥuṭṭī kalaman . . .*'

Hattam, still covered in the Mamluk's blood, glared at him. 'What evil spell is this? I seek refuge with God from your wizardry!'

Sarim laughed. 'My dear Hattam, it is no wizardry. The *abjad* is simply a matter of counting.' The Lions all looked at Sarim now. 'What do you think we Arabs did for numbers before we inherited the numerals of the Indians? We used letters. *Abjad* is merely the letters *alif, ba, jim* and *dal* – one, two, three, four, that is – made into a mnemonic word. And so on, up to *shin*, which represents a thousand.'

'Or rather, up to *ghayn*,' Haydar said, 'which represents a thousand in the Eastern *abjad*. Whether through innate perversity or in order to throw us further off the track, the Alchemist eschewed our Western system in favour of the Eastern one. I admit it almost put me off the scent.'

'But Haydar,' Layth said, puzzled and unconvinced, 'what makes you so sure?'

'It is more obvious than we realized, Shaykh Layth,' Haydar said. 'You see, the Alchemist's verse says black *is* a castle in Toledo . . . yellow *is* the mount of Cádiz, and so on. Not black is *from* . . . yellow is *from* . . .'

'Ah, Haydar, I never knew you had it in you!' Sarim exclaimed, smiling.

'Go on, then, explain,' Layth said, still looking dubious.

'What Haydar means, if I understand him correctly, is that because the verse contains place-names, we naturally expected those words to function as places do – as origins, or perhaps destinations, their place-like quality denoting their essences and attributes as locational or spatial entities *per se* . . .'

Layth raised a hand. 'On second thought, let us hear from Haydar.'

'Well, Shaykh Layth,' Haydar said, 'when I saw that the place-names made no sense as such, I asked myself what those series of letters could mean if they did not mean words. The only other possibility was . . .'

'Numbers . . . Yes, I see.' Layth frowned. 'But what makes you so certain?'

'Perform the calculation yourself, Shaykh Layth. I'd be glad of confirmation for my figures.'

Layth nodded, then raised his voice. 'What are you all gawping at, the rest of you? Go on, back to your tasks!' There was an unspoken hum of disquiet. 'I know it is almost time to eat, but that's no reason for wasting the interim in idle chat. Every second of our lives must be dedicated to our holy mission! Sarim, you're needed. And as for you, Hattam,' Layth added in an undertone, 'go and perform a full and diligent ablution. You stink of foul heretical blood.' He fixed the man with his green gaze. Hattam stared back at him, then turned and made for the ablution chamber.

Layth, Sarim and Haydar sat together in the torchlight. Sarim produced a penbox and a roll of paper from his waist-sash and began to write. First, he inscribed a column of letters and numerals, the complete *abjad* according to the Eastern system:

أ	a	1
ب	b	2
ج	j	3
د	d	4
ه	h	5
و	w	6
ز	z	7
ح	ḥ	8
ط	ṭ	9
ي	y	10
ك	k	20
ل	l	30
م	m	40
ن	n	50
س	s	60
ع	ʿ	70
ف	f	80
ص	ṣ	90
ق	q	100
ر	r	200
ش	sh	300
ت	t	400
ث	th	500
خ	kh	600
ذ	dh	700
ض	ḍ	800
ظ	ẓ	900
غ	gh	1000

He then wrote out the phrases from the verse:

قلعة بطليطلة	*qalʿah bi-Ṭulayṭulah*, a castle in Toledo
جبل قادس	*jabal Qādis*, the mount of Cádiz
رجم أرغون	*rujam Araghūn*, the graves of Aragón

and broke them down into their constituent characters, inscribing the numerical equivalents and calculating the sum of each phrase:

ق	100
ل	30
ع	70
ه	5
ب	2
ط	9
ل	30
ي	10
ط	9
ل	30
ه	5
Total	300

ج	3
ب	2
ل	30
ق	100
ا	1
د	4
س	60
Total	200

ر	200
ج	3
م	40
أ	1
ر	200
غ	1000
و	6
ن	50
Total	**1500**

'So, according to my calculations,' Sarim said, 'black is 300, yellow is 200 and white is 1500. It is beyond the laws of probability that all three sums should be round numbers.'

Haydar laughed nervously, and passed his own paper to Layth.

'*Charcoal 300*,' Layth read, '*sulphur 200, Chinese snow 1500 . . .* The figures are identical.'

'And that is what I feared . . .' Haydar said, still smiling.

'What do you mean, "what you feared"?' Layth asked.

'The Alchemist's verse gives us the very same proportions for compounding the Remedy that we having been using all along. They are precisely the proportions as given by the Syrian recipe. Three to two to fifteen.'

'So where is the Alchemist's great new discovery?' Layth asked. His voice sounded hollow.

Haydar shrugged.

'He was deceiving us all along!' Layth roared. 'Deceiving us and depriving us of our treasure! Damn his soul to everlasting Hell! He has duped and blinded us with words!' His whole body shook.

Sarim laid a hand on Layth's forearm. Even through the thick cloth of the sleeve, he could feel the heat of his rage. 'Shaykh Layth,' he said gently, 'there may be another explanation –'

'Explanations be damned!' He threw off Sarim's hand. 'I don't care any longer! We have enough of the Remedy to proceed, even without the accursed Alchemist's imaginary refinement. God will give us success!'

'But, Shaykh Layth, listen, I beg you,' Sarim pleaded. 'There is another possibility . . .'

Layth shut his eyes for a moment, then sighed. 'Go on.'

'The *matla*', the exordium to the Alchemist's verse . . .'

'Oh, tell us in plain Arabic, for heaven's sake!'

'The, er, opening lines lay out the poet's subject by means of simple similes – night, forenoon and so on.' Sarim paused. Layth motioned to him to continue. 'The central section of the verse, in which one customarily finds the main subject matter, the marrow so to speak, has now been shown to be an elaborate bluff, concealing from us that which we knew already, but did not know that we knew, on account of the . . .' Layth rolled his eyes. 'So we are left with the *envoi*.'

'The *what*?'

'The summation, the, um, ending, in other words.'

'That nonsense about turning flour into grain, or whatever it was?' Dirgham's pasty features edged into Layth's vision. The boy was dithering with a tray of couscous. 'Oh, put it down, you ape!' Layth yelled.

Sarim looked without enthusiasm at the shapeless mound of grains, glistening with a thin and greasy sauce. ' "*The final, fatal fire,*" ' he quoted, ' "*is lightning from the rain-cloud born, / He'll know, who grinds the finest flour . . .*" '

' "*. . . then turns it back to corn!*" ' Haydar cut in, gazing at the couscous as if it was manna from heaven, and then at Sarim. 'Sarim, I think you're on to something!' he exclaimed.

For a moment Sarim looked confused. Then an expression of near-beatitude lit his scholarly features. 'Oh, the elegance of it! *Al-sahl al-mumtana*'! Inimitable simplicity!'

'Will one of you tell me what the hell's going on?' Layth barked.

'I had at first interpreted those lines as an allusion to that proverb of inevitable failure,' Sarim said, his words cascading out with uncharacteristic rapidity. ' *"Whatever we ground turned back to grain."* But now the scales have fallen from my eyes, and I see that we should subject the ending of the verse to the most literal and exoteric exegesis, such as all right-thinking men apply to the book of God . . .'

Layth shook his head. 'Your literary criticism will be the death of us.'

'What Sarim is saying, Shaykh Layth,' Haydar said, smiling broadly, 'is that those lines may mean exactly what they say.'

'Indeed,' Sarim said. 'And what a rarity that is in our modern poetics!'

'What,' Layth said, 'you mean the Alchemist was telling us to turn flour into corn?' The two others nodded vigorously. 'Forget these impossibilities and eat, in the Name of God, for Whom, and Whom alone, nothing is impossible!' He rolled up his sleeve and dug into the couscous.

'So, Shaykh Layth,' Sarim said, 'this couscous, for example, is an impossibility? How was it made, but from the finest-ground flour, mixed with water "from the rain-cloud born", and shaped into grains of a uniform size?'

'*And then passed through a sieve!*' Haydar exclaimed, jumping up and almost overturning the tray.

'Haydar, possess yourself!' Sarim hissed. 'I was of course speaking purely theoretically, Shaykh Layth.'

'But why theoretically, Sarim?' Haydar exclaimed. The two other men stared at their fellow Lion, the quiet backroom-boy in his moment, his ferment of discovery. 'Don't you remember? She talked about her couscous sieves – the *qaynah*, the slave-woman . . . she said how the Alchemist had ruined them! By God, Sarim, I think you've done it!'

Chapter 24

The sleep of the dead, Lubna thought, raising her head from the hard ground. Sunrise gilded the graves of al-Bayyazin. *If only.*

Lying on her patch of dust by Ali's grave, she wasn't sure if she had slept at all. She was only aware of the cold in her marrow and the hunger that tugged and gnawed at her gut.

Would they have a search party out for her, the runaway slave? She'd kept away from the immediate area of the caves. Fear had told her they might come and look for her there. Why not here, too, little more than a furlong away? Yet something else told her that this spot, if anywhere, was a kind of asylum, a hallowed limbo between sleep and waking, life and death.

The trouble was, the cup of water that she'd begged from the gravediggers an hour or two before wouldn't keep her going long. She pictured their astonished torchlit faces when she'd loomed, a veiled ghost, out of the pre-dawn gloom. And then she thought of Jaime, that other living ghost; if he was even that.

Jaime is dead, her brother had said.

But she had to survive. She could forage for roots, leaves, anything digestible. After the Death had taken her parents, back in the other life – the other life but one – she'd kept herself and Jaime alive in those frowning sierras. Or should she leave this place, move up the valley, before the sun rose higher? But she remembered the city wall, glowering along the contour above the cave-line. No, it was safest to stay, protected by the sanctity of the ground and the anonymity of her veil. She could survive by rooting about and begging and the grace of God.

And here was her first chance: a bier, lurching at shoulder-height through the early morning light, coming along the path that led from the Alhambra, and a cortege, a big one. The procession entered the hillside cemetery, broke up and picked its way around the tombs to the new hole that the gravediggers had made on one of the higher terraces.

Lubna climbed towards the mourners. They'd all be men, of course, but she could cope with that. And she imagined the bereaved, with the hereafter on their minds, would be in a more charitable mood than most. But would they carry food with them? That's what she needed. Not money or prayers.

Lubna saw as she approached that most of the men were young and dressed alike, in blood-red jerkins and caps. *Mamluks.* Her heart somersaulted: Jaime might be among them! Then she thought of that ragged spectre of the day before and reasoned that he would not. And yet she felt – she knew – through some sense that operated beyond reason, that he *was* there.

The Mamluks formed rough ranks round the slot in the earth. Lubna slipped in among them. No one seemed to see her. As a beggar and a woman she was doubly invisible. She studied the bent heads, the grim set faces, looking for Jaime.

An older man in a turban was speaking, ' . . . to commit to the earth, from which God created him, our comrade, martyred in this place in the course of duty to his Maker and his Sultan– our comrade, our brother . . .' the voice faltered.

As a woman, Lubna had never been to a burial. She stared at the corpse as it was lifted gently from the bier and lowered slowly into the open jaws of the earth. She stared – and with the burial of this unknown soldier, veiled and anonymous in his winding-cloth, she buried her own dead. Her father and mother. Her childhood friends taken by the Death. Ali – how long ago and alien that life seemed now. Sinan, too, she shrouded in this stranger's winding-sheet.

' . . . our brother and our dear friend,' the turbaned man continued while the corpse inched down, 'whom God make to dwell eternally in the Garden. Wherefore keep ever in mind the grave and its torments, my brothers, and that which comes after the grave, for every soul tastes death, and . . .'

But the rest was lost in a stifled gasp from the crowd, for there was a movement inside the winding-sheet, and something heavy rolled out and lolled, and dangled – a head – and Lubna saw the plugs of scented cotton in its ears and nostrils, then saw for a fraction of an instant its nose, broken all those years ago, and then with great tenderness living hands tucked the head back in the shroud, and Jaime was laid in earth.

'I think I've done it,' Haydar said.

He had spent the night in his laboratory and was light-headed with sleeplessness and excitement. His moment of discovery was not yet ended.

'See, Shaykh Layth, how I've mixed the Remedy with a little water to make a paste.' He tilted a copper bowl to show Layth the black mixture. 'I first tried rubbing it into pellets between my palms, precisely as one does to make couscous. But it just ended up as a mess. Then I remembered what the slave-woman said, that the Alchemist had ruined her couscous sieves. After a certain amount of trial and error, I realized that he must have used the sieves to *extrude* the mixture, like this . . .' He took a spoonful of the mixture and pressed it through the mesh of the sieve. From the reverse of the mesh, small black worms of paste emerged. Haydar ran the blade of a knife across the mesh to shave them away, scattering them on to a tray as they fell.

Layth examined the tiny damp pellets, unconvinced. 'Why would doing this improve the Remedy?'

'I don't know, Shaykh Layth. I can only hypothesize that by super-adding the extra element, water, we are introducing moisture to the alchemical equation. Thus on ignition the Remedy, whose qualities are dryness and hotness, will have to react against *both* of its humoral opposites – the coldness of the surrounding air, plus the residual essence of the moisture.' Layth was still frowning at the black grains. 'This, in theory, could double its force.' Layth looked at him. 'Or more than double it.'

Now Layth was smiling. 'At last, dear Haydar, you are making sense. But, tell me, if you're right, then how do you think the Alchemist made this discovery?'

'God knows, Shaykh Layth. It was probably an accident. They say most great discoveries are.'

'Then they are wrong,' Layth said. 'Everything that has been and will be was decided at the moment of creation. *There are no accidents.*'

There was a silence between them, broken only by the sounds of the other Lions starting their day's work in the chamber beyond. 'So, what next?' Layth said at last.

'We have plenty of the Remedy in stock. And of course the recipe we have been using, the Syrian one, is exactly the same as the Alchemist's. As you can see, the "corning" process, as I term it after the Alchemist's verse, is straightforward enough. Even that oaf, Dirgham, would be up to it with a little supervision. Naturally we will have to carry out tests to make sure my hypothesis is correct. But if it proves to be so then, given enough hands the corning operation is not the problem . . .'

'What *is* the problem, then?'

'First, the drying time. Even if the humoral essence of the moisture remains, clearly the Remedy must not actually be wet, for how could it then ignite? How long it will take to dry I do not know. All we can do, Shaykh Layth, is wait and see.'

'Well, my dear Haydar, you have little more than a week. It all depends on you now.' He looked at the scientist and saw for the first time ever, beneath the high-strung, haggard lines of his sleepless face, an underlying confidence.

'I know, Shaykh Layth.'

'And what else?' Layth said, hearing a note of doubt from deeper still, beneath the confidence.

Haydar frowned. Memorized Latin words surfaced in his mind: *Si fieret instrumentum de solidis corporibus, tunc longe major fieret violentia.* 'There is the matter of the English monk's discovery: "If the instrument were of solid materials, then the violence would be far greater." I still do not understand the full import of these words, Shaykh Layth.'

'It is not for you to understand,' Layth said.

Haydar was not surprised by the response. He knew that Layth maintained control – and security – by ensuring that no one person, not even Layth himself, had the full details of their plot. Their conspiracy resembled the elaborate geometric screens that adorned, and concealed, the inmost chambers of the Alhambra: interlocking puzzles of precious wood and pearl and ivory, only when the last key element was inserted was their geometry complete. The Lions' plot was a puzzle, too, a screen designed to conceal the plotters – and to conceal itself. If any single Lion had held all the pieces and been taken captive, those pieces would have been extracted from him, one by one, along with fingernails and other body parts, by the Sultan's torturers: the entire geometry would fall, the conspiracy fail. So one Lion, one alone, held the last, key part that would complete the interlock. That lone Lion had no access to the other parts; the other Lions – even Layth – were ignorant of the precise nature of the piece he held, the part that he would play. There was, of course, a risk that the holder of the final crucial key – 'Asad', first and noblest of the many names of lions – would himself be found out. It was a risk they took; for they had calculated it and knew it was about as likely as finding an actual lion taking a stroll in the Sultan's pleasure-garden.

'It is not for any of us here to understand,' Layth added softly. 'But I will make contact with the Lion who walks by himself. With Asad. *He* knows.' Suddenly the fire in his green eyes flared bright. 'For the time has come, at last, at long, long last, for all that has been kept asunder to be joined together.'

Chapter 25

Beyond the alternation of light and dark, heat and cold, hunger and its bare and temporary relief at the hands of the charitable bereaved, time had ceased to exist for Lubna.

She was just about keeping body and soul, but not together. It was as if she had already set one foot inside the spirit world. When she made contact with the living who came to picnic and to pray in the company of their dead, they were all too ready to exorcize her with a crust of bread or a lump of cheese. Her thirst she slaked by lapping at the shallow water-bowls that were set into the graves and filled from time to time by visitors, for the benefit of birds and beasts and departed souls.

And then, one morning, time began again.

The peasants heard it first, out beyond the city wall in the higher reaches of the Hadarruh valley – a bolt from the blue, thunder from a cloudless sky that rolled down the valley, making men halt in their harvest tasks and oxen flinch with quivering flanks beneath their yokes, setting off a braying of asses and a barking of dogs, a screech of birds and a buzz of late flies that spread from hovel to hovel and hamlet to hamlet till the rumble reached the city wall where the guards looked at one another and wondered if another *zindiq* had been hauled down to Hell.

Lubna heard it too, from the far country she'd inhabited these past three days, and began her journey back.

Chapter 26

'Two days to go,' the Sultanic Secretary said, 'and everything is ready . . . Or so you say.' He stepped out from behind the screen surrounding the centrepiece of the new court. A workman with a sack entered the gap in the canvas.

Zayd, the auburn-bearded Clerk of Works, emerged. 'Yes, sir. The tests have been carried out. All is in order. We're just adding a few finishing touches.'

Ibn Zamrak looked about him. He hated to admit it, but the Grand Vizier's new court was the most splendid building he had ever seen. Indeed, it was hard to imagine that art or nature could produce a more exquisite prospect this side of Paradise. Light and shade played hide and seek among the colonnades and seemed to set the whole space in motion, an earthly mirror to the slow and ceaseless spin of the heavens. And at the centre of it all, the still-point of this firmament of marble, stucco and mosaic, Lisan al-Din's beautiful, blasphemous surprise for their master the Sultan.

'Well, you'd better be right,' Ibn Zamrak said softly, turning the waxen mask of his face to Zayd the Clerk. 'Because, if you're not, heads will roll. Beginning with yours, Master Zayd – last *head* of the house of Ziri the Berber – thus putting out of its misery the sorry history of Granada's former rulers. And then,' he shaped his lips into a sneer that passed for a smile, 'far greater heads than yours . . . All in all, a most lamentable de–' a large figure lumbered into view from the southern portico ' –*capitation*.' Ibn Zamrak raised his voice in the figure's direction. 'Ah, your eminence! I was just thinking of you. May your life be long!'

'And may yours be longer,' the Grand Vizier replied, batting the formula back in a tone that hoped the Sultanic Secretary would drop dead on the spot. 'What brings you here?'

'It being the prerogative of God alone, blessed and mighty is He, to ignore the usual constraints of time, and aware as I am of the fallibility of His creatures' temporal sensibilities, I merely wished to check that everything was on schedule.' He paused and looked about the court with studied superciliousness. 'All very . . . *pretty*, I must say. But what about that contraption of yours?' He jerked his chin towards the canvas screen. 'You will perhaps recall that my master – our master – will, on the morning after the morrow, condescend to grace the inauguration of this court with his blessed Presence. Naturally, I was curious to observe the progress made towards your eminence's . . . deadline.' His lips formed around the word with slow relish, like a python engorging its prey.

'I have absolute faith in our esteemed colleague the Clerk of Works,' Lisan al-Din said. Zayd bowed at the compliment.

'How I wish I could share in your confidence,' Ibn Zamrak said. 'But what I have seen scarcely engenders optimism. I shall not reiterate my main complaint, about the sacrilegious depiction of living beings . . . God can hardly be expected to bless with success a venture that apes so unashamedly His powers of creation. My lesser criticisms are concerned mainly with the inscription of my verses, with which you so wisely sought to redeem His Presence's surprise. There is an ugly bunching up of the characters in places, some diacritical points omitted . . . But then,' he turned on Zayd the Clerk a look that mixed saccharine and strychnine, 'what else might one expect from a scion of those rude unlettered captains of the house of Ziri? And – *ugghh* . . .' he pointed with the fastidious toe of his soft leather *khuff* at a scattering of droppings on the otherwise immaculate marble paving. 'Yet more evidence of rodent infestation.'

For a moment, Zayd stared at the droppings. 'I will deal with it immediately, sir,' he said.

'You'd better. Or have you forgotten His Presence's insistence on absolute hygiene at court? How do you think we survived the last visitation of the Death? Where there are rats, moles and other such vermin, the foul and noxious miasmata that cause the Death are sure to breed too, down in the bowels of the earth.'

'Evidently, my dear colleague,' the Grand Vizier said, 'you have not read my treatise on the Contagion Theory. I shall have a copy made for you forthwith. Zayd, you'd better get hold of some traps, or a cat or whatever. You've heard it: you have less than forty-eight hours . . . *If only,*' Lisan al-Din added in an undertone, turning his dark impassive jowls on the Sultanic Secretary, '*it were as easy to deal with the other, larger species of rat and mole that infest this noble palace.*'

As befitted his ambassadorial role, Abraham Ibn Zarzar had spent his first night in Granadan territory in the hospitable residence of the governor of Lushah, a gentleman he was acquainted with from his own days in the service of the Sultan. His accommodation had been comfortable, but he had not slept; or maybe only a wink snatched between the Muslims' dawn-prayer call and first light. Now, on the road again in the grey morning, relentless moors rolled past, and sparse olive groves. The rhythmic creak of harness and clank of weaponry from his escort of a hundred Berber horsemen, the attempts at conversation by his fellow envoys, a particularly stupid pair of *hidalgos*, and the soporific gait of his mule would all have sent him to sleep in the saddle. Were it not for the red nemesis at his back.

That brainchild of his moment of madness haunted him, taunted him – the Great Fake, the specious, trumpery 'Ruby' in its gilded casket, riding at the head of the baggage train, like him, upon a closely guarded and richly caparisoned mule. With every step that brought them closer to Granada, with every second ticked off the time till the feast-day of the Muslims' prophet – the morning after the morrow – the weight of Abraham's fear grew deader in the pit of his belly.

He recalled with a shiver Don Pedro's childlike delight when he'd first set eyes on the lump of red glass a week before. 'You artful Jew!' the king had exclaimed. 'You've out-alchemized the alchemists – changed the worthless into the priceless! Transformation! Transmogrification! Transubstantiation! But, *shhhh* . . .' he held a finger to his lips and whispered, 'Don't tell anyone it's a ruby for a booby.' Then an explosion of laughter: '*A ruby for a booby,* ha ha!' He clamped his powerful hand on Abraham's elbow, steered him round and round the palace pool, called him the saviour of thrones, the warder-off of wars. 'And as for Henry of Trastámara, brother of the wrong side of my late father's honourable blanket, he can go and screw himself. O my beloved Sultan Muhammad of Granada, with this Ruby I thee wed, and together we'll shaft the Bastard! Come on Abraham, you misery, join in,' the king said, gripping his confidant's arm so hard that he was silenced by the pain.

'*Together we'll shaft the Bastard!*'

The chant, repeated again and again, rang round the court and scattered the doves.

'But . . . your highness,' Abraham said when the king drew breath. He wanted Don Pedro to take hold of the fake, to feel its hollowness, to face reality before it receded forever. He turned square on the king and held it out.

Pedro did not take it. Instead he backed away, and words came from far off, from the past: 'I . . . never liked it anyway. Take it from me,

Abraham . . .' and then the sudden crazed blue ice of the stare and the whisper resounding round the court: '*Take the bloody thing away.*'

And now Abraham rode on to Granada, on to the Alhambra, knowing that if anything was going to cause wars and cost thrones, it was this blood-red bauble at his back.

Chapter 27

'Two more nights to go, my boy, and then we'll be out of this dump,' Abu Abdallah said. 'By the grace of God.'

The light was fading rapidly in their superior chamber in the hospital of al-Bayyazin. Sinan watched a musician wrapping up his lute down below in the courtyard, while two other players chatted beside him. It was strange, Sinan reflected, to listen as they did each day to music that was purely instrumental. But understandable: the passions aroused by the poetry of song would be dangerous to the inmates of the psychiatric wing. For Sinan, the space where the singer should have been was always filled with thoughts of Lubna, the *qaynah*, the singing slave. He wondered what her voice was like in song; if it had the rough-edged timbre of her speech, or whether melody rounded and polished it. In his mind that voice spoke to him for the thousandth time, ' "*We two are strangers here . . .*" '

But it spoke out of the past.

'I said, two more nights to go, *in sha' Allah*,' Abu Abdallah repeated, drowning out the remembered words. Sinan was his master's sounding-board, not his own.

'Yes, master.'

A chorus of melancholy musical lunatic shrieks and whoops accompanied the band's departure down below.

'And not a day too soon. Much more of this, and I'll be going as potty as the rest of them. And as for Lisan al-Din's whatever-they're-called . . . Hellenic diuretics, was it?'

'Galenic dietetics, master.'

199

'Yes, that stuff. Well,' he looked at the joyless remains of a platter of couscous with a bland vegetable sauce, 'give me a hunk of fat mutton and a good dollop of pickles any day. That's the sort of food that keeps *my* femurs in equilibrium. Anyway, less than forty-eight hours to go, and we'll be back in the fleshpots. Think of those stews Lisan al-Din's cook-slave does, with honey and green walnuts, and the almond soup, and the marzipan . . .'

For a while they both digested the imagined dishes. 'Master,' Sinan said eventually, then paused, wondering how to put in words what was on his mind – on both of their minds, if it were admitted. In addition to his roles of sounding-board, memory and occasional conscience, Sinan had realized that he'd always played an additional part – in the picturesque Nazarene phrase quoted by the Grand Vizier, that of 'Devil's advocate'. 'Master,' he began again, 'what if there's a hitch . . . if the Grand Vizier falls? What then?'

Abu Abdallah looked at him and drew a silent finger across his throat. 'In other words, my boy, it doesn't bear thinking about. So don't.'

But they both knew that, as the day of the ceremony at the Alhambra approached, it would be all they would be thinking about.

'Master, we must be realistic.'

'That's a good idea! Let's have a really good game of chess, then. Even if you're back on your old winning form.'

'Please, master, *think*. We know about the Remedy. We *must* get word to the Grand Vizier.'

'Look, you've been harping on about the ruddy Remedy all week. And you still haven't convinced me. Anyway, even if we did want to get word to Lisan al-Din, we couldn't. We've been sent to Waqwaq.'

'To Waq– . . . *where*, master?'

'Waqwaq. Haven't I told you about it? It's an island beyond China, on the edge of the world. From here, it's the furthest part of the inhabited globe. They say – and God is the most knowing – that virgin girls grow on trees there, and when they're ripe for the you-know-what – not that you *do* know, I sometimes think, but that's beside the point – they drop off the trees and float down, crying out, "*Waq-waq! Waq-waq!*" ' He flapped the sleeves of his *jubbah* and repeated the call at the top of his voice, making Sinan smile despite himself. There was an answering cry from one of their fellow-inmates in a nearby cell. 'Ahhh. Virgins growing on trees . . . I almost made it there myself,' Abu Abdallah added with a sigh.

'But, to return to the Remedy,' Sinan said, serious again. 'I don't know *why* you need convincing, master. Apart from anything else, the mathematical probability of those *abjad* totals adding up to round numbers by chance . . .'

' . . . is almost zero. Yes, Sinan. You have explained, with your impeccable logic, a hundred times. And, yes, my decrepit brain has taken it all in. So it's the Remedy. It's a plot. And I've told you a hundred times: even if they had a ton of the stuff, what are they going to do? Go *qahh qahh* with those fire-tubes and propulsor things until the entire Mamluk corps of the Sultanate of Granada run off and hide behind their mothers' skirts? Then turn them on door of the Sultan's vaults and make off with the Ruby? As Lisan al-Din said, the Ruby's as good as unstealable. I mean, it would be about as easy as pinching . . . oh, I don't know, the Black Stone of Mecca.'

'Master, the Carmathian heretics *did* steal the Black Stone of Mecca, back in the days of the caliphs.'

'Hmm. So they did,' Abu Abdallah said. He pursed his lips.

'Anyway, master,' Sinan said, looking out of the small barred window at the daylight fading from the Alhambra's walls, 'I'm not sure about this "red one" that they're trying to get at.'

'What on earth do you mean?'

'I mean, I'm not sure that it *is* the Ruby.'

'Oh, nonsense, boy. Whatever else could it be?' He studied Sinan's features, darkly impassive in the fading light. 'Come on, then. Out with it . . . I can feel another of your fiendishly clever theories coming on.'

Sinan didn't answer, but continued watching shadows welling up in the valley, splendour falling from the castle walls, darkness gathering its powers.

It was the time some call the Hour of Solomon. The time around the sunset prayer, when you feel the soft press of the incoming dark. *And the nights, as you know, are pregnant*, Sinan mouthed to himself. *Gravid, giving birth to all strange things.*

Even the lunatics had fallen silent.

'I wonder where she is,' Abu Abdallah said into the space left by sound. 'Lubna.' He smiled. 'Do you know, I used to say, "Plenty more gazelles on the plain." And there were. Then . . . Or was it just that I was better at catching them? *Lubna* – she might have been the One . . . There was a One before, back in the Maldives . . . Can you only have one One?'

The darkness thickened. For a while Abu Abdallah, who made noise even when he was silent, was truly silent.

He spoke again. 'But it was you she liked, Sinan . . . Poor boy. You didn't even know what was going on. In her head. Her heart. Her *liver* – that's where it really goes on.'

Sinan continued looking through the bars.

'Do you know, Sinan, I sometimes wonder if I'd be happier now if I'd been born like you. Like some . . . some idol of ebony, of basalt, all-seeing, all-knowing, but somehow at the same time – what? – without feeling. Without . . . self-awareness.'

Sinan closed his eyes.

'Would I be happy? I don't know, Sinan.' The voice had died away to almost soundless consonants. 'I just don't know.'

Across Granada fifty muezzins drew breath at the top of the twisting stairs of fifty minarets, inhaling the incoming night. For a long instant the city, too, and time itself, seemed to hold their breath.

In this suspended moment Sinan opened his eyes – and saw before him a blood-red scar along the valley side: the walls of the Alhambra, wallowing in the light of the dying sun, a deep and saturated red. Even as he watched, the colour began slowly to leak away, the daily death of light. Dry brick dust. Dead rose petals. He turned to Abu Abdallah, now a still and shrunken shadow against the whitewashed wall. 'Master . . . *Master?*'

The shadow didn't move. Then a small voice said, 'Don't worry. I'm not dead. Yet.'

'Master, how did the Alhambra get its name?'

'The Alhambra? Never thought of it.' Abu Abdallah sounded distant and weary. 'It's just called that. *Al-Hamra*. The Red. A feminine adjective. I suppose it's what our learned friend Lisan al-Din would call a . . . an apothegm.'

'I think you mean an *epithet*, master.'

'*Thank you*, Sinan.' Now Abu Abdallah sounded more like his usual jaunty self. 'You know – and yes, *you* probably do know – like they call Fez *al-Bayda*, the White, and Aleppo *al-Shahba*, the Grey, and the old Caliphal palace of Damascus *al-Khadra*, the Green, and so on. *Al-Hamra* . . . Have I heard that it's something to do with red mortar or red stone? I suppose it is quite red in some lights. Or maybe it was the only colour left when they were looking for that epi-thingie.'

'Master,' Sinan said quietly, 'do you remember, in the Latin message the Grand Vizier showed us, *rufa . . . rufi . . .* "the red one"? You know, the thing the plotters are trying to get at. And one of them was masculine, and the other feminine. Don't you think it could be –'

'The Alhambra? *The citadel itself?*' The shadow detached itself from the wall.

Now Abu Abdallah was over by the window too, gazing through the bars at the last faint stain of red leaking from the fortress walls.

'Hmm. I suppose you imagine that bump on the brainbox knocked some sense into it, for once. Well, boy, it's a thin thread that separates sense from nonsense . . .' He paused, as if listening to the suspended moment, the hush before the fall of the dark. Then suddenly, softly, he spoke: 'My God, Sinan . . . You could be right. We've been thinking . . . much too *small*, all along. This isn't about some piffling red pebble, even if it's worth a Sultan's ransom. It's about something beyond price: a citadel, a city in the sky, a symbol of power, a safeguard of peace . . . We *must* get word to Lisan al-Din. But how? *How?*' At the moment when the last sliver of the sun slid behind the horizon, the breath was released from fifty towers. A wave of sound broke against the valley side. The two men stared across at the citadel, the Red, now the colour of old bleached bones.

Chapter 28

The last call to prayer had ebbed away from the cemetery of al-Bayyazin. Lubna lay on the hard ground, listening to the snuffling of dogs around her inert body. Some aerial part of her mind rose, looked down upon herself and saw a shadow stretched out beside a grave with a stone as a pillow, like the mad graveyard-dwelling Sufis who saw chaotic visions.

But Lubna's visions were not chaotic. Since that second thunderbolt of four days ago, she had seen things with a detached and shocking clarity.

Beginning with the vision of her brother's head. In her mind's eye, she had watched him die so many times before that, in a way, she had been prepared for the sight of his actual corpse. She had heard the boy Jaime's screams on the day of their capture sixteen years ago, and heard in them the agony of his imagined death. Then, when word had come at long, long last that he had survived and been taken into the Mamluks, news of every border war brought images of Jaime's young body lying unburied on the battlefield. Jaime had died again in El Bermejo's coup against the Sultan, died in exile with the Sultan across the Strait, died in every visitation of the Death. So that sight of him, dead in reality, had been the latest episode of a recurring nightmare, a terror numbed by repetition.

What had been truly, newly terrifying was the intuition that she had been responsible for his death. 'Martyred in this place,' the turbaned man had said at his burial. She pictured Jaime's crazed look of fear when they had found him haunting the tombs that day, in the last hours, perhaps the last minutes of his life. Reason hadn't let her work out why; but instinct, in that awful moment when the head had stirred from beneath the shroud, had told her that – even if she wasn't the one who wielded the knife – she was her brother's killer.

How long she had spent in the outer darkness of that revelation she couldn't tell.

It had been that roll of thunder, that bolt unrolling from the blue, that had brought her to the light once more. The breaking of the storm, of her brain fever, took her back to the night of Ali's murder and to that other head, her lover's, his eyes beseeching her.

They still beseeched. But now they begged for vengeance, for them both: the lover and the brother, her two past lives, both severed in so bestial a way, both buried in this same steep acre of ground.

But how to avenge them? *How?*

While the moon ran its broad parabola across the sky, Lubna's mind ranged about the graves, around the tangled alleys of al-Bayyazin and the maze of events which had led her here, seeking the path that led to revenge. And when her mind at last returned to her, it was exhausted and unsatisfied.

The last thing Lubna knew, as always, when she finally entered the margins of sleep, was the flash of other eyes, green above a veil.

Not far away, in his chamber in the Sultan's guest-house, eyes haunted Abraham Ibn Zarzar's wanderings in the borderland of sleep: the frozen blue madness of Don Pedro's look; the deep brown gaze of his old master, Sultan Muhammad of Granada. In less than thirty-six hours, over a lump of red glass, he would come face to face with that second gaze, and he knew too well what dangers lurked in its placid depths.

He thought back over this last day of the journey from Seville, this flight towards doom. Fresh mounts had appeared in the late forenoon, horses to replace their mules, and had carried him, the counterfeit Ruby and the two dull *hidalgos* over the remaining leagues to Granada with the dreadful speed and inevitability of the four horses of the Christians' Apocalypse. A creeping paralysis had numbed his limbs on the final climb up to the torch-lit gate of the Alhambra, and there, under the eyeless gaze of those severed heads sent by Don Pedro so many years before, Abraham had almost dropped the casket when he handed it over to the commander of Mamluks.

Now the fake lay in the Alhambra's vaults, sleeping safe in the keeping of Allah and the Mamluks, awaiting its public restoration on the morning after the morrow. As for Abraham, both sleep and the Lord of his Hebrew forefathers had deserted him.

He tried, for the first time in many years, to summon them with psalms. But only one cold verse would come: *O my God, I cry to thee in the day-time, but thou hearest not: and in the night-season also I take no rest.*

'*Look on me not, my lord, my cloud, with brows of thunder.*'

The Grand Vizier, dismounting heavily at the gate of his palace, heard the words and turned, surprised, to the ever-present line of squatting petitioners. He had passed yet another sleepless night at the Alhambra, and was determined to spend an hour or two of the morning in his own private paradise before going back to the endless niggling supervision of preparations. And if things went wrong on the morrow, he reflected gloomily, he might be cast out of his paradise for ever.

He would not even have noticed the petitioners; they were part of the landscape, a vaguely human backdrop. But this voice he could not ignore. He saw at once who had uttered the verse: a woman, dishevelled and dusty but decently veiled. She looked at him with a level gaze. Then she continued, her Arabic impeccably classical, not so much an utterance as a chant, and with an edge of foreignness that played on his heartstrings like a bow on a rebec:

> 'Look on me not, my lord, my cloud, with brows of thunder,
> Look not askance with lightning glance that cleaves my breast asunder.
> You are the source with whose sweet rain to course my valleys thirst,
> And I the desert upon which your copious flood will burst.'

That friction in the voice, that frisson – it set off a resonance through Lisan al-Din's exhausted body that he had not known for years. He felt his extremities tingle with it, felt – *what?* – his old Mamluk, as Abu Abdallah had called it, bestirring itself.

'What a charmingly old-fashioned way of, er, gaining my attention,' he said. 'Who are you, woman?'

'I am – was – the slave of Ali the Alchemist, sir.'

The Grand Vizier stared at her for an instant, then turned towards his palace gate. 'Let her in,' he said to the guards.

Lubna sat on a bench in a dim antechamber, and went through her awakening once more: how she'd found herself sitting upright by the grave an hour or so before, eyes wide open to the cold light of dawn, but her mind still half in the dream that had woken her.

She had been in the old house, Ali's house, on that final evening, just before his murder and the thunderbolt had ended her second life. She was in the kitchen, preparing dinner and humming a song her mother had always sung when they were out on the sierra, in that even older life. A sudden hammering on the street door made

208

her jump. She turned to go and answer, but heard the creak as Ali opened the door himself.

And then she heard the conversation, ringing clear from the entrance-hall across the courtyard – and across a crevasse in time that was less than three weeks wide but seemed as bottomless as the pit of hell.

'You told me it would be ready,' an unknown voice said. It was a soft voice; but so cold that, refracted as it was by time and dreamscape, it made Lubna shiver even now. ' "In a few days," you said. You promised me. And you know what happens to those who break their promises.'

'But . . .I need more time,' Ali said. '*Please.* Just a little more. And the pressure . . . the debts. There's the coppersmith for a start. It would help if you could only . . .'

'Then take my gold,' the unknown voice said quietly. It then spoke in a whisper, but clearly audible across the courtyard, across that fissure in time. 'But know that from now on all you will earn from me is my wrath.'

The door creaked shut, even though Lubna had heard no departing steps. Was the unknown visitor still there?

'O God,' she heard Ali saying. She had never heard him call on God before. 'O God . . .if only I could undo what I've done. *If only.*'

And then the door of the dream swung shut too, and Lubna found herself awake, sitting bolt upright beside Ali's grave. There in the grey dawn light she knew that the dream was no dream, but a true clear memory. And she knew who the owner of the unknown voice was.

She knew, too, what she had to do. And the first thing was to kill her fears – of the beatings and violations she would earn from Ali's brother, and the other fear, faceless and formless, of the man who had spoken to Ali in the entrance hall that night, the veiled man with green eyes.

'So, to what do I owe the pleasure?' Lisan al-Din asked the slave-woman. He heard his words as if they came from the mouth of a stranger, and knew the reason: part of him was dead from weariness – it always was; but part of him was more alive than it had been for longer than he could remember.

Lubna told him everything. She told him of Ali's murder, of the thunderbolt and conflagration, of her brief sojourn in the cave to which she'd carried Ali's messages; of her captivity and interrogation by the man they called 'Shaykh Layth' in the other, bigger cave, and her further questioning by the Chief of the Night. She told him of the kind Moroccan gentleman and his gallant offers of help (the Grand Vizier, she noticed, smiled broadly at this); of her investigation of the first cave with Abu Abdallah and the subsequent attack on them in the suq of al-Bayyazin; of her long asylum in the cemetery and the dreadful witnessing of her brother's interment. Finally she told him of the dream that was no dream, but a memory – of that overheard conversation in the entrance hall. 'And sir,' she concluded, 'although I cannot discern the nature of the thread on which these disparate events are strung, I *know* there is a thread. And I know that it leads on further, to events and dangers that I cannot begin to imagine. And I know, sir, that the thread is held and controlled by the green-eyed man who interrogated me. So I beg you, your eminence, to find that man. Before it is too late.'

Lisan al-Din, who had listened as if in a trance to the slave-woman's strange narrative, wove his fingertips together beneath his chin and closed his eyes for a minute and more, until Lubna imagined he had fallen asleep. Then he opened his eyes and regarded her out of his fleshy face. 'So, before it is too late to prevent imminent and perilous happenings, the nature of which we are entirely ignorant, I must identify and apprehend a man known only as "Shaykh Layth", of whom we know nothing but the fact that his eyes are green, and who is to be looked for in an entirely unknown subterranean location. And all this on the say-so of a single witness who is not only a woman but also a slave.' He stroked a jowl. 'Forgive me, but the evidence is somewhat . . . *clouded*.' The word excited him even as he said: that poetic image of himself, the cloud pouring his sweet moisture on this woman's thirsting desert . . . He wondered if Abu Abdallah had made her new master an offer yet. He could outbid him; but would that be quite the thing to do to his old friend?

'Then, sir, I believe there is one person who can clear the clouds,' Lubna said. Then she added, looking down, 'Or rather, two persons. But I do not know what has become of them, or even if they are still . . . alive.' Her voice had trailed away.

'You refer to Abu Abdallah and his slave?'

Lubna looked at the Grand Vizier and nodded.

'Abu Abdallah is alive and well.'

'*And Sinan?*' Lubna asked. 'I mean, Abu Abdallah's slave?'

Lisan al-Din smiled gently at the unconcealable tone of concern and eagerness in her question. Gently, and perhaps a little ruefully.

'Sinan, too, is alive and well.' He saw her eyes brighten above the veil, and looked into them. 'Woman,' he said at last, 'God alone knows why it should, but your account moves me more than I can express . . . I . . . I . . .'

But words failed the Grand Vizier, and instead he clapped twice. An elderly slave appeared, his major-domo.

'Take this woman to the female house-slaves' quarters,' Lisan al-Din ordered. 'And have her fed and looked after. Then send word to the hospital. Tell them to release Abu Abdallah and his slave and have them brought here. With all possible haste.'

Chapter 29

Abu Abdallah screwed his squirrel features into a look of disgust. 'And as for those Hispanic emetics of yours that they kept giving us, Lisan . . .'

'Galenic dietetics, master,' Sinan said. Lisan al-Din smiled wearily through the gloom of his library. 'But master, we must tell his eminence about our discoveries. *There's no time to lose.*' Sinan knew all too well that barging straight to the point was the height of conversational bad manners. But when the point was a gunpowder plot against Granada . . . Equally well, Sinan knew that his master could be exasperatingly cool under pressure.

Abu Abdallah was looking at him as if from some icy summit of the High Atlas. ' "*Haste is to the Devil's taste,*" Sinan; "*leisure always wins, at God's good pleasure*". As I was saying, Lisan, with those horrible messes they kept feeding us, it was a toss-up as to whether I'd die of starvation first, or go bonkers like the rest of your inmates in the *maristan*.'

'My dear friend,' the Grand Vizier said genially, 'I am heartily pleased to see that God has preserved both your body and your sanity. Although . . .' He paused. 'Although I must say that it is only against my better judgement that I have released you from your protective custody. As a result, there is no little danger to us all, myself included.'

'So why *have* you released us?' Abu Abdallah asked.

'Intelligence, received from . . . let us say, a particularly well-endowed informant. Intelligence that touches on matters of the

213

very highest import. And not least upon the matter of the plot, doomed to failure though it necessarily is, to steal our blessed Sultan's Ruby.'

Sinan opened his mouth to speak, but was silenced by a glare from Abu Abdallah.

'And, apropos of this information I have come by,' the Grand Vizier continued, suddenly turning the dark lantern of his face full on Abu Abdallah, '*what do you know of a veiled man with green eyes?*'

'Oh, not a lot,' the little Moroccan said, looking nonchalantly around the manuscript-filled alcoves. 'Except that you wouldn't want to run into him in a dark alley at night. Hah! Do you remember that, Sinan? I said, "You wouldn't want to run into him in a dark alley at night." And we just had! Literally!' He chuckled at his own drollery.

Sinan did not smile.

'It was the night we got here, to Granada,' Abu Abdallah went on. 'Just a minute or two before that thunderbolt struck in al-Bayyazin. But Sinan can tell you more about old Green Eyes. Seemed to take a shine to you, didn't he, boy.'

'Sir,' Sinan said to the Grand Vizier, 'the attack on us in al-Bayyazin suq, shortly before we were taken to the *maristan* . . . The man who targeted me was that same person. He had green eyes and was closely veiled in a *taylasan*. But, your eminence, we have an even more important piece of information for you . . .'

'Indeed we do, thanks to my powers of deduction and inference,' Abu Abdallah interrupted, 'which as you know were honed by lengthy periods of study with the most renowned logicians of the Greeks, the Indians and the Chinese.' He frowned, scratched his beard and looked at Sinan. 'What was it, boy, the even more important piece of information?'

'The *Remedy*, master.'

'Oh, yes, absolutely. The Remedy.' With several confusions and interpolations of his own, Abu Abdallah explained their discovery of the conundrum hidden in the Alchemist's verse. The Grand Vizier followed his words closely, a slow smile spreading across his face. 'Sinan will crunch the *abjad* numbers for you,' Abu Abdallah concluded.

'Sir,' Sinan said, 'I'm almost certain that the system used is the Eastern *abjad*. Going by this, the numerical value of black, which we believe to signify charcoal – *qalᶜah bi-Tulaytulah*, "a castle in Toledo" – is 300. Yellow, or sulphur – *jabal Qadis*, "the mount of Cádiz" – is 200. And white, or Chinese snow – *rujam Araghun*, "the graves of Aragón" – comes to 1,500.'

Lisan al-Din was now nodding vigorously, his jowls quivering. 'Five to three to fifteen . . . the so-called Syrian Recipe, first expounded in *The Book of Horsemanship and Stratagems of War* of Hasan of Damascus, known as the Lancer; there's a copy over there, under Science and Technology. They are the very same proportions the Sultanic arsenal here in Granada has been using for years. Decades, in fact. We've all known that it would leak sooner or later . . .' He pouted, and wrinkled his brows. 'And between ourselves, although it's probably another open secret by now, the "Remedy" – yes, indeed, that is what some call it – is far from being the weapon of mass destruction that it is made out to be in certain quarters. Oh, there's all that propaganda about the recipe having been divulged by Satan himself and about propulsors belching hellfire and raining missiles like the birds in the Qur'an on the Day of the Elephant, and incurable wounds, and lingering deaths from the effects of toxic smoke. All utter nonsense, though of course there are plenty who fall for it.'

The Grand Vizier sat back. Sinan regarded him with surprise. But Abu Abdallah was nodding in agreement now. 'I must say, Lisan, that this all chimes with what I remember seeing in China, aboard one of those ships they call *junks*. For my benefit, as Ambassador Plenipotentiary and Extraordinary from the Sultan of Hind, they demonstrated some so-called anti-pirate weapons they'd developed. If you ask me, they were about as effective as a fart in the wind.'

'And to take a slightly less exotic example than yours,' the Grand Vizier continued, 'consider the king of Anqiltarrah's son, the one they call the Black Prince. In his great victory over the French – what, twenty years ago or more it must have been – he fielded propulsors, and those small hand-held weapons they call kohl-pots. But in the end it was his archers who won the day with those long-bows of theirs. And it was the same when he fought last year for Don Pedro, against Henry the Bastard. English longbows . . . that's the technology to have, not that we do. Or failing that, a crack corps of crossbowmen, which we do have. The Remedy is mere sound and fury.'

'Unless, sir,' Sinan said after a pause, 'the plotters have been able somehow to develop its potential – to increase its destructive power.' The Grand Vizier frowned, then motioned to Sinan to continue. 'I can't help feeling, sir, that there is some further enigma hidden in the ending of the Alchemist's verse: "*The final, fatal fire is lightning in the rain-cloud born . . .*"'

' "*He'll know,*" ' the Grand Vizier said, completing the couplet – and feeling haunted by images of rain-clouds, ' "*who grinds the finest flour, then turns it back to corn.*" Hmm. You could be right, Sinan. You just could be . . .' He shook his head. 'If only we did know . . .'

The words hung like book-dust in the silence of the library. For a while they sat and listened to the plinking of the fountain beyond the latticed windows.

'Sir,' Sinan said at last, sensing it was time to impart his other discovery, 'I believe we have gained an insight into another of the riddles – the one in the Latin message which you intercepted. I'm speaking, sir, of the "red one", the apparent target of the plotters.'

'Ah yes,' Abu Abdallah cut in, appearing to wake from a doze. 'Bless you, Sinan, for jogging my memory. I was about to come to that, the second of my momentous deductions. Having applied the strictest principles of Aristo . . . *Aristocratic* logic to the conundrum, I realized that the plotters may be planning not only to steal the Ruby, but also to launch an attack on the Alhambra itself, the *Red Palace* of the Nasrid dynasty.' He paused to let the words sink in. He didn't need to: Lisan al-Din looked immediately astonished. 'And how, you may well ask,' Abu Abdallah continued, 'did I arrive at this portentous conclusion?' He looked round the room, as if searching for the answer in the voluminous stacks. 'How indeed? I ask myself.' He looked at Sinan. 'Sinan,' he said through clenched teeth, '*how?*'

'It is a question of the grammatical genders used in the Latin message, your eminence. If I remember the words right, *rufi*, I believe you said, sir, is masculine. *Rufa*, though, is feminine – like *al-hamra* in Arabic. I just wondered . . . if it might be a possibility.' Sinan cleared his throat. He wasn't even certain that he had recalled the alien words correctly. And in any case his concussed brainwave in the madhouse suddenly seemed dreadfully muddled and implausible in the academic cool of the Grand Vizier's library. 'Or rather,' Sinan said, shooting a look at Abu Abdallah, '*my master* wondered. It was his "Aristocratic" train of thought that brought him to the conclusion; although I believe he meant to say *Aristotelian*.'

'Thank you, my boy,' Abu Abdallah said, nodding in vigorous agreement.

For the second time this morning, Lisan al-Din wove his fingers under his chin and closed his eyes for a long time. 'So,' he said at last, 'we are certain almost beyond any doubt that the putative plot we have uncovered involves the use of the Remedy. As for the target of the plot, it may be the Ruby, or the Alhambra, or both. But in all cases we have nothing to fear. The Ruby is ensconced deep within the Alhambra. It is as safe as it was when it yet lay undiscovered in the bowels of the earth.' A bird shrieked in the brightness beyond the lattice. 'As for the Alhambra, it is heavily garrisoned by the elite of the Mamluks, and further guarded by squadrons of crack Berber cavalry and patrols of regular infantry. In view of the importance of tomorrow's ceremony, I have stepped up security to a level never seen before in the Sultanate of Granada.'

'But don't forget they've got the Remedy, Lisan.'

The Grand Vizier raised his weighty statesman's chin. 'Even if there were half a thousand plotters, equipped with the latest firearms, they would scarcely be able to make pockmarks in the Alhambra's noble walls before being cut down to a man. Do you know how long it takes to reload even one of those puny "kohl-pots"? A good four minutes – during which a trained crossbowman can loose a dozen bolts.' He paused to savour his speech. 'No,' he went on. 'We have nothing to fear. Unless . . .'

'Unless what, Lisan?'

'Unless your brilliant and subtle slave is right, and there is a further enigma buried in that final couplet.' His head sank, then he sighed deeply, and was silent.

'Or unless,' the Grand Vizier continued abruptly, looking up again, 'there is some . . . some chink in the Alhambra's defences. As there was back in the year sixty.'

'The year sixty, sir?' Sinan asked.

'When El Bermejo, if you recall the red-headed gentleman up on the gate, staged his first coup. Hmmph. We were repairing a bit of the wall, and they climbed up and strolled through the breach in the masonry . . .' Suddenly the Grand Vizier rose, dark and towering as a *jinni* set loose from a bottle. 'Enough! An end to complacency! *I shall search the entire Alhambra.*'

'Goodness, Lisan,' Abu Abdallah said, 'you look as if you're going to storm the place. Black as thunder, you are.'

The Grand Vizier eyed his friend. Black as thunder . . . *brow of thunder* . . . He allowed his mind to wander for a moment over to the slave-women's quarters, to the Alchemist's *qaynah* – and felt a pathetic prick of jealousy at the thought of leaving Abu Abdallah

218

so near her. 'You'd better come too, my friend. And you, Sinan. We could do with your powers of observation.'

'But I thought we were meant to be under suspicion of murder, Lisan.'

'Suspicion be damned! I am the Grand Vizier of Granada, and you are under my protection!'

By the end of an afternoon in which the Grand Vizier swept through the Alhambra as irresistibly as a weather system, Sinan felt he had explored every corner of the mighty palace-citadel, from the massive western Watchtower they had ascended that first morning – so long ago, it now seemed – to the far eastern bastions that beetled over the chasm separating the main acropolis from its dependant pleasure-garden of Jannat al-Arif. They had combed colonnades and corridors, scoured bastions and bath-houses, and had beaten the towering bounds, half a league in length, of the Alhambra's curtain wall. From his vantage point at the eye of this human storm, Sinan saw it all – all except the Sultan's private apartments, whose inspection Lisan al-Din entrusted, with extreme reluctance, to Ibn Zamrak the Sultanic Secretary and a team of eunuchs. Now the two search parties met up in the completed new court, where Sinan marvelled at the finished paintings of the Nazarene decorators and was dizzied by the sheer crowning richness of it all.

Ibn Zamrak alone seemed immune to the magnificence, which he regarded with an unconcealed sneer. 'No rodent excrement, I am glad to see,' he said, surveying the gleaming marble pavement. 'But I cannot fail to note the presence of two larger species of vermin, as our dear Grand Vizier would put it, one of them of the most dangerous variety of all – the *Black*.' He shot Abu Abdallah and Sinan a scowl of undisguised contempt, then looked at Lisan al-Din. 'What in God's name are you up to, *your eminence*? These two are the prime suspects in the murder of one of His Presence's Mamluks!' Ibn Zamrak's eunuch henchmen turned their fleshy faces on the two men; Sinan tasted the venom of their stares.

'They are in my charge,' Lisan al-Din replied quietly, 'and, in case it has escaped your notice, I would remind you that, as Grand Vizier of Granada, I am your superior.'

' "The most honourable of you," ' Ibn Zamrak said, quoting the Qur'an, ' "in *God's* view, are those who are most pious . . . " And, in case it has escaped *your* superior purview, it is only the Almighty Himself who remains superior forever. In this world of creation and destruction, vizierates come . . . and vizierates go. Even the grandest ones.' He slid silently to the edge of the court, to pace the colonnades with his silent eunuch escort.

Sinan could feel the Sultanic Secretary's stare piercing him through the pillars. He tried to distract himself by pondering yet again the puzzle in the centre of the court. The new palace – for that was what it was: an entire new royal residence – now stood revealed in all its magnificence; all except that one focal point of the whole design. He noticed that the canvas screen around the centrepiece had been replaced with a much grander sort of tent, a small but gorgeous pavilion of brocade. The Sultan's surprise remained a secret, now royally wrapped.

Sinan also noticed a pair of cords running out from inside the pavilion; they were half hidden in one of the four shallow drainage channels that divided the court into four quarters, like the quadripartite design of a formal garden. The cords had also caught the Grand Vizier's attention, for Zayd the Clerk of Works was explaining them to him. 'You see, your eminence, I grasp the cord, the cords, and pull smartly – and the pavilion falls away, revealing our surprise within.'

'Might we have a little demonstration?' Abu Abdallah asked. 'Just in case we don't get a good seat at the ceremony tomorrow . . .'

'No we might not,' the Grand Vizier said with absolute finality. 'Now, Zayd,' he continued, addressing the Clerk, 'you have joined us at an opportune moment. We have been performing a thorough inspection of the Alhambra, for reasons of security. We have looked into every nook and corner of every part of the palace and its dependencies, and I am glad to say we have found nothing amiss.' He recited the long list of locations which they had searched. During the recitation, Sinan saw Ibn Zamrak sidle back; he remained at the edge of the group, listening. 'I wonder, however,' the Grand Vizier went on, 'if in your capacity of Clerk of Works you might know of any places of concealment in this glorious Alhambra, places which may have escaped our notice.' He looked carefully into Zayd's fair Berber features.

The Clerk, Sinan noticed, passed his hand over his face, as if concentrating his thoughts. 'I believe, sir, that you have, as they say, left no stone unturned.' He paused and thought again. Then a faint smile lit his eyes. 'At least, not *in* the Alhambra. But there are other places, your eminence. Places unknown even to yourself.'

'Not *in* the Alhambra . . . What do you mean, man?' Lisan al-Din said, frowning. 'Where?'

'*Under* the Alhambra, your eminence.' Zayd was now smiling.

Only Sinan saw the infinitesimal moment of horror that possessed the waxen face of Ibn Zamrak, the Sultanic Secretary.

Chapter 30

'And the sovereign prophylactic against subterranean miasmata, the foul airs that cause the Death,' Sinan heard the Sultanic Secretary say to the chief eunuch, 'is this.' Sinan turned and saw Ibn Zamrak holding a dark and glistening bolus in his pallid fingertips. If anything, it resembled a lump of donkey manure, freshly excreted. Ibn Zamrak raised it portentously to his nostrils and inhaled deeply. 'A *pomander*,' he explained, 'compounded from camphor, pepper, sandalwood and rose petals, all ground up and mixed with rosewater, gum Arabic and bole Armeniac.'

'And to think he falls for that quackery,' the Grand Vizier said loudly to Abu Abdallah. 'God, you can smell the thing from here. And the stink of that vinegar he's doused himself and his eunuchs with. All to fend off his blessed *miasmata*.'

The shadows were lengthening and the sunset prayer fast approaching when they passed the Sufi shrine on the south-east slope of the Alhambra hill. Zayd the Clerk, in the lead, turned off the main track and made for a gap in a high and mossy wall. The rest of the search party followed him with evident reluctance. Sinan heard a murmur passing round the men, in which one word was clearly audible: *jinn*.

'Is it not strange, sir,' Zayd the Clerk said to the Grand Vizier, 'how invariably the *jinn* are said to take up residence in abandoned places such as this old garden?' A smile spread over his fair Berber face. 'But at least it meant that, when we were young, we used to have the whole of it as our own private playground.'

'And these ... underground places we are supposedly inspecting?' Lisan al-Din asked. 'My concern is not your childhood memories, Zayd, but the security of His Presence. Woe betide you if you are wasting my time.'

'All will become clear soon enough, your eminence,' Zayd said, calmly, entering the gap in the wall. 'Given your encyclopaedic historical knowledge,' he continued when the Grand Vizier was through, 'you will know, sir, I am sure, that when my ancestors the sons of Ziri ruled Granada, they built some modest fortifications at the far end of the Alhambra hill. In the course of the surveys preceding these works, a number of natural caves and fissures were discovered, piercing the hill. My forebears gradually enlarged them, and used them to store munitions and, it is said, treasure. This was long before the Nasrid Sultans ...'

'*Whose dynasty may God prolong,*' hissed Ibn Zamrak, who had edged up to listen in.

' ... before they built the noble palace of the Alhambra.'

By now all the men were through the breach in the wall. Forced into single file by the narrowness of the descending path, they penetrated the tangled and twilit wilderness of collapsing terraces that had once been a garden. Only the occasional whisper of a prayer against the *jinn* broke the silence, or the odd curse as roots and thorns tripped feet and tugged at robes or weapons.

'Just as the risen sun of the Nasrids eclipsed all former dynasties, sir,' Zayd eventually resumed, addressing the Grand Vizier in a low voice, 'the peerless glory of the Alhambra caused people to forget the existence of the vaults that lie beneath it. But knowledge of these crypts and tunnels passed down through our Zirid family. I used to come here ...'

A castrato shriek came from a eunuch caught in a thicket by an imagined *jinni* – '*It's got me!*' – followed by a nervous laugh from the Mamluks.

' . . . I used to come here,' Zayd went on, 'when I was a boy, with my elder brother, may God rest his soul. We would roam the underground chambers and tunnels, looking for the lost treasure of the sons of Ziri. We used to daydream . . . about restoring the fortunes of our family.' He smiled sadly. 'We never found the treasure. And then the Death, that first and most terrible visitation of it back in 'forty-eight, took my brother, and my only remaining cousins. As you know, sir, I am the last of the sons of Ziri – '

He pulled up short. They were standing in a small clearing in the wilderness. In front of them, set into the hillside, was a door. A door with no handle and no lock.

'This . . . the door . . .' Zayd said. 'It wasn't here before. Or only an old wrecked thing, hanging off its hinges.'

Lisan al-Din looked at him. 'There is no other entrance or exit?' Zayd shook his head. 'Break it down!' the Grand Vizier commanded. A group of Mamluks made for the door.

'*NO! Don't touch it!*' Every head turned. It was the Sultanic Secretary, a look of terror on his face. 'This is folly! You will unleash the untold miasmata of the Death that lurk in the subterranean bowels of the hill!' The Mamluks hesitated, looking from Ibn Zamrak to the Grand Vizier.

'If you had cared,' Lisan al-Din said softly, fixing Ibn Zamrak with his doleful gaze, 'so much as to glance at the copy of my treatise on the Contagion Theory that I sent you, you would know the truth about the Death. You would know that the only *miasmata*, dear colleague, are in your own brain. You would know that the Death is spread not by foetid air but by human agents. You would know that groups who are isolated from their fellow men, such as nomads deep in the desert and prisoners in confinement, do not succumb to the infection. You would know, in short,' he continued, his voice growing in volume, 'that the folly is yours alone, for clinging to outmoded, unscientific and irrational myths worthy of old women! *Break it down, I said!*'

225

The Mamluks laid into the door with their fists, then their boots, then their shoulders; to no effect. Then their comrades found the small trunk of a fallen tree, and with this as a battering ram, the door at last began to give. Ibn Zamrak stood before it, rigid with fear and fascination, flanked by Lisan al-Din on one side and by Abu Abdallah and Sinan on the other. Zayd, peering between the onlookers, kept mumbling to the Grand Vizier, ' . . . inexplicable, your eminence . . . I cannot think who might have sealed the entrance thus . . . no idea at all . . .'

At last the central plank of the door began to crack, and a rim of darkness to appear within the frame. Between alternate inhalations of his pomander and of another object – a bunch of myrtle twigs, Sinan realized – Ibn Zamrak was now nibbling at something greyish and slippery-looking. 'A pickled onion?' the Grand Vizier exclaimed. 'For heaven's sake, man, you live in the age of science and reason!'

'As if science and reason will protect you from the inexorable will of God!' Ibn Zamrak replied, still staring at the door. 'You will soon see what it is that you are letting loose, and I shall be vindicated!' He laughed – a laugh that had an edge of madness to it – then began reciting from the Chapter of Noah: ' "*Give warning to your people before a woeful scourge overcomes them . . .* " 'Another sniff of the pomander, another nibble at the onion. ' "*My people, I come to warn you plainly. Serve God and fear Him, and obey me!* " Stop! Stop, I say, while there is yet time to save yourselves!'

But at last the door broke free from its frame, and for an instant seemed to hesitate, unsupported in mid-air – and then fell inwards with a dull whump and a puff of dust. Involuntarily, the Mamluks ducked, and the other onlookers swayed backwards as if impelled by some escaping force. Ibn Zamrak leaned forward and peered in, mesmerized, now holding a linen pad soaked in vinegar to his mouth. Within, there was . . .

Darkness. Silence.

Only Sinan saw it: a flash of eyes, of inexpressible anger and hatred and violence, as of a beast cornered in its lair. A flash – he was almost sure – of green.

But they all heard it, in that moment of silence – the word, soft yet poisonous, that was flung out of the tunnel mouth in the face of Ibn Zamrak, spat out like a viper's venom: *kha'in*.

Traitor.

'So, my dear colleague,' the Grand Vizier said, turning to Ibn Zamrak. 'Your "miasma" addresses you with a human voice.' Then, to the Mamluks, 'Pray escort the Sultanic Secretary away. Take him to a place where he will be safe from his Death ... Until *I* can come and deal with him. As for whoever is within, and whom he has so helpfully betrayed–' Lisan al-Din permitted himself a small but triumphant smile, '–they are caught in a trap of their own making.'

Ibn Zamrak's waxen features looked set to melt. His mouth opened and closed repeatedly but no sound came out. A brutish-looking, lantern-jawed eunuch made as if to step forward and defend him; but the Mamluks flicked him aside, and the Sultanic Secretary was marched off, still gasping for words.

'Follow us,' Lisan al-Din said to the remaining Mamluks and eunuchs, who were lighting their torches. He took the lead into the tunnel mouth, with Zayd the Clerk, Sinan and Abu Abdallah behind. 'Search every twist, every nook. Try to take alive anyone you find. But if they resist, have no mercy. There must be no escape.'

Sinan felt himself swallowed by blackness. The tunnel narrowed, like a sphincter. He smelt damp and decay. Then his other senses began to adjust – last of all his eyes. Torchlight conjured enemies from shadows. He jumped at a tap on his shoulder.

It was his master. 'So, my boy,' Abu Abdallah whispered, 'it looks as if we're out of the woods and into the light at last.' Sinan turned to him: given their situation – a cave in a forest at dusk – it was a strange turn of phrase. 'I mean, Lisan al-Din's got his vole, or his mole, or whatever you call the beast. Never liked the look of him, that Ibn Zamrak. And now we've got the other rats trapped here.'

'Master, don't be complacent. When you've just got the first one . . . that's the moment of greatest danger.' Suddenly his father's voice sounded across the years. They were out with the men, hunting lion, had just killed a big full-maned male. Sinan saw his boyish self perched on the corpse, laughing, as he did in those days. *This is the moment of greatest danger,* his father whispered, *just when you've got the first one . . .* And almost as he spoke there was a roar and a rustling and a rushing and the bushes broke and a female charged – on to his father's waiting spear.

'The moment of greatest danger . . . Honestly, Sinan, don't be so melodramatic,' Abu Abdallah was saying. He cupped his hand round his mouth and spoke in even softer tones: 'With Ibn Zamrak out of the picture, there's bound to be a reshuffle. Think positive. *Think vizierate!*'

Sinan raised his eyebrows and nodded. He was about to jog his master's memory about his secret secretaryship when, in the fitful light of the Mamluks' torches, something unexpected caught his eye. It was a pattern so regular as to conceal itself by repetition: from as high as a man could reach down to floor level, the walls of the tunnel bore the marks of having been carved, or rather scraped, with deliberate regularity. The marks appeared to have been made by picks or chisels. 'Master, look . . .' He pointed out the methodical striations to Abu Abdallah.

'So what?' the old man said. 'You heard Zayd the Clerk telling us how his ancestors had the original caves enlarged.'

'Yes, master. But that was centuries ago. These marks look as if they've been made recently. I was just thinking about what you told me . . . about Chinese snow. That it's scraped from the walls of cellars and latrines and so on. Don't you think we should remind the Grand Vizier – I mean, that we're dealing with men who have the Remedy? God knows how much of it they've produced. Don't you think we should counsel caution?'

Abu Abdallah cut short a laugh. 'I thought you were meant to be the intrepid hero who rips villains' arms off . . . So, they come at us with their repulsives, or chamber-pots, or whatever the things are called. I told you. I've seen them, these . . . these *firearms*. They're hardly fit for scaring scarecrows.'

Sinan realized that, as Abu Abdallah was speaking, the tunnel had risen and the scrape-marks had disappeared from the walls. Then, without warning, they emerged into a spacious chamber. From somewhere ahead the faintest whisper of a breeze blew. The scent of damp and rot had gone. The chamber was dry; dry as a hayloft. And silent as a sepulchre.

Abu Abdallah's voice cut through the silence: 'Don't you remember, boy? It's like the Grand Vizier said – the Remedy's nothing but sound and fu . . .'

They saw it too late: another torch, flying at them out of the dark in a blazing arc and landing in –

A blinding flash. A wall of flame.

Then silence again, and the reek of roasted men.

Chapter 31

'As I was saying,' Abu Abdallah resumed, speaking between choking coughs, 'this Remedy's nothing but sound and fury.'

The chamber was filled with evil-smelling smoke and with the splutters of two dozen men – not roasted, but only lightly toasted. Sinan, dazed, amazed to be alive, flicked frizzled fragments from his beard and eyebrows and spat out the acrid taste of the fumes. By the light of a lone torch that had not been blown out by the blast, he saw the Grand Vizier brushing his own singed beard and turning to Abu Abdallah. 'I believe the technical term is . . .'

But it was lost in a yell that rang through the chamber and through Sinan's head: '*Al-mawt al-ahmar!*'

Red death . . .

And then they were on them – shades materializing into men, coming at them from half-seen tunnel mouths and side-caverns. And another battle-cry: '*Fight like lions!*'

They did. They were outnumbered, but in the smoke and dark and confusion they were the ones who knew the layout of the chamber. Sinan went for one of the approaching silhouettes – and realized he was unarmed. He struck out, hard as he could, with both fists, felt one of them connect, heard a crunch – then caught sight of the face of a youth, a bloodied pudding, before it sank. The boy tried to rise but was felled by a swishing blow from a Mamluk's sword.

Sinan saw the glint of a dagger in the dying boy's hand, wrenched it free and plunged into the scrum of attackers. He felt the blade enter flesh and organs, felt it grind on bone, heard a groan – and then another scream: 'Hattam! *Get the Black!*'

Just in time he dodged. But now he was up against the rock wall and a tall, cadaverous man was bearing down on him, a crazy death's-head grin on his face and a giant curved blade, half-sickle half-scythe, in his double-fisted grip. *God*, Sinan thought, *this is it*. He lunged at the apparition with his puny knife, but his assailant dodged each thrust and laughed, the grin getting nearer and bigger. A voice came out of the grin: 'I cut off heads . . . Never done a Black before, though.'

The end was swift. The mad rictus was on him, and the grinning blade – and then a miraculous bolt from a Mamluk crossbow transfixed the man's neck, fixed the grin for ever.

Sinan heaved off the falling corpse and panted, smelling the sharp mineral-animal stink of sweat and piss and gore that mingled now with the hellfire fumes of the Remedy. For an instant as he caught his breath he looked about for Abu Abdallah – and picked out the small figure of his master, wielding the sword of a fallen eunuch, laying about himself like a windmill in a gale. As he watched, the sword sliced into the neck of a scholarly man who had been making fluttering and ineffective stabs at Abu Abdallah with a small poniard. Sinan saw too the look of utter surprise on both faces, then a jet of blood spurting from the other man's jugular.

'Well I never . . . Beautifully balanced, these Granada blades,' Abu Abdallah called across to his slave. 'Come on Sinan, stop gawping, get fighting.'

But the pace of the fight was slowing as, one by one, overwhelmed by the training of the Mamluks and the brute weight of the eunuchs, their opponents fell. None surrendered, except to Izrael, the angel of death.

At last the chamber was quiet again, but for the gulping breaths of the victors. But Sinan could also hear low voices, speaking, and realized they were coming from a lit passage. He made his way in – and found himself in a side-cave illuminated by candles in glass-shaded sconces.

In the middle of the space was a sort of stone work-bench, on which stood cauldrons, mortars and other vessels of more obscure purpose. One large bowl, he noticed, was filled with jagged and misshapen pieces of metal – copper, by the look of them. And there was an even more puzzling stack of couscous sieves. For a moment Sinan was reminded of the Alchemist's laboratory. But it was the scene to one side of the cave that drew his attention. There stood the Grand Vizier, and a small arc of Mamluks, all with weapons at the ready, all looking at something on the floor; no, *someone*. 'Gently now,' Lisan al-Din was saying in a soft voice, 'gently. If we could take just this one alive . . .'

Sinan looked over the Mamluks' shoulders, and saw a small, precise-looking man with a scholar's penbox in his waist-sash, kneeling on the floor. There was terror in his eyes and a lighted torch in his hand. On the ground between him and the Mamluks was a large brass tray covered in some kind of black grain, of a sort Sinan had never seen before. In the flamelight it resembled Malabar pepper, although the corns were somewhat elongated. The torch hovered near the tray, and shook.

'Come on matey,' one of the Mamluks said, almost kindly, but with an unconcealable note of nervousness, 'give us the torch. It's all over now.'

The torch shook harder, so hard that a blazing ember fell from it and the Mamluks took an involuntary step back. They were all so mesmerized by the flaming brand that none of them seemed to see what Sinan saw – or, rather, what he realized he'd seen when it was already done: the man's free hand, quivering, reaching down for his penbox, flicking open the lid, drawing out a small glass inkpot, easing out the cork and in one swift fluid motion –

They all saw it now, too late: the little bottle going to his lips and the liquid pouring down his throat.

For a long moment nothing happened. Then the torch in his hand became still and the terror left his eyes. He smiled as if to himself, and spoke, strange, slurred words that Sinan guessed were Latin: '*Si fieret . . . de solidis corporibus . . . tunc . . . tunc . . .*' The man's head shook sadly, then lolled. Then his face turned black and clenched into a mask that was not human.

Sinan was in the deep past, with his father, in a painted hut, before the *boliw*. *Remember, son, don't look them in the face,* his father was saying. *You'll never rid yourself of what you see.* But he had stolen a glance, and one of the faces he saw then he saw now.

The kneeling figure sank, the torch fell – on the ground – and the Mamluks sprang. They picked the man up, patted his blackened face, slapped it, punched it, shook the inert body. Then they threw it down. It twitched once or twice and then was still.

'Damn,' the Grand Vizier whispered. '*Damn.*'

Back in the main chamber they did a body-count. One Mamluk. One eunuch. And nine . . . but what to call them?

'So, with our suicide in there,' the Grand Vizier said, 'that makes ten of them. Whoever they are.' He went round peering at the dead faces. 'Hmm. I think I recognize this one,' he said, stepping over a coagulating pool of blood and levering the head of Abu Abdallah's victim over with the point of his *khuff*. The dead face, Sinan saw, still bore its look of utter surprise. 'Turned him down for a job once . . . But come on. We must comb the rest of the tunnels. There could be more of them. Split into pairs. Abu Abdallah, Zayd and I will remain here to guard the entrance tunnel. You two Mamluks, stay with us.'

Sinan found a fallen torch, relit it and, with a eunuch, set off down one of the passages that radiated from the main chamber. He heard Lisan al-Din's voice receding behind him: ' . . . quite enough heroics for one day, my friend. I never knew you had it in you . . . Dear me, what a display of swordsmanship: you looked just like one of those Indian idols you described to me once, those ones with all the extra arms . . .' The Grand Vizier's creaking laugh grew faint.

Single file, each with a torch in his left hand and a drawn sword in his right, Sinan and the eunuch stole into the silence and blackness of the tunnel. They trod on tiptoe – pointlessly, as the torchlight gave them away. It also set shadows in motion, made limbs of darkness grope at them out of the rock walls. They rounded a corner and descended. Sinan, in the lead, saw once more the scrape-marks on the tunnel walls. He wondered how much Chinese snow they'd gathered.

The hairs had risen on the back his neck: there was a presence, a third one – sensed, not seen; as in the lion-haunted thickets of his past. A presence *behind*. He swung round at the clatter of a falling sword, saw the eunuch writhing on the ground, a streak of magenta blood on the rock beside him. And then a shadow sprang.

Sinan ducked the lunge of the dagger-point but felt it kiss his bare neck; felt an ooze.

'Poison.' The shadow had spoken out of the shadows. 'Wolfsbane. With a touch of strychnine. It is swift, and fatal. Against it your sword, your . . . irresistible strength, are nothing.'

Sinan did not dare to take his eyes off the shade. His heart pounded at the words; he waited for a numbness, for a fire to spread. But the liquid on his neck was cold. There was no blood. The tip of the dagger hadn't even grazed his skin.

'Yes,' the shadow said softly, taunting, cajoling, 'only . . . a *kiss*. To begin. But come . . . come to me, and I will give you more. Aah . . . I will pierce you, so gently . . . I will send you into an ecstasy . . . *Of agony*,' the voice added, all but inaudibly.

Sinan gripped his sword tighter, burned to attack. But stood his ground.

'No?' the shadow said in a thin voice, disappointed. '*Then I will come to you.*'

The shadow leapt at him again, transformed into a man. Sinan wrenched himself aside, dodged the blade by a whisker. His own weapon was pointless in the narrow passageway. He threw it down and faced his attacker, armed now with nothing but his firebrand. Again the green eyes glinted, hated, lusted. For the third time. For the last time: for he knew that this time one of them would die.

The dance of death began, a nightmare thrust and parry of blade and brand, fire and poison. Sinan longed to cry out, to summon the others, and knew that even that small lapse of concentration would mean death. On went the duel, for seconds that seemed infinite. And, suddenly, by that instinct honed on boyhood hunts, Sinan knew the man was going to make his final, fatal move.

Fatal to whom? He had his own dark eyes locked on the other's green, judging the direction of the spring . . .

. . . and judging right. He caught the wrist when the point of the blade was still inches from his breast – caught it, twisted it with all his power, felt the rip of sinew. The dagger fell and he kicked it hard, sent it skittering down the tunnel.

Now they were all but in the dark, the torch glowing feebly where it had dropped, and they fought by feel alone in a savage lock of limbs, until at last Sinan felt the strength of his opponent begin to give under his own greater mass. There was one last surge of effort from his opponent, a sheer shock-wave of animal force. But he summoned the remaining energy from his own flagging muscles, wrestled him to the ground, straddled him, gripped him in the vice of his thighs, pinned him down by the shoulders, felt the body under him arching and thrusting, panting and burning. Saw the eyes loathing and lusting. *All I need to do is hold him.* At last he yelled out to the others with the shred of strength that still remained in him. And, looking down again, he knew now where he had first seen these eyes.

In a painted hut, in the deepest past.

It happened quicker than a blink. The man still had a hand free. There was a movement down at his side, the faintest glimmer in the ember-glow, of *another blade* –

Sinan raised the shoulders and smashed them back on to the ground, heard skull crack on rock. The head split open like a rotten gourd, spilling brains.

For a few moments the eyes looked up at him, the hatred gone; Sinan looked down into the bottomless opaline green, and saw tears.

But the green was clouding.

There was a sound of voices, of hurrying feet, approaching.

Beneath him the last of the light in the eyes dimmed and died.

Again, in frustration, he smashed the lifeless head on the rock.

And again.

In exorcism.

Chapter 32

'They'll take a little getting used to,' the Grand Vizier said. He screwed his eyes up in the morning sunlight and peered at the top of the great gate.

Sinan and Abu Abdallah followed his gaze. Above the main entrance to the Alhambra, the heads of the eleven dead Lions had replaced those of the usurper El Bermejo and his followers.

'But a fresh set of heads always sends the right message,' Lisan al-Din continued. 'Especially when you have important visitors. And in any case, El Bermejo and company were well past their prime. Mind you, the department of execution and torture were up all night patching up the middle one.' As if on cue, a raven landed by Layth's head and pecked hungrily at one of his green eyes. 'They said it was almost too damaged to go on display . . . I don't think you know your own strength, Sinan.'

Sinan said nothing. In the silence, broken only by the stiff rustle of official robes and the clink of Mamluk weapons, he studied the reception party. Gorgeous as a flock of exotic birds, the courtiers were variously draped in Sicilian brocade, Syrian damask, Egyptian velvet and *zardkhanah*, and all the textile wealth of Andalus itself. Each wore sleeves bearing elaborate inscriptions embroidered in Kufic characters. The Grand Vizier was stately but subdued in a robe of cobalt blue, while Abu Abdallah was in regal purple with gold lightning-bolts, and sported a large sky-blue turban as befitted his status as a scholar and a judge. Sinan, in a plain grey *jubbah* and green Granadan cap, felt like a pigeon among popinjays; but then, he was fated to stand out whatever he wore.

'What I just don't get, Lisan,' Abu Abdallah said eventually, 'is what those so-called Lions were hoping to achieve, hidden away like that so

239

deep under the ground. And with that pathetic amount of the Remedy. I mean, they didn't even have any of those jam-pots or expulsors or whatever they're called. All their Remedy did was go *whoosh*.'

'Indeed,' the Grand Vizier said. 'Oh, and the technical term for your "whoosh", as I was about to say when we were so rudely interrupted by the Lions, is *deflagration*. As for their Remedy, it wasn't even proper powder. Did you see it? A mass of little lumps, like peppercorns. I think they must have broken the first rule of the modern arsenal: keep your powder dry.'

'Perhaps they were running a clandestine couscous factory,' Abu Abdallah said. 'Did you see all those sieves they had?'

Lisan al-Din smiled. 'No doubt my colleague the Sultanic Secretary will be able to enlighten us, before his head joins the others up there. The department of execution and torture are, I believe, applying a little psychological pressure as we speak. But I doubt whether they'll need to go on to the physical stage. I gather the man's a gibbering wreck already, and driving them mad with his miasmata.'

The reception party were beginning to grow restive with the wait. Sinan heard other low conversations breaking out among the courtiers. Only the Mamluks maintained their disciplined ranks, standing to attention in the growing warmth of the morning.

'At least we can all sit back and enjoy today's ceremony with clear minds,' Abu Abdallah said.

God willing, Sinan whispered to himself. In other circumstances he would have warned his master of the dangers of complacency. Not that Abu Abdallah had ever paid heed to that counsel.

'It must be extremely gratifying,' Abu Abdallah went on, 'to know your resident plotter's safely locked up.'

'Yes, we have trapped our mole. And to change the metaphorical species, we have, so to speak, bearded the Lions in their den.'

'But not without the Lions bearding *us*, first,' Abu Abdallah said, stroking the frizzled remnants of hair on his chin. 'I never had such a close trim as I got from their Remedy.'

The Grand Vizier's broad cobalt shoulders began to quake, and he emitted that strange wheezing and creaking sound which was his particular expression of laughter.

'I imagine,' Abu Abdallah said hesitantly, when Lisan al-Din's fit began to subside, 'that now, at this moment in time, the situation being as it is, I mean with Ibn Zamrak out of the picture, there'll be a, hmm, hah, to coin a phrase, a *vacancy* . . . At vizieral level.'

The Grand Vizier was suddenly still. In the stillness Sinan heard the distinct sound of his master's hint hitting stony ground.

'My dear, my peerless Abu Abdallah,' the Grand Vizier said slowly, turning to his friend with a sad smile, 'if only we could run to a Diwan of Diversions, a Vizierate of Witticisms, an Office of Irrepressible Optimism, you would be appointed to it on the spot . . . But hark!' The knots of courtiers stood straight, the Mamluks even more stiffly to attention. 'Here they come, at last.'

Sinan had already felt it before he heard it – the kerrump of kettledrums, the shriek of shawms, the clangour of clarions, cutting through the still air. But now the sounds were clear, and getting louder, coming up the track, until at last around a bend the cavalcade appeared, all nodding helmets and plumes, diagonals of trumpets and banners and lances, weapons and pennons glittering and hooves and harness twinkling in the morning light, caparisoned in crimson and purple and malachite. And, framed by this panoply, flanked by a pair of oafish *hidalgos* and almost lost between a robe of stiff brocade and a yellow Jew's turban, the small and worried-looking face of Abraham Ibn Zarzar, ambassador of His Most Noble Highness Don Pedro of Castile.

' "*Was it the memory of neighbours in Dhu Salam*
That made you blend your flowing tears with blood?" '

At the sound of the thin sharp voice cutting through the hush in the new court, Abu Abdallah turned to Sinan. '*The Ode of the*

Mantle,' he whispered. 'You know, the famous eulogy of the Prophet. Just the thing for his birthday, peace and blessings be upon him.'

> ' "Was it the wind that blows from Kazima?
> Or did lightning flash in darkness over Idam?" '

A second voice, similarly reedy but subtly different, had picked up the next verse from somewhere on the opposite side of the packed court. Sinan's neck prickled as the unearthly antiphony fell into rhythm, ebbing and flowing back and forth across the shimmering space, and the whole assembly fell beneath the spell of the words.

He looked around the standing ranks of courtiers and scholars and captains, gorgeous and multi-coloured in their robes. When he and Abu Abdallah had first taken their places here, he had felt a thousand eyes on him, staring at the mark of Cain bequeathed him by the black assassin of the old Sultan. But now, poetry was softening their stares. So too was a thickening drizzle of rosewater and musk water, sprinkled by page-boys wandering through the assembly. It mingled with other scents, of civet and ambergris, as if all the perfumes of the world had shed their fragrance on this spot. The only ones apparently unaffected by this intoxication of scent and sound were the two lumpen Castilians and their Jewish fellow-envoy, who seemed visibly to be shrinking in his robes.

> ' "Muhammad, lord of both universes, lord of men and jinn,
> Lord of the two peoples, Arabs and foreigners." '

And together with the cloud of scent, a cloud of smoke was growing denser too, from great braziers that belched Arabian frankincense, benjamin of Java, eaglewood of Champa.

> ' "How in this world can his true nature be grasped
> By a people of sleepers concerned only with their dreams?" '

And like a dream himself, vivid but insubstantial in the smoke, was the Presence: the Sultan, sitting beside his surprise, the still-hidden centrepiece. Enthroned cross-legged on cushions of flame-striped silk beneath a rich red ceremonial canopy and backed by red standards embroidered with the Nasrid motto – *No one wins but Allah* – he looked more Nazarene than Arab; generations of Castilian concubines on the female side, Sinan assumed. And he looked younger than his thirty years and his many tribulations – overthrow, flight, exile, war – should have allowed.

> ' "Fresh as blossoms, grand as the full moon,
> Generous as the sea, unflinching as Time." '

On and on, back and forth the ode flowed, telling of the Prophet's glory, his smile, fragrance, nobility; of the chagrin of the fire-worshipping Magians on this the day of his birth, for whom

> ' "Fire flowed like water out of grief
> And water flamed like fire," '

until at last the whole court seemed to be quite literally entranced. And when Abu Abdallah suddenly prodded him in the ribs and mouthed a verse at him, it took Sinan a few moments to see the import of the words:

> ' "When they meet those helped by the Prophet of God
> The lions of the thicket are stunned." '

Sinan saw the exchange of smiles between his master and the Grand Vizier.

At last the ode wound down and the audience wakened from their trance, then rustled and coughed and shifted in preparation for an even longer eulogy, this time to the Sultan. Sinan told himself that all this stiff and courtierly standing was training for the day he'd be his master's Secret Secretary; whenever that day would come.

But Abu Abdallah leaned towards him and said, 'Lisan al-Din tells me he's giving what he calls "a very short speech" in praise of His Presence. The Sultan doesn't want to upstage the Prophet of God on his birthday, you see. Of course, where Lisan's concerned, "very short" is a relative term.'

By the standards of Arabic oration and its foremost practitioner in the Western world, the speech was indeed short – little more than thanks to God for the successful completion of the new court, for the preservation of the realm from 'a certain plot very lately confounded', and prayers for the continued health and prosperity of the Sultan; albeit including a litany of his titles and genealogy back to the founding father of the dynasty that made Sinan's mind glaze over.

It was the very last word of the litany, the name of the stern dynastic progenitor, that broke through the glaze and made Sinan come to with a jerk: ' . . . Ibn Nasr, also known as Ibn *al-Ahmar*.'

Eyes wide, he turned to Abu Abdallah. 'Master, you never told me the Sultan's ancestor was called "the Red One".'

'Oh, didn't I? Probably because it's common knowledge. I think he had red hair or something. Why do you think the dynastic colour's red?' He pointed to the scarlet banners that hung about the Sultan. 'They generally prefer to be known as Banu Nasr, the sons of Nasr. They think it has a more sultanaceous ring to it, what with *nasr* meaning "victory" and being an ancient Arab personal name as well. But outside Granada most people call them Banu 'l-Ahmar. Hmm, "the Red Sultans" . . . it probably explains why they're so fond of rubies.'

Sinan stared at Abu Abdallah. 'But, *master* . . .'

His words were cut short by a din of drums and trumpets.

'Keep your eyes on that tent thing,' Abu Abdallah shouted through the noise.

The thousand eyes were on it. Suspense hung over the court, palpable as the pall of incense.

'*Master* . . .'

But Abu Abdallah wasn't listening.

Standing near the tent, the Grand Vizier wore a look of sombre satisfaction, the nearest his public face ever came to a smile. Almost imperceptibly, he nodded in the direction of a small pavilion that projected from the colonnade into the court, at its eastern end. Sinan followed the direction of the nod. At first he could see nothing through the smoke belching from a battery of outsize incense-burners that bordered the pavilion. Then, for a moment, the smoke parted and he glimpsed the fair face of Zayd the Clerk of Works, framed by columns, returning the signal then dipping down.

Sinan recalled Zayd's ingenious plan – the twin cords that, when pulled, would reveal the Sultan's surprise – and scanned the marble paving. Yes, there were the cords, running along the shallow channel in the marble.

Something was wrong: only one of the cords twitched . . . But no; there was a gasp from the crowd as the brocade walls of the tent fell away – then silence as the multitude took in the sight before them – then a cry of '*Allah!*', and cheering, and shouts of '*God save the Sultan!*'

What Sinan saw revealed before him was a curious and exquisite assemblage of sculpted marble. In the centre of it was a broad, shallow bowl, twelve-sided, superbly carved and painted – he could just make out the verses, highlighted by gilt, which the disgraced Ibn Zamrak had composed. He could also see that the bowl rested on a marble cylinder, but in such a way as to appear to hover, unsupported, above the most remarkable feature of the composition: a guardian phalanx, one beneath each side of the bowl, of twelve carved and painted beasts, each standing to attention and with a bronze tube or spout emerging from its mouth. Seeing the tubes, Sinan realized what the centrepiece was: a fountain – but one of such originality and beauty that he doubted if its like existed anywhere on Earth. He also recalled Ibn Zamrak's continued railing against the evil it embodied – the evil of aping God's creation. Now he understood: here, at the epicentre of Islamic power in al-Andalus, and in three dimensions, was a whole herd of graven images.

But, herd, or flock, or pack, or what? For, to be honest, Sinan could not tell what it was that the twelve creatures were supposed to represent. Wearing pugnacious expressions and what might have represented short tunics of chain-mail, if they resembled anything it was . . . dogs. Hounds. Mastiffs, perhaps.

'Master,' he said when the cheering had died down a little, 'is it not inauspicious . . . I mean, to portray unclean animals like dogs in so hallowed a spot?'

Abu Abdallah looked at him for a moment then spluttered with laughter – just when the general cheering had subsided to a hushed buzz of approval. A few of the nearer courtiers shot looks of disgust at the little Moroccan and his Black. *Blood brother to the regicide*, Sinan could feel them thinking. *Murderer of Mamluks.*

'Dogs? *Dogs?* Don't be ridiculous, boy!' Abu Abdallah said, the words slicing through the hush. Sinan gestured desperately to his master to keep his voice down. 'For heaven's sake,' the old man went on, quieter but still piercing. 'You're from the Negrolands! From what you tell me, you were brought up with these creatures gambolling round your crib.'

'But master, what are they meant to be?'

Abu Abdallah looked up, imploring the heavens for patience. 'Don't you know a *lion* when it's staring you in the face, boy?'

Sinan looked at the twelve raised heads around the fountain. Something in their stiff, sightless stares brought back the image of the heads on the gate. Twelve lions here; there, eleven, plus . . . '*Master* –'

He saw it even as the thought was forming – saw it, alone, of all the hundreds in the court, the hundreds with their eyes still fixed on the fountain, waiting for it to explode in jets of crystal: saw Zayd the Clerk, wreathed in smoke, holding a pair of tongs, taking a coal from an incense-burner, dipping down again . . .

Faster than thought Sinan was off across the court, a black bolt racing the flame that tore along the second cord, unseen fire and all-too visible man converging on the fountain, on . . .

'The Sultan! *The Black's going for the Sultan!*'

Sinan had eyes only for the flame that flashed and ripped towards the fountain base, but he heard the cry and knew the flash of blades was closing in on him.

Chapter 33

In the three seconds it took Sinan to sprint across the diagonal of the court, Abu Abdallah had three thoughts:

that negro spirits had finally got the better of his slave;

that any wisp of hope for a vizierate was gone;

and, as a bristle of blades rose round the Sultan like the quills on a porcupine and another hackle of steel aimed itself at Sinan, that the young man who had taken the place of all his own lost sons was going to die.

And then it happened: Sinan fell.

But no . . . Abu Abdallah, pushed forward by the surging crowd, realized that Sinan had not fallen, but had *thrown* himself, in a wild lunge, away from his collision-course with the Mamluk guard – thrown himself on to one of the channels that bisected the court, and was now smashing his bare fists at something on the marble paving, again and again and again.

And Sinan's dive had wrong-footed the Mamluks just long enough for them to hear a roar of command that shook the courtyard, clear even in the tumult: '*Leave the Black!*'

It was the Grand Vizier, parting the steel-crested red sea of Mamluks and striding over to where Sinan lay prostrate, his body heaving. 'Get up, Sinan. You're safe.'

Sinan rose painfully, tugging at something as he did so, then holding out the object for the Grand Vizier to see: it was a scant cubit of cord, and one end of it was blackened and smoking. 'Your . . . eminence,' he panted, 'I think you will find that this

fountain ... was intended not for water ...' a great gulping breath
' ... but for *fire*.'

A shock-wave of disbelief swayed the now-silent crowd.

Sinan reached down to one of the marble lions' mouths, and pulled
at something in the bronze pipe. Abu Abdallah strained to see what
was happening. Something – a wad, or bung – came out in his slave's
hand. And was followed by a stream, not of water, but of *black grains*.

Lisan al-Din stared at the black cascade falling on white marble ...
'Step forward, you Mamluks,' he ordered. 'Remove the top of the
fountain.'

Three dozen men laid down their arms and took hold of the
heavy marble bowl. With a little effort, it began to move, to rock,
until at last it parted from the cylinder beneath. Gently, the men
lowered the bowl to the ground.

Abu Abdallah looked on, astonished, as Lisan al-Din plunged his
hands into the hollow interior of the cylinder, raised them, and let
fall a stream of more black grains. He then turned to the Sultan, who
was still sitting, enthroned and unperturbed. The monarch raised a
quizzical eyebrow. 'Your Presence,' his Grand Vizier announced, 'by
the hand of this Black, the ever-living God has saved your life –
may He for ever prolong it!' A shout of '*Amen!*' rose from the
multitude and ricocheted about the columns. Lisan al-Din gestured
for quiet, then continued. 'And not only that. He has saved all our
lives. He has saved Islam in al-Andalus!'

In the moment of silence in which the crowd took in the words,
a small anguished voice could be heard from the east side of the
court:

' "*Fire flowed like water out of grief*
And water flamed like fire" '

All turned at the sound – and saw the fair, auburn-bearded Berber
face of Zayd the Clerk of Works, still wreathed in incense-smoke and
holding a pair of tongs that grasped nothing. ' "*The jinn screamed,*" '

another voice replied, picking up the Clerk's verse from *The Ode of the Mantle,*

> ' "*the lights rose high,*
> *And Truth appeared in meaning and in word.*" '

It was the voice of the Sultan.

The whole court held its breath.

'Come, slave,' he said to Sinan, rising from his cushioned throne. Hesitantly, Sinan walked over to him, felt the Sultan's hand take his and draw him to his side. 'Behold this Black,' the Sultan said to the assembled court. So silent were the multitude now that Abu Abdallah could hear the minute patter of the grains of the Remedy, still falling from the lion's mouth. 'One of his kind killed my father, may God have mercy on his martyred soul. But *this* Black, by the will of the Creator who endowed him with strength and with wits, this man has preserved *my* life. And by so doing he has washed away the blood that, in your eyes, had stained his race. *Sinan,*' he said, glancing at the Grand Vizier, who nodded at the name, 'Sinan,' the Sultan said again, now beaming to his saviour, 'I have a proposal: that you should henceforth serve me as the . . . the *sinan*, the spearhead, of my bodyguard!'

Abu Abdallah felt a rift open in himself, between pride, and grief.

Sinan stared at the blank white marble at his feet, dumbstruck, it seemed, by the Sultan's magnanimity. Eventually he spoke, quietly and clearly, still looking at the ground: 'Sire . . . *I cannot.*'

A subdued thrill passed through the onlookers.

Now the Sultan looked lost for words. 'Then . . . then, at least, let me grant you your freedom.' He smiled suddenly. 'I will make your master an offer that, unlike you, *he* cannot refuse!'

The crowd laughed and looked at Abu Abdallah, who acknowledged them with a grin and a nod of his turban.

Sinan's gaze had not left the ground. But now he turned to the Sultan and spoke. 'Sire . . .' Once again a thousand eyes were on him, a thousand ears waiting on his words. 'Sire, I thank you for Your Presence's noble graciousness. But I do not want freedom.' Another thrill, felt rather than heard, coursed through the court. 'Not for myself. However . . . there is another slave. A female slave. I humbly petition your royal Presence to purchase *her* freedom, in place of mine.'

A third frisson thrilled through the crowd, audible this time, and followed by an undertow of incomprehension.

'It shall be as you ask,' the Sultan said. 'For, today, *I am your slave.*'

'So, master,' Sinan said, when the stare of the crowd had finally left him for Zayd the Clerk of Works, who was being escorted out of the new court with bowed head, 'we have found the real twelfth Lion.'

Abu Abdallah nodded slowly. 'And we've found out what the red target really was – not the Ruby, not this Red Palace of the Alhambra, but the Red Sultan. Hah, you were wrong on that one, weren't you, Master Know-all. Not that you haven't made up for it, I suppose . . .' He looked at Sinan and shook his head. 'Well, I told you you'd be moving in high circles when you came travelling with me, didn't I. Never thought they'd be quite *this* lofty, though. Dear me, my slave having the Sultan of Granada as his slave . . .'

Sinan shrugged.

Suddenly Abu Abdallah frowned. 'But don't look so damned pleased with yourself, boy. You think you're clever, don't you – but, honestly, turning down a job offer from Himself . . . Don't you know rule number one for hobnobbing with potentates? Never say No to them. It's very bad manners. And then, on top of that, turning down an offer *I* couldn't have refused! What in God's name were you up to, Sinan?'

Sinan bit his lip.

Abu Abdallah looked at him, still frowning, then continued: 'Don't you realize you've just lost us the very crock of gold we came here looking for in the first place?' He groaned, looked down and slowly shook his turbaned head.

'But master,' Sinan said, 'I'm happy as I am. Besides, you'll be a vizier one day, somewhere, and you won't be able to move for crocks of gold. I'm sure of that. And as you yourself are always saying, when that time comes, who else but me could be your Secret Secretary?'

Abu Abdallah looked up at him, still shaking his head; but he was almost smiling, and his eyes were brighter even than usual. Then he quickly looked away. Sinan could think of nothing more to say.

A sudden hoarse fanfare split the quiet of the court, followed by a thunderous drum-roll. Abu Abdallah cleared his throat. 'Now for the second climax of the ceremony,' he shouted over the noise. 'Or should I say the *anti*-climax, after you single-handedly saved the Sultan and Islam, redeemed the entire race of the Blacks . . . *and* lost us a fortune.'

The drum-roll stopped. Once more the Grand Vizier looked gloomily around, commanding silence. Then he began to speak – of the great and no such Ruby, stolen six years before by the cursed usurper, now restored to its rightful owner,' . . . by our neighbour Don Pedro, infidel tyrant of Qashtalah, may God guide him to the religion of truth, as an earnest of his eternal loyalty and amity to His Presence, our blessed Sultan, Commander of the Muslims. *And furthermore,*' he continued – then paused, and seemed to turn his melancholy gaze on each one of the hundreds present in turn, daring disagreement –'and furthermore, to disprove, once and for all, the pernicious and irreligious rumour that has circulated among the ignorant these several years past, namely that such an object as this Ruby might exert an adverse or evil effect on the course of events – events which are guided by God alone, Almighty and Omniscient is He!'

Another pause. Then the Grand Vizier inclined his head towards the ambassadors. Slowly, stiffly, they shuffled towards the enthroned

251

Presence, Abraham Ibn Zarzar bearing the casket in hands that shook so hard that Sinan could hear the Ruby rattling inside. Lisan al-Din looked on, evidently satisfied by the dread inspired in infidel hearts by the Presence of the Commander of the Muslims.

Along with the thousand other eyes, Sinan looked on. In some strange inversion of perspective, it seemed that the ambassador grew smaller the closer he drew to the Presence. At last, when he was directly before the sultanic dais, he bent down and, after an undignified struggle with the catch, opened the gilded lid of the casket.

The Sultan peered in.

And then the placid royal expression changed. The Sultan's brow furrowed. His eyes narrowed. He reached out to the Ruby – then abruptly withdrew his hand, as if from something disgusting, polluting.

For a moment nothing happened. Then the Sultan, his face now dark with anger, spoke to the shrunken figure that crouched and quaked before him. 'Take it back to Pedro,' he said, '*and tell him he can keep it.*'

Chapter 34

'There is something else, Sinan, that you accomplished by your quick thinking and action yesterday,' the Grand Vizier said, 'but which I could not spell out in public.'

The red standard of the Nasrid dynasty slapped a brisk rhythm above them in the gusting wind. Abu Abdallah looked at his friend. Sinan surveyed the view from the Watchtower: the green ocean of the plain with its far shoreline of hills; Jabal Shulayr, glittering with the season's first fresh snow. The hopes that had blossomed when they first stood here – dreams of vizierates and secret secretaryships – had withered and died with the coming winter. In this clear cold dawn that had followed the extraordinary day in the Court of the Lions, they had both known it was time to go; to chase the dreams elsewhere.

Lisan al-Din continued: 'You averted war, Sinan. War between Granada and Castile.' Sinan turned to him, surprised. 'The death, Sinan, not only of our blessed Sultan but also of Don Pedro's envoys, representatives of the honour of the crown of Castile, would have torn our two kingdoms apart. For ever.' The wind dropped for a moment, but the climbing sun did not dispel the chill. 'As you know,' the Grand Vizier went on, 'behind the well-worn rhetoric that brands our neighbour "tyrant" and "infidel", our two states are closer than many that share the same faith and tongue. But there are always those, on both sides, whose perverse logic leads them to strive for separation – for "purity", as they see it – at any cost. They were the ones behind the plot.'

'But sir,' Sinan said, 'Zayd the Clerk of Works did not strike me as being a misguided zealot.'

'I do not believe he was. Although we will never know for sure. He was dealt with ... rather too summarily. But I suspect that some kink in his nature, connected with his descent from the former Berber rulers of Granada, the sons of Ziri, caused him to hate our beloved Nasrid – and Arab – dynasty. He was, after all, the last of the Zirids. He had nothing to lose but himself. His unnatural alliance with the so-called Lions was of inestimable benefit to both parties.'

'But, Lisan,' Abu Abdallah said, 'why did he lead us to the vaults? Why on earth did he sacrifice his fellow-plotters?'

'I can only suppose,' the Grand Vizier said, 'that he was putting us off his own scent ... that he was making use of my well-known dislike – for which God forgive me – for the Sultanic Secretary. Did you see how Zayd hid behind Ibn Zamrak at the door of the vaults? How he literally used him as cover? It was at *Zayd* that the accusation of treachery was aimed. My prejudice against Ibn Zamrak blinded and deafened me to the truth.' He sighed.

'So you think Zayd knew his companions would be killed?' Abu Abdallah asked.

'I am sure that is precisely what he intended. In Zayd's eyes, the Lions had done their work. With us still crowing over their defeat, he knew he would be able to perform his final act – to light that ... *wick* – completely unsuspected. To Zayd, the Lions were expendable.'

'Like the marble lions of the fountain, sir,' Sinan said.

'Indeed,' the Grand Vizier said with a smile. 'And what a perversely pretty fancy they turned out to be! Lord, I can already hear Ibn Zamrak beating me with *that* stick: "You see, your eminence, I told you so! The depiction of living creatures ... oh, the insufferable *sinfulness* ..."'

Sinan and his master laughed at the imitation of the Sultanic Secretary's sibilant voice.

'That,' Lisan al-Din continued with a shake of his head, 'is the price I'll have to pay. Still, *sticks and stones*, as they say ... And *I* shall give him stick for his "rodent excrement" – though I admit that the new Remedy does look remarkably like rat droppings.'

For a while they listened to the wind.

'Forgive me for being dense, Lisan,' Abu Abdallah said at last, 'but I still don't see how that fountain trick was going to be so dangerous. I mean, that rat-shitty Remedy would have caught fire, there would have been a *whoosh*, and the Sultan would have had his blessed beard singed – God preserve it, and its owner too – and that would have been that.'

The Grand Vizier stared out over the plain. 'My dear Abu Abdallah, did you not hear the thunder-clap that echoed over the city yesterday afternoon?'

'I did, now you come to mention it. A huge great bang, out of the blue. It seems to be the season – come to think of it there was another one, nothing like as big, mind you, about a week ago. It quite took us back to that night in al-Bayyazin, didn't it, Sinan – the night the Alchemist was killed.'

'Well,' Lisan al-Din said, 'that was the sound of your "fountain-trick". You see, I had them remove the Remedy from the base of the fountain and take it well beyond the city walls. The charge of powder, or grains, I should say, was packed tightly into an interior copper lining that had been carefully incised with grooves, so as to fragment into sharp flying pieces with the force of the deflagration . . .'

Abu Abdallah looked puzzled.

'The technical term for your "*whoosh*", if you recall,' the Grand Vizier explained. 'But no; "deflagration" is not enough to describe the terrible forces released. One might better use the term "plosion"; or more accurately "*explosion*", to coin a word. I gave strict orders for the Mamluks who ignited the instrument to retire to a distance of fifty paces and take cover. But, unfortunately, one of them was killed and another severely injured by the flying fragments of copper.' He frowned and shook his jowls. 'Cut to pieces.'

Sinan looked at his master.

'As for that curious version of the Remedy,' Lisan al-Din continued, 'formed deliberately, as I now realize, into grains, its power – God knows why – is quite extraordinary. Far greater than that of the usual sort. We tried a small amount as a charge in one of those hand-held firearms, and it burst the barrel. Like a banana skin. Another Mamluk killed.'

'"*The final, fatal fire is lightning in the rain-cloud born,*"' Sinan recited. '"*He'll know, who grinds the finest flour, then turns it back to corn.*"'

'Yes,' the Grand Vizier said softly. 'That was the Alchemist's infernal discovery . . . In that packed new court, the bursting of the copper sheath, and also of the marble casing of the fountain, would have caused a truly horrendous loss of life.' The wind had dropped again. 'By the way,' he said more cheerfully, turning to Sinan, 'we have decided to preserve the lion fountain – to return it to its proper use, since all the necessary hydraulic appurtenances are already in place. It will be for ever a reminder of divine providence . . . working through you, Sinan.'

Sinan shrugged. The sky darkened suddenly as a cloud engulfed the weak morning sun.

'And so, my heroic slave has saved Granada from the War of the Sultan's Fountain,' Abu Abdallah said. 'Only for it to be plunged into the War of the Sultan's Ruby.' He looked at Lisan al-Din.

'So it seems. "*Kings have gone to war for less*" . . . It looks as if those words of mine were prophetic. Well, I'll no doubt find out more after the noon prayer. I have a private audience with His Presence. Between ourselves,' he said in a lower voice, 'I'm not looking forward to it one bit. I've known him almost since he was born, and I've never seen him look so angry as he did when they gave him the Ruby.'

'I know what you mean. Anyone would have thought that casket contained a fresh-laid turd, not a precious stone. Honestly, you'd think they'd tried to pass off a fake on him.'

Sinan looked at his master, surprised.

'Hmm. The thought has crossed my mind, too,' the Grand Vizier said. 'Although the audacity, the stupidity of counterfeiting so famous a stone would be beyond belief. Such a slight to His Presence's honour and intelligence could indeed ignite war . . . Ah, war, foul and unholy war, must you come to blight and blast once more this blessed land?' He turned to Abu Abdallah, his face darker than the sky. 'Your imminent departure from Granada may be well timed, my friend.'

They emerged from the dark dog-leg of the great gate to the crash of a farewell salute. Abu Abdallah turned in his saddle to acknowledge it with a sideways nod. Sinan, on foot beside the mule, turned too, and as he did so a cheer rang out – a shout of joy that spread along the walls above in a ripple of waving arms, until the battlements were alive with limbs and acclamations.

'Enjoy it while it lasts, my boy,' Abu Abdallah shouted over the cheers. 'You'll never be as popular again.'

'Look, master,' Sinan said. He pointed to a twelfth face on the crest of the gate. The sun was catching its neat auburn beard.

'A pity,' Abu Abdallah said, squinting up at the severed head of Zayd the Clerk of Works. 'I rather liked the chap. In fact I almost wish it *had* been Ibn Zamrak's slimy noddle up there instead . . . But come on.' He twitched a rein. 'I've seen enough heads to last a lifetime.'

The cheers followed them as they made their way along the track beneath the walls. But Sinan's thoughts were elsewhere. At last, when they turned into the wooded gully that separated the citadel from Jannat al-Arif, he spoke. 'Master, think back to that first night . . .'

'The night of the thunderbolt in al-Bayyazin?' Sinan nodded. 'If it really was a thunderbolt. I don't know what to believe anymore, what with possibly fake rubies and possibly fake thunder.'

'Well, master, I think I know what happened. Do you remember what she said – Lubna – that morning in the *majlis* of the Chief of the Night?'

For Abu Abdallah, the scene was as vivid as a miniature in a book. But the words had gone. 'Of course I don't remember. My brain's filled with two thirds of a century of junk. Why do you think I rely on you to remember for me?'

For a moment, there was only the sound of the stream that ran through the gully, and of the stream of wind riffling and loosening the autumn leaves. 'What she said, master, was that she saw a strange copper vessel in the Alchemist's laboratory. She thought it was some new kind of lamp. And then he asked her to bring a good length of wick . . .'

'That's it: "The evenings are drawing in,"' Abu Abdallah cut in, softly. 'That's what she said.'

'I believe she did, master. And then she said he told her he was going to his vineyard for a few days . . .'

' . . . to try it out! He'd made one of those instruments. Yes, it makes sense, boy. But then the instrument plosed, or exploded, or whatever Lisan's word for it was . . .'

' . . . and the copper fragmented . . .'

' . . . and a piece of it cut the poor bugger's throat! Yes, I remember now: I found a nasty jagged piece of copper stuck in the wall of the laboratory.'

They ambled on in silence for a while.

'What I don't understand, master,' Sinan said at last, 'is how – *why*– the Alchemist's instrument was ignited.'

'That's what I'm wondering too, my boy. And I believe we'll never know the answer. Let us say it was an act of God, accomplished through the agency of a person or persons – or for that matter, of *jinn* – unknown.'

Or, Sinan thought suddenly, remembering the streak of grey that had shot through the lattice instants before the bang, *of a cat called Jinni.*

The path emerged into the open. To their left was the cramped valley of the Hadarruh, and beyond it the plain, dark under a lowering sky.

'What a way to die,' Abu Abdallah murmured. 'Like a foretaste of hellfire. And those Mamluks, too . . . You know, Sinan, they're the first; but they won't be the last. Perhaps there'll never be an end to it. I don't think the Alchemist knew what he was letting loose. It's like that old story about the bottle of brass.'

'The story you used to tell me, master, from *The Thousand Nights and a Night*, about the fisherman who let the evil *jinni* out?'

'That's the one. With the difference that I don't think this evil will ever be tricked back into its bottle.'

On they went through the sombre noonday hush, both thinking of the night, the winter to come.

It was only when they turned at last on to the track that led to the Spring of Tears and the Grand Vizier's palace that their melancholy was dispelled – and replaced with another sort of sadness, a darkness struck with light, as the two men's thoughts both turned to Lubna.

'Go on. You give her the news,' Abu Abdallah said to Sinan when at last he handed the reins to a boy at the Grand Vizier's gate. 'After all, her freedom is your gift to her.'

'And the other news, master? Of how the Alchemist died?'

'That, too, is a gift of sorts for you to give. The knowledge may bring her some peace.'

Strange, Abu Abdallah thought as they rode and walked up the ascending lane soon afterwards. *As soon as we went through the gate I felt she wasn't there.* Perhaps, with age, memory weakens but intuition wakens.

He'd sensed she wasn't there; and when they said she'd 'borrowed' a pot of basil from the kitchen garden, he'd known for sure where she would be.

He was right. There she was, by Ali the Alchemist's grave in the cemetery of al-Bayyazin. She had placed the basil on the grave and was carefully watering it from a small waterskin. The stream caught the sunlight that had broken through. But the flow ceased. She had felt their presence, and now turned.

'Go on then, boy. As I said, they're your gifts to give her.'

Abu Abdallah held back, and paced the paths between the low tombs, head bowed. For how long he didn't know; graveyards are pools that punctuate the rapids of time.

They squatted, wordless, side by side, looking down the valley to the spreading plain, aware only of the inches separating their bodies.

Something caught Sinan's eye: drops of water sparkling on the basil leaves. Then the sky darkened once more, and the light went, and before he knew it he was telling her, slowly and softly, how her lover died.

When he finished Lubna said nothing. There was no sound at all. Only the hum of the wind in the graves.

At last he turned to her and saw that she was rocking – no, nodding, very slowly, eyes closed above her veil. As if she'd known it all along. Then she turned to him – and smiled. A faint smile, like a wan dawn; but still a smile. *Sunrise pale above her veil* . . . Sinan sighed inwardly at the phrase from some old poem, sighed at the shedding of his burden, and smiled back. 'There's more,' he said, too quickly, suddenly finding the silent language of their eyes unsettling. Her gaze widened. 'Don't worry. It's good.'

And now the words flooded out as he told her of the events at the Court of the Lions, the Sultan's magnanimity, her freedom. 'Oh, and you'll never believe the last thing the Sultan told me,' Sinan said as the flood petered out. 'He said, "Today, I am your slave." ' He smiled at the ground, shook his head at the memory, then looked back at Lubna.

She was staring ahead, stunned. When she spoke it was scarcely more audible than the wind. 'But why? Why *me*?'

He shrugged.

'The gift of freedom . . . It was the only thing that was ever truly yours,' he heard her whisper. 'And you gave it away.'

She turned to him again, asked the question with her eyes: why? *Sunrise pale above her veil . . . and night beneath her gown.*

'Why, Sinan?' she was saying aloud again. '*Why?* So that I can be with – with you?'

He caught the falter in her voice, followed the fall of her eyes to the basil on the grave. The leaves had dried in the thin cold air.

'My master . . .' he heard himself saying, ' . . . he would have to decide.'

They looked at each other, shocked back to silence by the clash of loyalties and loves. *And* – they both realized in the same instant –*lust*.

Lubna looked away from him.

When finally she turned back, that pale dawn fire had left her face. 'Do you remember, that first time we were alone, what we said? "*We two are strangers here . . .*" '

' " *. . . and strangers are to one another kin.*" ' The words that then had been so full of solace now rang hollow.

'Perhaps that is what we are destined to be,' she said. 'Strangers. Not more.'

Her fingers slid from his. He didn't know how long they'd been there. But now he felt them, cool and smooth, brushing a tear from his cheek, and saw her smile again, and felt the flow of time once more, back to the Great River.

Not since then had he been so close to someone, or so far.

When at last he heard Sinan's soft stride approaching through the dust, Abu Abdallah looked up – and there was Lubna, still by Ali's grave, gazing at them. Her unveiled face was bright; whether with tears or light he couldn't tell. He raised a hand, palm towards her. It hovered, between greeting and parting.

Lubna knew its meaning, even if Abu Abdallah did not. She stood where she was. For a long moment she looked about for words, then she called out, strong and clear: 'Sir, I . . . I wished to express . . .'

261

That foreign, siren catch to her voice . . . Abu Abdallah looked at her over the intervening distance. 'You have said it, without words.' He heard his own voice calling across to her as if it came from someone else.

'Then, sir . . . *May God go with you . . . both of you.*'

He had no more voice to respond, so he waved to her once across the graves, and turned away.

The road rose beneath them, carrying them upwards, high above the plain. Every so often, Sinan's grey mare and Abu Abdallah's chestnut would seem to pause in their paces and sniff the thinner air. Higher still, above the folds and pleats of hillside, clouds scudded in the gusting wind – a wind that seemed to have a catch in its voice, to call them back. But they'd known they had to go, to leave then and there.

In what remained of the day they would hardly cover a half-stage. But they would make al-Hammah on the morrow, and then the pass that led down from the uplands. Another day would see them on the coast. And then where?

His master had been silent on the matter. On all matters. In fact, Sinan had never known him so silent: at first, even the inaudible buzz of vivacity that the old man always seemed to emit had fallen silent. It was as if Abu Abdallah had died some kind of preliminary death.

There had been a few monosyllabic instructions as they had prepared for the journey. But it was only when they'd left the city gates, and Sinan had reported his farewell conversation with the Grand Vizier, that his master began to show any real signs of vitality. Abu Abdallah had nodded, knowingly, when he'd learned that there were plans afoot to offer Lubna a position at the palace, as a sort of literary tutor to the women of the Sultan's household; he had even mumbled something that sounded like, 'You cunning old bugger,

Lisan.' Since then his silence had become one of repose, or at least of resignation.

And now, at last, at the rolling crest of the hill above the plain, Abu Abdallah halted, turned his mount to look for the last time on Granada, and spoke. 'That's the trouble with travel, my boy . . . You know what they say? *Travel is travail.* But it's not the sore feet. It's the sore hearts. It's the farewells.'

They both looked over the great vista, the Alhambra riding above it like a ship, the Watchtower its forecastle. 'You know,' Abu Abdallah continued, 'I've always wanted to *possess* a woman. Not in the sense of owning a slave-girl. God, I've done that enough times. I mean, I've always wanted to possess a woman's heart and soul, not just her body.'

'I know, master,' Sinan said. 'But don't you think what you really mean is that you want *her* to possess *you*?'

Abu Abdallah turned to him. 'And since when do *you* know anything about being possessed? You're only a slave.'

Sinan frowned at him.

'Don't look so bloody offended!' Abu Abdallah said with a bitter laugh. 'You're the one who turned his freedom down . . . and lost us that crock of gold.' The chestnut snorted. 'Still, at least good old Lisan al-Din's given us that going-away present. Enough to keep body and soul together for a while. And when that runs out . . .' He looked Sinan up and down. 'Yes, the price of black slaves must be going up nicely, what with news of your heroics spreading abroad. And – that's a point – it's you who's the hero! You'd be worth a dinar or two, my boy, even still attached to your balls.'

Sinan did his best to look offended again.

Abu Abdallah shook his head. 'But something tells me I'll always be stuck with you. You, and the road ahead.'

They sat there in silence, the horses twitching beneath them, longing for the off. Abu Abdallah could feel the old itch too. But Sinan spoke.

'Master . . . I've been thinking. About money. I mean, this new version of the Remedy . . . anyone who possessed it would have unimaginable power. And anyone who had the secret to sell could make crock upon crock of gold.'

'*And that*,' Abu Abdallah said, quietly but with a vehemence that made Sinan shiver, '*is a road that I will never take. Be* sure: the secret will spread. There's no remedy for the Remedy. It's as unstoppable, as incurable, as the Death. But *I* will not be the one to spread it. And nor will you, Sinan. The choice is clear: going poor to Paradise, or going rich to Hell.'

The thought silenced them.

'God, we must be off,' Abu Abdallah said, suddenly. 'Take it all in, my boy. One of the finest prospects on all God's Earth. And to think I could have been a vizier there . . . I think I might permit myself a last sigh.' He groaned, long and deep.

'But, master,' Sinan said gently, 'if I may be frank, I could never see you fitting into the Alhambra. You are too . . . independent of spirit. And could you honestly work with the likes of the Sultanic Secretary?'

'Uggh, that ghoul Ibn Zamrak and his vinegar, and his phantasmata or orgasmata or whatever he calls them? Yes, you're right there, Sinan. And there's something about the place . . . With all its beauty, all its splendour, there's a darkness to it. Not something you can see, exactly. More a darkness you can feel.'

'And that darkness will gather, master, with the coming war.'

'*The War of the Sultan's Ruby.* Yes, I can see it now. The Mamluks riding off to raid the marches and to die . . . Don Pedro's knights encamped down there, on the plain . . . siege, starvation, misery, death . . . And all for the sake of a stupid red stone.'

Sinan stared out across the plain. 'But master, if Granada can use the new form of the Remedy, can make stronger firearms and those exploding instruments, will she not gain the upper hand in a war?'

'She will indeed, Sinan. For about five minutes. And then, as I told you, the secret of the new Remedy will break out, however

264

hard they tried to contain it, and war will spread about this good Earth like the plague.' Abu Abdallah's fingers tightened on his rein. 'Come on, let's be off.'

But before he could tear himself away the horses' nostrils flared in the direction from which they'd come, and their ears pricked. Then Sinan heard it, and finally Abu Abdallah too: the beat of hooves coming up the track, towards them. The two men looked at each other, then turned as a lone rider appeared around the bend, a smile on his face and his mount in a lather.

'It's the Grand Vizier's confidential clerk, master. You don't think . . .'

' . . . Lisan al-Din's changed his mind about the . . .' Abu Abdallah stopped himself, and mouthed the magic word ' . . . *vizierate*.'

'Thank God I've caught you sir,' the clerk called out when he was within earshot. 'I come with a most urgent letter from his eminence the Grand Vizier.' He reined in his horse beside Abu Abdallah's and handed him the scrolled Venetian paper with its triple tie-strings and heavy red seal. 'By your leave, sir,' he added, then turned away.

'Oh . . . Is his eminence not expecting an immediate reply?' Abu Abdallah said, puzzled.

'Apparently, sir, he knows what it will be. Forgive my informality. But I am instructed to give you the letter and return forthwith. May God keep you, sir.' And with that he wheeled about and trotted off, back down the hill.

Abu Abdallah stared wide-eyed at the letter as if his name on it, written in Lisan al-Din's own elegant hand complete with honorific titles, belonged to someone else. Then he passed it to Sinan. 'Go on, then boy!'

Sinan broke the seal, unknotted the ties, unrolled the sheet and read:

'In the Name of God, the Compassionate, the Merciful

'Pleasant salutations. And to continue:
My most beloved friend, I trust you will forgive my haste, and the consequent

lack of formality and eloquence, but I have tidings of such gladness that to keep them to myself would be to risk an explosion of joy . . .'

Sinan looked up. Abu Abdallah was grinning and nodding vigorously. 'Go on! Go on!'

'The nature of the news is such, however, as you will see, that I can share it with no one in our divinely-guarded Sultanate of Granada . . .'

Sinan frowned and looked up again. One of his master's eyebrows was cocked.

'In return for my imparting it to you, I am confident it will go no further. I write immediately following my meeting with our beloved Sultan, in which His Presence vouchsafed me the following, namely, that, having been saved from the red death . . .'

'Master, by "red death" he means violent . . .'
'For God's sake, Sinan, I *do* know. Stop interrupting yourself.'

'. . . having been saved from the red death, by divine providence, acting through your excellent slave, while yet not yet in possession of the supposedly cursed Great Ruby, His Presence's illuminated wisdom caused him to reconsider the possible actuality of the supposed curse attaching thereto. In consideration of the fact that the three former possessors of the Ruby since its arrival in Granada – namely, his martyred father the late Sultan Yusuf, his misguided brother the late self-styled "Sultan" Isma'il, and his usurping cousin of damnable memory known as El Bermejo – all died exceedingly red and violent deaths while in possession of the said Ruby, and in a moment of logic worthy of the great Aristotle and of inspiration such as is rarely granted but to poets, nay, to prophets . . .'

Sinan glanced up. His master's mouth still bore a grin, but it seemed not to belong to the mask that was rest of his face. 'Come on, boy,' he mumbled, as if half-paralysed, 'get to the point.'

'. . . His Presence decided to present the Great Ruby, formally and finally, to the tyrant Don Pedro, hoping thereby to cement relations between our two

neighbourly states, or – in the case of there being any foundation of truth to the alleged curse of the Ruby – trusting that this curse will work to the detriment of the said infidel tyrant Don Pedro, either of which two outcomes must needs redound to the benefit of the blessed Sultanate of Granada in particular and of the Muslims in general.

'And, to conclude: once more, most esteemed and beloved friend and brother, I trust you to communicate this joyful intelligence to no one. May your road be easy, and may God be ever with you.

'Farewell.'

Gingerly, Sinan looked up at his master. But Abu Abdallah's mask had softened into a smile, and the old man was nodding slowly and twinkling. Sinan cleared his throat. 'Master, what shall I do with it?'

'With what?'

'With the letter, master.'

'Well, as every would-be Secret Secretary knows, there's only one safe way to dispose of a confidential document.'

Sinan looked at him.

'Eat it, you fool!'

Sinan stared at the thick polished sheet in his hand. 'But, master . . .'

'Oh, for heaven's sake, boy . . . Just tear it up and forget you've ever read the thing.'

They looked one last time over Granada as the words flew away on the wind, then turned their horses' heads to the road.

Appendix
Arabic and Spanish Place-names

Araghun	Aragón
Ayn al-Dam'	'the Spring of Tears', Sp. Ainadamar
al-Bayyazin	Albaicín (Rabad al-Bayyazin is 'the Suburb of the Falconers')
Funduq, the New	the extant *funduq* or warehouse-*cum*-inn known today as Corral del Carbón
Hadarruh, Wadi	Rio Darro
al-Hammah	'the Hot Spring', Sp. Alhama
al-Hamra	Alhambra
Jannat al-Arif	probably 'the Garden of the Architect', Sp. Generalife
al-Jazirah	in full al-Jazirah al-Khadra, 'the Green Peninsula', Sp. Algeciras
Lushah	Loja
al-Mudawwar	Almodóvar
Qadis	Cádiz
Qashtalah	Castile
Shulayr, Jabal	from Latin Mons Solarius; Sp. Sierra Nevada
Tariq, Jabal	'the Mountain of Tariq' (eighth-century Muslim conqueror of Spain), Sp. Gibraltar
Tulaytulah	Toledo

Afterword

The seed of this story came from my first reading of Abu Abdallah Ibn Battutah's *Travels*, many years ago. During his last recorded journey, to West Africa, he stayed in 1353 in a town on the Niger between Timbuktu and Gao with a high-ranking commander of the Empire of Mali. 'A five-span-high slave-boy came in,' Abu Abdallah remembered when he wrote his travel book. 'The commander called him and said to me, "This is your welcoming gift. Keep an eye on him in case he bolts." ... The boy he gave me is still with me to this day.' Over the years, that boy grew in my imagination into Sinan. I realized he would have a tale or two to tell. It was while staying in different circumstances further up the Niger (under house arrest in a hotel-*cum*-brothel in the Guinean town of Siguiri, just before the military coup of 2008) that I decided to lay down the staff of travel, as Abu Abdallah would put it, if I ever got back home, and tell Sinan's tales.

At the time, Abu Abdallah had been my invisible but ever-present travelling companion for over a decade, as I followed his footsteps through his book and over three continents, through the many lands he visited. My own books about these travels make up the *Tangerine Trilogy* (*Travels with a Tangerine*, *The Hall of a Thousand Columns* and *Landfalls*). Over this time I became fond of the old Moroccan and his foibles, and was loath to say farewell. The single report of his death is so woolly – 'he lived till the year 770 [1368–9] and died holding the office of judge in some town or other' – that I began to wonder if he might not have had another, secret life beyond his unknown grave. So I took him travelling again, this time with Sinan.

The relationship between Abu Abdallah and Lisan al-Din, Grand Vizier of Granada under Sultan Muhammad V, was suggested by surviving correspondence between them, and by a satirical but fond pen-portrait by the Grand Vizier of his friend that I discovered. Although chiefly remembered as a bellettrist and historian, Lisan al-Din did indeed write the pioneering work of empirical observation, mentioned in the story, on the Contagion Theory. Ibn Zamrak, Sultanic Secretary, poet, and plotter, I have perhaps made even less likeable than he was in real life; I do not apologise to his memory (see below). El Bermejo's absconding with the crown jewels of Granada and his subsequent killing by Don Pedro of Castile are in both the Arabic and Spanish histories. Among the jewels appropriated by Don Pedro was the great balas ruby, or spinel, later known from the name of its recipient as the Black Prince's Ruby.

Otherwise, apart from Abraham Ibn Zarzar, whose historical career – like that of other enterprising Jews of the time – straddled the kingdoms of Granada and Castile, the other characters are my inventions; or rather, pieced together from fragments of real-life people who appear in the histories, and particularly in Lisan al-Din's *Ihatah* – 'The Encompassing' – his great biographical dictionary of Granada. Lubna, for example, was suggested by aspects of Subh – 'Dawn', the concubine and poetic protégée of a fourteenth-century alchemist – and of an earlier poetess called Nazhun, from whom I borrowed the actual encounter with the blind poet of Almodóvar (its filthiness toned down for genteel modern readers).

My historical backdrop is faithfully painted, as subsequent events show. Don Pedro was finally overthrown and killed by his illegitimate brother, Henry of Trastámara, within five months of the end of my story. Two years later, it was largely the machinations of Ibn Zamrak that led to Lisan al-Din's second exile in Morocco and eventually, in 1374, to his judicial strangling on charges of heresy; Ibn Zamrak, who is said to have headed the execution squad, succeeded him as

Grand Vizier of Granada. As for *al-Dawa* ('the Remedy'), as it is often called in Arabic texts of the period, the 'corning' process that makes it so much more powerful is first mentioned in writing in the early 1400s. Corning allows the 'Chinese snow' (saltpetre) partially to dissolve, and as a result to coat the inner micropores of the charcoal much more thoroughly than by mechanical mixing alone. It led to the development of truly effective small arms, revolutionized artillery and permitted the exploitation of gunpowder as an explosive, rather than just a propellant. It is not known who discovered the corning process. It might as well have been Ali and Lubna's cat as anyone else; as Novalis famously said, novels arise out of the shortcomings of history.

As for the Black Prince's Ruby, following further adventures at the battles of Agincourt and Bosworth in the fifteenth century and its sale under the Commonwealth in the seventeenth, it now resides in the Tower of London, set into the Imperial State Crown of the United Kingdom.

The translated verses from al-Busiri's *Mantle Ode* on pp. 259-62 and 268-9 come from Stefan Sperl and Christopher Shackle (eds.), *Qasida Poetry in Islamic Asia and Africa*. Christopher Tanfield kindly provided the Latin text on p. 145. All other translations, real or imaginary, are mine.

Finally, regarding poetry, fourteenth-century Granada might come across from this story as a particularly poetical time and place. In fact, most Arabic speakers have been fascinated by poetry, everywhere and everywhen. 'If poetry could be exhausted, then it would already have been so,' said one of its masters, Abu Tammam. 'Rather,' he went on (in the translation by Geert Jan van Gelder and Gregor Schoeler),

> *'it is the rainfall of the mind: some clouds*
> *may vanish, only to be followed by more clouds.'*

Abu Tammam lived in the ninth century. The clouds still follow on today, and always will.

Fourteenth-century Morocco and Granada were, however, particularly saturated with poems. And even if the pool of poetic inspiration had become, as later critics claim, a little stagnant, the thirst for verse was unquenchable. A versifying cousin of Sultan Muhammad V, Abu 'l-Walid Isma'il, used another metaphor to describe the poetic obsession of the age. In his anthology of contemporary verse entitled – and with what panache! – *Scattered Pearls From Poets With Whom Time Made Me Rhyme*, the lyrical prince wrote that poetry 'clung to its high station among the intellectuals as tenaciously as a chameleon to a treetop'. It is a strange image, but strangely apt. Like the chameleon, poetry came in every shade imaginable, according to the setting. Most of it, as the critics say, was rather dull; but sometimes it could take on pleasing shades of meaning. More rarely still, it caught the light of genius – and came out in colours unimaginable, scintillating with truth that couldn't be expressed in any other words or ways.